MY DE

"I would not tease, my dear. I have every intention of kissing you," Valentine Wharton vowed.

He did just that, an infinitely gentle kiss, just one, and then his lordship pulled back, lingering close enough that, resolution wavering, Elaine closed the gap, bowing her forehead to rest upon his chest, hands clutching crisp white shirt linen.

He laughed, and pulled her close, his fingers sending fresh shivers down her spine, plucking at the bow tied beneath her left breast, loosing her wrap. As his lips sought hers he murmured heatedly, "I am a man of wicked reputation, my dear."

"I know," Miss Deering said, and lifted her lips that he might kiss them again.

"Well deserved," he admitted, and trailed his fingers along her spine so that she arched her back, fitting her body more tightly to his.

Valentine's Change of Heart

Elisabeth Fairchild

A SIGNET BOOK

SIGNET
Published by New American Library, a division of
Penguin Putnam Inc., 375 Hudson Street,
New York, New York 10014, U.S.A.
Penguin Books Ltd, 80 Strand,
London WC2R 0RL, England
Penguin Books Australia Ltd, 250 Camberwell Road,
Camberwell, Victoria 3124, Australia
Penguin Books Canada Ltd, 10 Alcorn Avenue,
Toronto, Ontario, Canada M4V 3B2
Penguin Books (N.Z.) Ltd, 182–190 Wairau Road,
Auckland 10, New Zealand

Penguin Books Ltd, Registered Offices:
Harmondsworth, Middlesex, England

First published by Signet, an imprint of New American Library,
a division of Penguin Putnam Inc.

First Printing, January 2003
10 9 8 7 6 5 4 3 2 1

 REGISTERED TRADEMARK—MARCA REGISTRADA

Printed in the United States of America

PUBLISHER'S NOTE
This is a work of fiction. Names, characters, places, and incidents either are
the product of the author's imagination or are used fictitiously, and any
resemblance to actual persons, living or dead, business establishments, events,
or locales is entirely coincidental.

BOOKS ARE AVAILABLE AT QUANTITY DISCOUNTS WHEN USED TO PROMOTE
PRODUCTS OR SERVICES. FOR INFORMATION PLEASE WRITE TO PREMIUM
MARKETING DIVISION, PENGUIN PUTNAM INC., 375 HUDSON STREET, NEW YORK,
NEW YORK 10014.

To the courageous, who leap,
and especially to those who get back up again

Chapter 1

A wall of mist pressed in on Valentine Wharton, hemming in the landscape of intent into which he rode, wetting his cheeks, dripping from hat brim and limp locks on this, his birthday. His rebirth day. A thin flag of mist flew from his mouth when he loosed a laugh. Not a white flag of surrender. Never surrender. *Dragon's breath.*

His best friend Cupid had dubbed it so on the battlefields of France, the fighting spirit of the dragon in each of them, drifting from noses and mouths in the chill rains. The notion had bolstered their courage, fired their imaginations.

Val was in need of a bit of bolstering this Valentine's Day. He missed Cupid's company, his quiet good cheer. He had not seen much of him since the wedding, since the night his fellow marksman had shot him in the leg. The old wound ached from the damp, reminding him of a dark night, a harder rain. With gloved hand he rubbed at the knot in his right thigh. Cupid's arrow. His enemy not the French but a friend.

No! My enemy is the drink, mock courage. Mustn't forget. Mustn't let down my guard.

Would it always trouble him? Always serve to remind

him? Cupid's best shot, the one that had turned his life—
and his thinking—inside out.

The bay's neck gleamed in the pearly morning light, its
mane, flung against his face by the wind, stung like the
memory. Behind him, an embodiment of the past that
meant to catch up with him, the carriage rumbled and
splashed.

Val remembered another gray Valentine's Day, and on
the road a young woman in a violet cloak. Penny.

"Val!" Joy in her voice. A spark of light in her eyes.
How in Heaven had she found it within her to be glad to
see him when he had left things so badly?

*Penny. Pretty Penny. I thought to pocket you again, my
misspent coin.* He closed his eyes, shut out the vision, sadness permeating him like the mist, a chill that seeped down
to bone. He longed for a drink, with sudden, gut-wrenching,
mouth-souring urgency. Something to put fire in his belly,
warmth in the cracked stone of his heart. He did not want
to recall all that he had done, and said, and ruined.

Her words haunted him still. *"How much of your life is
forgotten, Val? Lost? Remembered falsely?"*

He tipped his head, a rivulet of water dousing his neck.
He shook wet hair out of his eyes, raking it under the hat
with a resolute sweep of his hand. Blast the past! He was
intent on building a fresh future.

*I make this journey in search of freshly minted coin, in
search of . . . the spirit of the dragon. Penny Foster, now
Penny Shelbourne, is spent. Lost. Like the trees in the mist.
Like the tenderness in me.* His own fault. He had gone
about it all wrong—not realized the implications of his own
actions, his dagger sharp tongue. He and the damned spirits.

He spurred the horse through the gateway to the old
Elizabethan manor. Gargoyle dragons, imbibing too freely,
spewed rain rather than fire. *Heads and stomachs of stone.
That's what it takes. I am not made of stone. I only thought
I was.*

He stepped down from his horse, splashed through puddles, burst through the door, wet boots slipping on the flag-
stones—unsteady on his pins, as he had been many a time
before, throat wet, feet dry. An oath slipped his lips, entirely inappropriate in this learned atmosphere. He laughed
at the thought, a dry, sardonic laughter that echoed in the

empty hallway. Children sang in one direction; a young girl recited poetry in the other. The place smelled of wet wool, chalkdust, moldy book leather. He closed his eyes and drank it in.

Different dragons here, the dragons of innocence. He could remember in some distant past his own innocence. The odors brought it rushing back without fail, the same way the smell of rain, gunpowder, and wet horse brought back France, the singing state of heightened awareness that had ruled his every waking moment there, until the burn of too much rum allowed him to forget the anguished cries of the dying.

He brushed a gloved hand across his moisture-beaded mouth, reaching, out of habit, for the embossed hip flask no longer carried, a silver dragon, its tail wrapped around a castle's turret. No more warm burn of forgetfulness to fire his veins. No more breath of the silver dragon to offer false courage. He would need the real kind to do what he had set out to do. He would need sounder foundation than an imaginary silver castle.

It was harder than he had anticipated. Saying no, and no, and no, while need raged, and anger rose, scalding, to the back of his throat. He licked his lips, and swallowed the ragged edge of thirst, once more, with renewed resolve.

Felicity. His daughter. His castle.

The headmistress's office looked the same: green blotter upon the desk, striped aspidistra in porcelain pots by the window, a painting of two children and a pained looking spaniel behind her, an outdated globe near the door—the realm's horizons expanding, as were his own. A new world, a new Valentine Wharton. Something larger than the wing-backed chair Mrs. Northgate bade him sit in, the leather gone scaly.

"You are certain you wish to take her with you, sir, on such a long journey? A child her age may prove a burden."

A burden too long shirked. He veiled his sarcasm. "I've no doubt."

The headmistress blinked at him, as if unclear what part of her remark he met with such certainty. With a wave of her hand, she summoned passing footsteps from the hallway.

"Elaine."

"Yes, Mrs. Northgate?" The voice was that of a young woman: gentle, subservient, agreeable. With the words came a cool whiff of almond-scented soap, and the vibration of a presence immediately behind his chair.

Val turned to look into dark, guarded eyes, soot-dark hair pulled severely away from porcelain-pale cheeks. Her lips were pressed tight. Those quickly averted eyes seemed fearful or shy, he could not be sure which. Here was a background sort of creature. *Timid tabby.*

Not at all the sort of woman he was drawn to. He might have passed her by a half dozen times without noticing anything but those eyes.

He recognized evidence of intelligence there, a spark, as if a fire lurked in the depths of her. Recognition? Disapproval? He blinked, surprised. *Do I know you, puss?*

"Miss Deering will fetch Felicity," Mrs. Northgate assured him.

He knew the name at once, stared at her a moment longer than was polite. She bowed her head, dark hair parted down the middle, raven dark wings pulled over her ears, a neatly woven braided style wound in a tidy knot at the nape of her neck.

"Yes, of course," she murmured as she turned to leave.

Her every movement was carefully contained, understated, designed to go unnoticed. She avoided eye contact, and yet she knew he stared at her. The faintest bloom of raspberry stained her cheeks. She slid a wary look from beneath a dark fan of lashes. "If you will be so good as to wait," she suggested.

I am neither good, nor patient, and I do not care to wait.

He rose from the wing-backed chair and briefly clasped the headmistress's hand. "A pleasure. I shall just tag along if you do not mind."

Before Mrs. Northgate could object he was out the door and discreetly following Miss Deering, two ees. Not Miss D-E-A-ring always mentioned in Felicity's letters, but dearest Miss D-E-E-ring. Her stride was almost soundless, and swift.

A deering on the run, a younger doe than imagined. She will do, Miss Deering. I've a proposition for her.

"Miss Deering reminds me of Penny," Felicity had written. And then she had crossed out the "Penny" and written in above it "Mrs. Shelbourne."

The carefully scribed words had left him thirsty. He had stood a long moment considering the craving, his hand clawlike, crimping the page. Just one glass of wine, just one to take the edge off. He had rung for Yarrow. The old man had met his request with baleful eyes.

"There is no wine in the house, sir. No spirits at all, not even for cooking. As per your request, sir."

A request made the night the not-so-well-mannered Cupid had shot him in the leg.

The night you almost killed your daughter. The unspoken truth hung in the air. Yarrow would never say it, but the thought had to have crossed his mind as clearly as it had crossed Val's.

Val's heart ached to think of her. Penny, his bright Penny, who had not given up hope when hope was, he had been convinced, lost forever. He had forsworn both, Penny and drink, for Felicity's sake—sweet Felicity, the careless mistake of a child he had been ready to die for. He had sent her away to school, this child he barely knew, while he battled spirits, and memories, his daughter better left to another's care, another's instruction. *Her own personal dragons.*

A sweetness had marked her every letter home to him— dutiful letters, written because he had asked her to, not because she longed to communicate with the stranger who was her father. In those letters Miss Deering had often found mention.

"Clever Miss Deering: She speaks five languages fluently, plays three different instruments, and knows the most interesting details about the farthest flung places.

"Miss Deering makes Gatehouse feel like home," Felicity had confided, reminding him how far away he'd sent her, how great her homesickness must be. Miss Deering, he was told, knew when students were bullied and intervened. She took time to counsel each of her girls individually. Val suspected Felicity had confided in this woman much of her troubled history. *And thus she knows the worst of me.*

He quietly followed in her wake, certain she held him in low esteem. It ought not to have bothered him—a mere governess. He had been scorned by far better, far more important and influential people in his life, and yet, in watching the demure sway of her hips, in studying the gleaming twists of tightly braided hair, he did not want this young woman to despise him, as Penny Foster had grown to despise him. He never wanted another woman to have sufficient reason to revile him.

Besides, she meant too much to Felicity.

There was, deep within him, a reluctance to offend anyone who in any way reminded Felicity of Penny Foster. Too much offense had already been generated in that quarter.

The resemblance was not physical. Miss Deering's backside had a less pronounced curve than Penny's, her shoulder blades were sharper, her waist smaller, indeed her entire frame was slighter, more delicate. Could there be something similar in the quiet, self-possessed stride? The tilt of her chin? The fluid grace of her movements? No stray curls tempted a man's gaze to linger, and yet his did, searching for a glimpse of Penny, whom he should have married, could have married, would have married. *Had you been a different man, a wiser man, a more sober one.*

Miss Deering shot a quick glance over her black-clad shoulder, an impression of guarded concern. Concern that he followed her? But no, her dark brows furrowed at the sound of a woman scolding, the voice like an unoiled hinge.

"Willful child! You must put it back on."

With a horrible clanging of iron came a second voice from the same distant classroom door, one that made him hasten, the voice of a child.

"I will not. It pinches. I cannot breathe, and my neck and shoulders go all stiff."

Felicity!

Miss Deering passed through the doorway as the woman gave a contemptuous laugh, saying, "How else are you to obtain regal bearing, stupid child?"

And here was Felicity's voice again, sharp, strong, completely uncowed. "There is nothing whatsoever wrong with my posture."

Just as it had been the day he had introduced himself.

"You are not my father. My father is dead!"

He was her father. The two of them, cut from the same cloth. He had never denied her that, once he was aware of her existence. Val stopped just outside the doorway, head cocked to listen. Did his daughter regularly misbehave at school? Was she always so wayward and headstrong? As her mother had been wayward, as he had been headstrong?

"Unmanageable! You are an entirely unmanageable young man! I've no idea what to do with you."

His quiet, even tempered mother. How sorely he had tried her patience. How many times had she wrung her hands over his behavior? Did it explain why she had never sought to care for Felicity in his absence? Her only granddaughter. Her illegitimate granddaughter. She had to have turned a blind eye on the resemblance, a deaf ear to the gossip. They had never spoken of the matter. Would they ever?

Had his unmanageable daughter battled wills with Penny throughout her youth, without his knowing?

"Felicity Wharton."

That sharp voice again! As mean-spirited and biting as the voices of his childhood. His lip curled.

"Would you live without benefit of stays, Miss Wharton, in an age of dumpling-shaped girls?" The woman's bark was sharp. "I think not. Your father has paid for the privilege of a proper education, and that includes proper posture obtained by the use of the proper posture device. Now put it back on, at once."

Val peeped inside the doorway in time to see Felicity, looking taller than when last he had seen her, arms folded obstinately across her chest, regarding with contempt a pile of metal bands and leather straps strewn upon the floor.

"It is torture, Miss Bundy," she stated belligerently. "I refuse to willingly succumb to such a device."

No surrender. No defeat, Val thought.

Someone sniggered. Val shifted position for a better view. In the row of desks behind Felicity the strangest sight met his eyes. Young women, children really, like Felicity, ten to twelve he guessed their ages, sat like stiff-backed, life-size automatons, trussed up in metal bands and leather straps that forced their shoulder blades together. Metal rods with semicircular chin props kept their gawky, girlish heads artificially high.

Clapping a hand over his mouth he stepped back out of the doorway. It would not do to simply burst out laughing at them. Visions of his Latin professor, Mr. Barrow, rose at once to mind, slapping a rule against his palm, frowning at him most severely.

"You take things far too lightly, Wharton. Another outburst of unnecessary laughter and I shall . . ."

His hands tingled with the thought of his ill-met response. *"Risio, risor, risus."*

Miss Deering said something he could not make out. He turned his head, the better to hear, stifled amusement shaking his shoulders.

What is this nonsense?

"Miss Deering," Miss Bundy spoke with haughty disdain. "Can you not see I am in the midst of chastising a wayward pupil? As for you, Felicity Wharton, why, when I was your age I was hung by a ceiling ring and straightlaced to the point of fainting. Our shoes were lead weighted to strengthen our legs, and we gladly swung by our chins to stretch our necks, that we might stand proud, recognized as ladies!"

Bloody nonsense! He was fully prepared to defend his daughter, but Felicity, his outspoken, sensible nine-year-old going on twenty, beat him to the punch. "How foolish!" she stated flatly. "I would rather forgo being a lady if neck stretching and chin propping are required."

Hear! Hear! he wanted to crow.

"Ill-mannered child!" Miss Bundy barked. "Pick up that posture perfecter and apologize at once." Pikestaff stiff with a persimmon twist to her lips, the woman circled his child, cracking a rule against her palm.

Felicity stood her ground without cowering. Pride surged through him. Brave and beautiful, his wayward seed. It was time he intervened.

His daughter's silence infuriated Miss Bundy. "You do not belong here, Felicity Wharton, amongst so many well-bred young ladies."

Felicity took the words like a blow, body braced. Her chin fell. Her defiant gaze did not. Val's blood rose.

"You did not think I knew of your disgrace, did you now, Miss High and Mighty? Well, I do know. We all know . . ."

Miss Deering interrupted. "Miss Bundy! Miss Wharton has a visitor. Can this reprimand wait for a more appropriate time?" Dark eyes, dark winged brows, a generous mouth above the sharp little chin. So serious she looked.

Not a beautiful face, Miss Deering's, but aware, so very aware.

Bundy turned on her, spewing vituperation. "Appropriate? Your continued interference is most inappropriate and impertinent, Miss Deering. I do not know how you were allowed to behave in your last position, young woman, but as a governess at Gatehouse you must learn to demonstrate better manners. You are an example to these girls, Miss Deering."

The younger woman's cheeks flushed rosy. Hands clasped, a picture of demure reason, she murmured, "As are you, Miss Bundy."

Val cocked his head. An unexpected comeback from the not-so-timid tabby. Bundy's back went posture perfecter rigid.

He drawled acidly, "Would you hold the child guilty for her father's sins?"

Miss Bundy's head snapped round. Color flared in sunken cheeks.

"Papa!" Felicity turned, uncertainty in her eyes, in her demeanor. "You will not make me wear it, will you?"

It tore at his heart to see his defiant daughter lose backbone at sight of him. He eyed the proper young girls who stiffly stared back at him. *They know my daughter's shame. My shame.*

With a cynical bark of laughter he said, "In the Far East women's feet are bound in youth, that they might be small and dainty, if completely deformed. We consider that barbaric."

With all the grace of lamp posts, the girls glanced from him to their governess, confused. They did not grasp his meaning. Miss Deering's manner remained as quiet as ever, hands clasped, fingers caged in her own grip, guarded amusement in the curve of her lip! Pretty lips. She was quite attractive, dearest Miss Deering.

Miss Bundy did not look at all amused. "This is quite different."

"Is it indeed?" His brows rose. The cynical bite of his voice deepened. "Well-bred young ladies trussed up like Christmas turkeys?"

The turkeys awaited her response, wide-eyed. Felicity stood a little straighter.

"B-b-but, sir . . ."

"Do not, I beg of you, waste time or breath in trying to defend such a ridiculous contraption." He waved a negligent hand at the students.

Miss Deering bit her lip. Miss Bundy blinked at him in dismay.

He smiled at his daughter. "Care to go on holiday, poppet?"

She hesitated a moment, as he had known she would. Penny shouted at him, from the fells, from the past. *"She does not know you, Val. I told her you were dead."*

"On holiday, Papa? Where? When?"

"To Wales. As soon as you apologize to your governess."

Doubt and rebellion hung like a cloud before the sky blue eyes. *Like mine. She has my eyes. My temperament.*

"Your teachers are due your attention and obedience." His father's words spouted from his lips. How strange the sound.

Miss Bundy's head rose abruptly in surprise. Miss Deering looked up, head cocked. His borrowed wisdom met with startled approval.

The language, the duty of fatherhood were unfamiliar to him—uncomfortable. Felicity stared at him belligerently, angry and resistant. He stared back, implacable and unyielding in his expectation. Her gaze fell. She frowned at her shoes, lower lip out-thrust. *She might refuse. I would have refused, given such a come-lately, shirk-thy-duty father.*

But his dear, illegitimately born daughter was blessed with a far more obedient heart than he. Fair head lifting, her blue-eyed gaze met his with a trace of angry, betrayed defiance for a long silent moment, before swallowing her pride, she said, "I apologize for my rudeness, Miss Bundy."

The room held its breath.

"Back to your studies!" Miss Bundy curtly ordered her students.

Stiff-necked and wide-eyed the students directed their attention to pages that whispered their obedience.

Unappeased, Miss Bundy said curtly, "You had best go now."

Dreadful woman.

Felicity nodded, turning toward him, crestfallen, the pain of her disgrace written clear in every feature. He wanted

3 1833 04317 3431

to sweep her into his arms, to shout "Bravo!", to assure her all was forgiven, but she would suffer no such unexpected public display of affection. He clutched his hat and fell into step behind her. *Like a dog. Like Penny's man-eating dog.*

Miss Deering brushed past him to tap Felicity upon the shoulder. "Well done, my dear. I shall miss you. Do you need any help in gathering together your things?" She held out her arms.

With a stifled whimper, Felicity fell against her bosom.

Have I only to throw wide my arms? Would she respond, or simply stare at him, uneasy, uncertain what he wished of her? As uncertain as he had been with his father's occasional stiff embrace, the pat on the shoulder, his mother's kiss on air.

Val licked his lips, mouth dry. For most women he had only to throw open his arms with a certain smile. This governess would be easier to conquer than his own daughter, a young woman he had no idea at all how to rule. The dragon stirred. Desire stirred. It surprised him. She was not the sort that usually caught his eye, Miss Deering.

Have I only to throw wide my arms?

Chapter 2

Elaine Deering hesitated to approach the headmistress's office. Fear slowed her steps, and yet she could not look away, could not retreat. Wharton had seen her. The monster waited—no—lounged was the more appropriate term—one arm propped along the plain oak benchback provided for students, muscular legs crossed at the ankle, one expensively shod foot swinging with nervous energy, flinging raindrops. *Father of Felicity's illegitimacy. As careless of his seed as he is with wet boots.*

She could see why women were drawn. His presence filled a room. He was undeniably attractive, even thoroughly drenched, but more than a handsome face and muscular grace, his gaze mesmerized one.

This man of monstrous reputation intently watched her approach, raindrops coursing damp tracks along weathered cheeks, his eyes glittering and cold, piercing and yet shuttered, as if he gazed down from unbreachable arrow-slitted battlements, as if for all his relaxed stance he sat coiled—waiting.

For who? Or what? A shift of the light in his eye, the slightest adjustment in the tilt of his chin, gave her the strangest feeling it might be her—a ridiculous notion—and yet the very idea made her heart flutter.

Did he turn such a look on any woman who crossed his path?

He does not look like a monster. Nor had he behaved like one in Miss Bundy's classroom. *Monsters seldom do.*

Her former employer had fooled her. The distinguished and respected Lord Palmer had presented himself more innocuously than Wharton did, for Palmer was neither so handsome, nor so bitingly witty, and he had seemed a happily married man, a good provider, and an excellent father, not a man of questionable past and moral character.

She had heard stories of Felicity's father, Valentine Wharton, a heartbreaker if ever there was one. Dreadful tales if they were true, far more scandalous than poor, pitiful Palmer's sins. And yet, these tales reminded her all too much of the desperate haste with which she had abandoned her latest post, the breathless panic of her leave-taking.

I have no very high opinion of men. Valentine Wharton is not the sort of fellow to restore my faith. The eye-catching looks, barbed humor, and delving gaze of this uncontested rogue proved at the same time attractive and repulsive.

How confusing when an ugly character came handsomely wrapped. This monster had abandoned the mother of his child. He had stolen his illegitimate offspring from the tender, loving care of another young woman. He was a danger to any single young female's reputation—a sharpshooter of violent history, reputed to imbibe too deeply in spirits.

Everything Elaine had heard of Valentine Wharton made her wish to avoid him. Indeed, she wished she might refuse him his daughter's care—sweet Felicity—such a father would surely pervert her goodness.

And yet, he had shown himself remarkably sensible to his responsibility in confrontation with Miss Bundy and her ridiculous posture perfecter. He had supported his daughter's good sense in rebelling and yet attended to Felicity's apology for her rudeness.

Small seeds of hope.

He stirred her curiosity, this detestably comely creature. He watched her, as she approached, one eye half closed, as if he measured her, as if he had the right to examine her like any horse or a dog whose performance he judged. It made her wonder if this second summons to the headmistress's office had aught to do with him, or if she were merely to be scolded for too rudely interrupting Miss Bundy's class.

He addressed her as she went to pass him, "Felicity speaks highly of you, Miss Deering. Tell me, do you suffer motion sickness?"

She stopped, nonplused. *An odd question.* Was her monster the Sphinx with such a riddle? She unquestionably turned to stone for a moment, before responding evenly, as if she were asked such questions every day by her pupil's parents. "No. Why do you ask?"

He tipped his head at an angle, eyes narrowing, raindrops glittering in his lashes, the aloofness she had first noticed in him undiminished, despite the light of interest that lurked in his changeable gaze. "I wonder if you would care to go to Wales?"

Chapter 3

He awaited her response with a sardonic lift to chiseled lips, a lazy watchfulness in hooded blue eyes.

Elaine considered him carefully. Snide and handsome young men generally took advantage of gullible women. She knew that all too well, and yet there was nothing flirtatious in his gaze, nothing suggestive or lewd—only that testing, watchful fascination.

"Wales?"

His lips curved upward, his mouth wide and full and mischievous. A mouth to make a woman think of kisses, of this rogue's reputation for freely dispensing such favors. "Wales. You have heard of it, I trust?"

Impertinent question. Impertinent smile. She would not be beguiled by a handsome face. By bold blue eyes. By rain-starred lashes. By enticing lips. She must not feel either flattered or offended that a handsome young man invited her to go away with him. *That the monster remembers my name.* This was a business arrangement. Surely it must be.

"Are you in need of a governess, Mr. Wharton?"

"I am in need of governing, yes." Valentine Wharton's

lip curled. He seemed to laugh inwardly, as if in private jest, as if he had some sense of her unwilling fascination.

Her breath caught in her throat.

"I've need of many things, Miss Deering."

The words hung between them, like the droplets that hung above his brows, in the rain-soaked, honey-colored forelock. Elaine frowned, swallowed hard. He meant to be suggestive, meant to see if he could rattle her. Well, she would not be rattled.

"For Felicity?" she asked in the calmest of voices.

He paused a moment. "She claims you are her . . . favorite."

Innuendo.

"I am pleased she should say so." She chose each word carefully. "And it is kind of you to offer Wales."

It would not do to offend a man of his position. *Or the monster he is said to be.*

"But, kind sir, I do not think . . ."

"Do not think." He changed her words' meaning, making them a firm directive rather than her waffling attempt to refuse him. "You have only to act. To say yes. I will double your current salary."

He means to tempt me. It was tempting. She could use the money.

A flicker of heat warmed his gaze. Impatience, not desire. She frowned. "I fear . . ."

"Fear?" He pounced on the word, as if she chose it unwisely.

"I might prove a liability."

He tilted his head, raindrops glinting like diamonds on his lapel, trickling in a crooked path toward damp lips that echoed, "Liability? Would you present yourself in a negative light, Miss Deering?"

"I am conversant in five languages, but Welsh does not number among them."

He regarded her a moment as if she baffled him. "I am in no need of an interpreter. I speak the language fluently."

She clasped her hands, stared at her feet. *Am I foolish not to jump at his offer?*

Mrs. Northgate came to the office doorway. "Miss Deering?"

Nothing yet settled between them, Elaine said, "If you will excuse me, sir. I am summoned."

Relieved by the interruption, she followed Mrs. Northgate, surprised to find her office occupied. A gentleman sat in the chair before her desk, all she could see of him his sleeve, one well-shod foot, and his lividly scarred hand. She knew the hand. She was the reason for that scar. Her stomach lurched in anticipation of fresh disaster. *Another monster.*

"Miss Deering, I believe you know Lord Palmer." Mrs. Northgate made an obsequious gesture toward her visitor.

Her former employer regarded her with a distant expression, chin high, as if they were barely acquainted, as if she stood miles beneath him. And yet, feeling smoldered in his gaze, gave hint in the weakened purse of his lips.

How dared he show his face? Did he mean to apologize? Or was it trouble he was after? Elaine drew a deep breath. "Do you mean to school Jennifer here, my lord?"

Mrs. Northgate answered for him, tone chill, as if Elaine's question were in some way inappropriate. "Lord Palmer comes upon another matter, Miss Deering."

"Oh?"

"Yes, I am most disappointed to hear report that contrary to Lady Palmer's recommendations you were regarded unsatisfactory in your handling of their children. Lord Palmer regrets the need to set the record straight. He voices concern that you seek employment again in a situation that involves young ones."

Elaine stared at him, a sinking sensation in the pit of her stomach. Revenge. Of course. He meant to sully her name, to leave her without references. No hopes of finding a position of any standing. No hope at all.

Palmer eyed her with unguarded satisfaction, no pity, no heart.

"It is a lie!" she blurted.

Mrs. Northgate wrung her hands. "I very much regret, Miss Deering, that so serious and derogatory are the nature of these reports that I cannot keep you on here at Gatehouse."

Elaine regarded her with dismay. "You give me no opportunity to defend myself? What are these trumped up charges?"

Mrs. Northgate licked her lips uneasily.

"I can think of no good reason why a gentleman of Lord Palmer's standing should wish to slander you, Miss Deering. I must accept his word as truth."

Elaine's heart broke all over again. Mrs. Northgate's mind was already made up. The truth did not matter. Her future teetered, poised to plunge into an abyss of ignominy.

"Lady Palmer supported me in my going. She knew my reasons—found them both honorable and valid. She liked me, as did the children."

"And Lord Palmer?" Mrs. Northgate pressed. "Would you accuse a gentleman of doing this out of spite? He did not like you?"

Elaine pressed her lips together to still her shaking chin. She must not allow her voice to quaver, her growing sense of terror to overwhelm her.

Palmer's brows rose. How smug he looked. *The beast.* He knew this was the reception his accusations would meet, that he might with the snap of his fingers ruin her chances for gainful employment.

"Have you no answer?" Mrs. Northgate demanded.

His hands! The looks. The whispers. How to explain?

"He liked me too well!"

A moment's shocked silence, and then Palmer murmured coolly, nostrils flaring, "You flatter yourself, my dear."

Mrs. Northgate shot him a measuring glance.

He sat, straight-backed and well-groomed on the edge of the chair, the picture of a proper English gentleman untouched by English rain—or the sordid breath of scandal.

Elaine met Mrs. Northgate's delving look, chin up.

Pity welled in the headmistress's eyes. She pursed her lips and shook her head regretfully. "I am terribly sorry, Elaine."

Elaine braced herself.

"I cannot take your word over a gentleman's. You do understand?"

Elaine closed her eyes, heart sinking.

"You will be so good as to fetch your things?"

So good as to avoid making a scene. So good as to avoid involving the school in a legal proceeding.

Elaine turned, knees shaking, her future undone. She stopped beside Lord Palmer's chair, gaze fixed on his bald spot. With every inch of self-respect she could muster she said calmly, "You are, in every way conceivable, a profoundly little man, my lord."

His head twisted, that he might shoot her such a look of malevolence she was tempted to fall back, tongue stilled. But she had nothing to lose now in speaking out, and so she stood her ground and said, "I pity your wife, sir. Your children. On you I waste no such tender emotion. For you, sir, I feel nothing but contempt."

Invigorated by her own nerve, she turned her back on him, turned her back on security and income, on the certainty with which she had regarded her future at Gatehouse, and sailed out the door.

Valentine Wharton still waited on the bench, a puddle at his feet. The Sphinx once again stopped her in her tracks. His hair curled wild and wet, as disarrayed as her emotions. His sky blue gaze rose to meet hers, fair brows raised, as if in question.

He heard! Oh Lord, he heard the whole. And now this monstrous man will judge me. She paused to catch her breath, to stiffen her resolve, her back, the wobbly condition of her knees.

What was this look in his eyes? This warmth! Here sat the picture of a profligate man of dreadful reputation, and she found in his formerly chill regard nothing but an invigorating blaze of admiration.

He said, ever so quietly, "My offer still stands."

She frowned. *Do I misjudge him?*

"Elaine."

Palmer's voice. He spoke from the doorway behind her. Without turning she said, voice strong. "Miss Deering to you, my lord."

"I've no desire to see you cast onto the street."

So sympathetic his words, so snide his tone.

Hypocrite! Snake!

In Valentine Wharton's gaze hovered a moment of understanding, a quick, flickering look of distaste for Palmer, a mirror of her own feelings.

She whirled to face her former employer. He looked her over contemptuously, head to toe, his gaze sliding past her to the figure who lounged upon the bench.

To think that she had trusted him! Admired him. Envied his wife such a husband. *How could I have been such a fool?*

Her anger flared. "Is the street not exactly what you intended for me in producing such a pack of lies?"

He held wide his hands, palms up, as if he were harmless, blameless. In the most urbane and unobjectionable of tones he said, "I offered you a position once. I stand by that offer."

"What? Beneath your thumb?" she snapped, and then surprised herself by saying, "Or is it another part of the anatomy you had in mind?"

He laughed. "You disgrace yourself, my dear, with such a suggestion. Where will you go?"

She said nothing.

"Penniless," he pressed.

And you would leave me so.

"Without proper references? Where in heaven's name will you go?"

She had not imagined him such a cruel man. He had once professed to love her, to need her. And now, he seemed set on breaking down every wall of defense, that he might destroy her, destroy every option save the one that would break her spirit, pride, and self-esteem completely.

I shall not fall prey to your guile. I will not.

Wharton's gaze shifted from one to the other of them and back again. "You could come to Wales," he drawled lazily.

Palmer was left temporarily speechless.

Elaine found herself tempted to smile at Palmer's thunderstruck expression. It did her heart good to see all glee, all confidence fade from his features. The rogue's plan, destroyed by another of his kind.

She could not trust this father of a bastard child to treat her with any more respect than Palmer had—and yet, she felt grateful. The notorious Valentine Wharton made it seem she had options.

He stared at Palmer with the most amused and congenial of expressions, a perfect reciprocal for Lord Palmer's sudden frown.

Theater masks. Quite a little drama played out between

the two of them in the moment of silence that stretched and grew.

Palmer's scowl shifted, redirected at her. "You would offer your services to a known profligate?"

"You presume to know me better than yourself, Palmer?" Wharton murmured. His light tone provoked a murderous glare from her former employer.

She said nothing.

Valentine Wharton regarded her again, nothing remote or distancing in his gaze this time, mischief sparkling in his eyes one moment, profound understanding the next. "And so it would seem you are caught betwixt the devil and the deep blue sea," he said quietly.

Between two monsters.

"I must gather my belongings," she said, her situation appalling, her future bleak.

Without another word she turned on her heel and left them.

Chapter 4

Val eyed the gloomy black carriage across the courtyard. Palmer's coach, Palmer in it, stood waiting, black horses rain sleek. *Miss Deering's dragon. Are we all beset by them?*

Bags safely stowed on top, Val leaned in the window to insist Felicity must not stick her head out. He told her yes, he meant to go and see if dear Miss Deering wished to come with them. He turned away to find his subject watched them from the entryway's arch—her gaze measuring him—as Penny had measured him that day he rode toward her across the lonely fells—the empty fells.

"Penny, pretty Penny. You wanted me?" He had twisted the words, her reason for coming to see him. She had looked about uneasily, at the empty road, afraid—he had never meant to make her fear him—as this governess feared him. She looked pale in unremarkable black wool. A cape. A bonnet. She carried a heavy; well-stuffed valise in each hand.

Through the soft fall of rain he went to her, the question on his lips silenced by the question in her eyes, so solemn that gaze, so serious.

"Is this everything?" he asked, assuming she meant to join them.

She glanced toward Palmer's coach, then to his own mud-splattered vehicle, where Felicity sat, nose pressed to glass. She drew herself up, clutching the bags fiercely, the angry resolve in her eyes outshining the rain that beaded the edge of her bonnet.

"He wanted more than a governess, Mr. Wharton."

But of course he did.

"Do you?" So fierce the look in her eyes, the hard edge to her voice. "I will turn you down as soundly as he if . . ."

He stopped her with a look, the slightest gesture, knowing her fear, knowing what she had heard of him, why she stood searching his eyes.

He spoke carefully, gently, afraid that with a single wrong word or gesture she might bolt, "I made the mistake once, Miss Deering—of assuming the dreadful gossip I had heard in connection with a young woman of my acquaintance was true."

She blinked, digesting this.

"I hope you will not refuse this position assuming all the dreadful gossip you have heard in connection with me is also true."

She studied his face as if she might read his history there, the trustworthiness of his character, the demons within. A good thing she could not hear the chorus of women in his head, the women of his past. Penny had seen the good in him, but the bad had drawn so many other women—flies to honey. He studied this prim, rather aloof tabby cat of a governess, unblinking, wondering if curiosity might draw her to him, wondering what his life might have been like had he always played the role of gentleman, no danger to any of the skirts he so skillfully lifted.

He had resolved to learn the difference, for his daughter's sake—for his own.

She asked, "Where in Wales do you mean to go, Mr. Wharton?"

He schooled his features, reluctant to reveal the sudden surge of hope that welled within. "St. David's. Do you know it?"

She shook her head, still doubtful, still confused. He felt a pang of pity, of regret for all the women he had confused throughout the course—or was it the curse?—of his life.

"A friend of King Arthur, was he not?" How much the

governess she sounded. How like a lost child she glanced at Palmer's coach.

"Patron saint of Wales," he said.

She dragged her gaze away. "Why there?"

He looked up, at dragons spitting rain, and remembered the sun, the warmth, the difference within himself, the sound of his father's voice, the carefree innocence of early childhood, seashells in a bucket, sand between his toes, the rush of the tide.

"I've fond memories. Of the sea. The islands. Sand-castles."

Something changed in her eyes. She seemed in some way to see him for the first time, to see that part of him that clung to innocence, to childhood, to seashells in a bucket. It startled him, that delving look. He had not expected it of her.

He tipped his head, closing his eyes, seeing it in his mind. "There is an island . . . where gannets nest." Raindrops pelted his hat, cascaded from its brim, and yet he could feel the sun's heat, hear the waves, the seals barking, birds crying. His voice tightened with anticipation. "Thousands of them, big as swans, with ink-dipped wings and Egyptian eyes. Such a din they make. There are seaweed nests by the hundreds upon the ground. Their fishing takes one's breath away." He opened his eyes.

Raindrops glittered in her plaited hair, trembled on her bonnet's brim, braided straw glowing golden in the rain. Penny's bonnet, Penny's eyes, but the light in these eyes shone brown, not blue.

He caught his breath. She was beautiful. He had not thought her beautiful, only useful. He shook his head, re-membering. "Ever seen gannets fish?"

"I have never seen the sea."

"I have never seen the sea." Penny's words. Miss Deer-ing's voice. He blinked, nonplused. Odd how life, and words, repeat themselves. "Never?"

She ducked her head, hiding her eyes' dark mysteries.

His hand soared upward, thumb and pinkie finger making wings, the movement drawing her gaze. "Gannets fly high." He turned his face to the cold pelting of the rain. "Then they fold their wings." He drew his fingers together, let his hand fall, as he had fallen that rainy night, the burn of the ball in his leg, the child clasped in his arms.

"Plummet—as a tern will, but from a great height. Straight into the sea." His bird hand smacked his flat open palm, cracked like gunfire, like Cupid's best shot. His thigh twinged. He rubbed it.

Her gaze followed the movement of his hand, stirring heat. *Breath of the dragon. Breath of desire.* She seemed intent upon his every word, her interest genuine, and yet there was a bleakness to her expression.

"Surely you remember." Penny had worn just such a look.

"In they plunge—these great white birds"—he had plunged. Reckless—"with such force, such a splash, one wonders if they have broken their own necks." Into love. Into war. Into fatherhood. Reckless plunges. "Then up they pop, fish wriggling in their beaks."

Her bonnet tilted, an arrested expression in possession of her features. Like birds, her brows. Up they soared.

"I should like to see that," she murmured.

"Leap of faith." His mother's voice. She had stood, hand raised to shade her eyes. Watching.

"Leap of faith my mother called it, and I was impertinent enough to correct her in saying they do not leap, they fall." He paused, watching white wisps of breathy stream rise from Miss Deering's nose and mouth. *Dragon's breath.* "Will you brave such a leap?"

Uncertainty plagued the eyes that glanced away, fear of falling. She looked toward Felicity, who drew a question mark in the steam her breath made upon the coach window.

"To question is a sign of wisdom." She ventured a nervous smile.

"Yes. To question my motives demonstrates your wisdom. You would not be the first."

Smile fading, she eyed him intently beneath the peak of her bonnet.

He glanced toward Palmer's coach. "I know my own reputation. I do not deny it."

She went very still. Not a rabbit. Not a tabby cat, but a brown-eyed bird—watching the fox, poised to fly.

He exhaled heavily, a fluttering white wing of breath.

"I vow I am changed by my own foolishness, Miss Deering." So hard to read, that demur, dark-eyed visage. "Will you come with us, Mistress Governess?" He arched his brows in question.

She drew her cloak more closely about her and eyed the dark coach across the courtyard with misgiving. Then she frowned at the sky, bird-like brows arching, falling. *Leap of faith.*

"A long walk to Leeds in the rain. Might I offer transport?"

She seemed taken aback. "You are very kind."

His lip curled. "You do not really believe that, or you would agree to go to Wales."

"I will accept a ride to Leeds, and I thank you."

He reached for her bags. For a fleeting moment fear darted in her eyes. *Silly puss. What has Palmer done to you?*

She regained her equilibrium, her sensible manner, as she relinquished the bags. "Thank you," she said again.

He glanced at Palmer's coach as he followed the dark sway of her cloak, as he swung wide the door. The black horses were whipped into motion. Palmer's coach wheeled out of the courtyard. A dragon flown.

Felicity squealed a welcome. Miss Deering stilled his child with a word, arranged her skirts with practiced hand, and squinted at him through the misted windowpane as he slammed the door shut.

"He does not mean to come with us?" he heard her ask.

His daughter knew his habits. "He always rides in the rain."

Mrs. Olive, his housekeeper, hard of hearing, spoke loudly as he swung into the bay's saddle. "Enjoys the elements since his French tour."

It is the stillness I enjoy. The sound of my own breathing. The pounding heat. Life between my legs. He watched his breath drift white upon the breeze, heard Cupid speak softly, giving him courage.

The footmen who clung to the back of the coach eyed him balefully beneath dripping hats, caped coats buttoned high. They hated this sort of weather. No dragons among them. He spared them no pity. It was nothing to survive a bit of wet when one knew a warm fire, hot food, and a dry bed waited. Not like serving time in a wet tent, not knowing if the morning's light would bring victory or death. He nudged the horse into motion. Cupid would understand.

He could not think of Cupid without thinking of Penny. *Mouth dry, reputation soaked. Lord, I need a drink.*

As if God heard, it started to rain harder. Val turned his face to the sky and opened his mouth, catching raindrops on his tongue, the droplets teasing his thirst rather than quenching it. *A drink. A proper drink. Just a mouthful would do. A tongue-nipping swallow of whiskey, a throat-warming brandy.*

But no. He would not, could not. Especially not now, with Mrs. Olive just returned to him, Felicity in his care, and dear Miss Deering watching his every move with her bright, dark eyes through the coach window. So Palmer had wanted more than a governess! Palmer, who prided himself on being better than everyone else, with his perfect home, perfect wife, and three doting children. Palmer had wanted the doe-eyed Deering?

The want within him burned fiercely. Not for this Deering, but for a misspent Penny. Foolish to yearn after that which he might not have, not ever again. No better than Palmer.

The pounding of the horses' hooves seemed bent on pounding that truth into his skull. No drink. No Penny. He vowed he would not think of her again and found, as he raced along the lane, legs wrapped around the bay's surging, muscular sides, that his mind would fix on nothing else. *Penny. Pretty Penny. Touch-me-not. Touch-me-never.*

Chapter 5

Elaine had not expected to find a woman in the coach. She had seen no sign of her through the rain-fogged window, though it made sense that Valentine Wharton would bring entertainment for the child, a companion.

She was a buxom woman going gray about the temples, with fly-away hair of a particularly undistinguished shade, her most attractive physical aspects a merry mouth and laugh-lined gray eyes. Her lap was full of knitting. The needles in her hands flashed rhythmically.

"Mrs. Olive, my father's housekeeper." Felicity made introductions as the coach jerked into motion, suspending momentarily the clicking needles.

"Do you mean to join us then, dearie?" Mrs. Olive asked in a rather overbearing shout, compensating for the rumble of the wheels.

"I go as far as Leeds," Elaine said.

Mrs. Olive leaned forward, hand cupping her ear, the knitting balled in her lap. "What's that, my dear?"

"Leeds." Elaine said again louder. "I mean to get out at Leeds."

"Leeds?" Felicity stared at her in amazement, an expression that quickly gave way to furrowed brow and pouting lip.

"Oh my dear!" Mrs. Olive sat back, looking both surprised and disappointed. "I have been counting on your company ever since the suggestion was made that a governess would ensure Miss Felicity not fall behind in her studies. Is there nothing we can say to change your mind?"

And so it was a governess he wanted, just a governess. Mrs. Olive set to work again.

Felicity demanded, "What is in Leeds? I thought you meant to come to Wales. Papa said he would ask."

"And so he did."

"But why do you say no? Did he not tell you how most particularly I asked for you?" So worried she looked, young Felicity.

Elaine smiled and patted her hand. "You are kind to have done so."

"Please, Miss Deering. Please come with us." Felicity clung to her fingers. So serious, for one so young. Such a contradiction of outspoken independence and need.

Elaine sighed, searching for words. "I . . . I do not know if it is appropriate for me to accept your father's kind offer, my dear."

"But of course it is. Why would it not be?"

Elaine's gaze met the older woman's. One could not explain a monster to the monster's daughter.

"I know so little of the circumstances," Elaine skirted the truth.

"Well, my dear, if that is the only obstacle," Mrs. Olive shoved aside her concerns as swiftly as she shoved aside her stitches. "I can tell you anything you need to know. I have been with his lordship's family since he was in nappies. He is a good master. In fact, you could not choose a better time to serve him."

Was there ever a good time to serve a monster? "Oh? How so?"

The older woman's gaze flickered toward Felicity and back again. "The child brings out the best in him," she said, and then clamped her mouth shut and yanked smartly on her ball of yarn, as if there were quite a bit more to be said, but not in front of the child.

"Please, Miss Deering. Say you will stay," Felicity pled.

"My dear." Elaine held her arms open, and when her former charge had flung herself into them, she whispered into her hair, "You must learn, my dear, that it is not at all dignified or ladylike to beg."

"I've no wish to be ladylike if it means you are to go away."

"Sounds just like her father, she does," Mrs. Olive said jovially. "Always claimed he'd no desire to be the gentleman his father would make of him."

Elaine held Felicity gently at arm's length. "Felicity. Do not say one thing when you mean another."

"You sound just like—" She shot a nervous look out the window.

Elaine crooked a finger beneath the unhappy chin. "But you do wish to be a lady, my dear. And dignified. I know you do." She turned her attention to Mrs. Olive. "What was he like as a boy, Felicity's father?"

Felicity sat forward, hunger in her eyes. "Yes. What was he like?"

Mrs. Olive smiled, all of the lines in her face engaged. "Well, my dear, your father was in many ways very much like you: headstrong, full of energy, convinced he was right and the rest of the world entirely wrong. His poor parents did not know what to do with him. Not at all of the same temperament, you see."

"What else? What did he like to do?"

"Riding. No one in the county had ever seen a lad take so fast to a saddle. Neck or nothing, over walls and fences, after foxes and hares. Rough and tumble. Up he'd get after every fall, dust himself off, give it another go. A fine figure of a lad, turned the head of many a local girl."

Elaine turned away from the window, away from the view of Lord Wharton on horseback. *Does he turn my head? Does he mean to turn my head?*

Felicity wore a serious expression. She echoed Elaine's thoughts. "Did he turn Penny's head? My mother's?"

"Aye, no denyin' it." Mrs. Olive tapped her plump chin, with the blunt end of a knitting needle, thinking, lips pursed.

Elaine felt that once again they had touched upon a subject Mrs. Olive did not care to plumb. There was an indefinable tension between the woman and the girl.

"Archery." Mrs. Olive aimed an imaginary bow at Felicity, her knitting needle an imaginary arrow. "He was very good at targets—your father—and firearms. Learned to load ball and shot ever so fast."

"Just like Cupid," Felicity said, and pretended to shoot back.

"Cupid?" Elaine asked.

Felicity nodded, eyes sparkling. "Papa's best friend."

It sounded too fantastic to be true—a Valentine and a Cupid, friends. Elaine turned a quizzical eye on Mrs. Olive.

"Yes, indeed." The arrow became knitting needle again as she cast off a fresh row. "They came back from fighting Bonaparte together, Valentine and Cupid."

"Cupid married Penny," Felicity confided, as if it were important Elaine should know.

Penny. Felicity had spoken more than once of Penny. "She cared for you as a child, did she not?"

Again the uneasiness in Mrs. Olive.

Felicity nodded, and tipped her head so that her hair fell down over her face. "His name is not really Cupid, of course."

"Shelbourne," Mrs. Olive said, and then waved her knitting needles, so that the long swathe of stitchery danced in her lap. "Shells."

Felicity regarded her with puzzled expression.

"Another of your father's interests as a child." Mrs. Olive delved into a fresh band of color in the knitting. "Brought back a huge collection of the dirty, sand filled things, he did. Learned all of their names, even the Latin. Poured over books for weeks. Made his father proud. Mounted the best in boxes, with labels. I wonder what's become of them."

What is to become of me? Elaine clasped gloved hands together, worrying over a loose stitch on her pointer finger, worrying about the loose stitch of her future. Both best mended quickly.

They drove through the crowded, bustling, befogged streets of Leeds. A regular warren of narrow lanes led through the eastern half of the city, the street changing names from York, to Quarry Hill, which curved into Lady Drive, which became Lady Lane, ending abruptly in North

Road, which doglegged down into Lowerhead Road, which turned into Upperhead Road.

The street names were hard to read in the rain, hard to find on the sides of the buildings where they were posted, but Elaine made a game of it, the good governess—for the moment at any rate.

Felicity called out each find, spelling the words.

We must stop soon. I will have to get down. Get out in the rain. No references. Dear God. No references! And new gloves needed. What am I to do?

The coach stopped at the corner of Guilford Street and Park Row.

Wharton opened the door and opened it to splattering rain. "We mean to turn south here and cross the river."

Without me. They will go on without me. What will become of me without references? So keen those blue eyes, so handsome. A monster has no right to look so appealing in the rain.

His lips were moving. Wet lips. Raindrop beaded. His manner unassuming. Gentlemanly. "Will you go on to Manchester with us, Miss Deering? The city is larger than Leeds, and might offer better opportunity for a position."

"Do not leave us, Miss Deering. Please." Felicity sought her hand, wrung it in a child's urgency of wanting, as if it were a life-line.

Elaine said nothing for a moment, considering her charge's desperation, considering Wharton's glistening jaw as he regarded his daughter's wheedling with evidence of distaste. She considered, too, how a man might wish to offer her better chance of a position when she had refused his offer—not a monster.

"You are too kind."

He tipped his hat, rain in a river, wet locks and dry, golden hair that turned to dross when drenched. "Not at all." His gaze was steady, keen, his tone undeniably playful. "I would but give you chance to change your mind, and my daughter additional opportunity to grovel at your feet."

He meant to reprimand the child with such insult, but she was too young to comprehend his sarcasm.

"Oh, yes. Do stay." Her clutching fingers were hot.

"Indeed, my dear," Mrs. Olive coaxed, clicking off stitches with the same persistent rhythm as the rain on the roof. "You cannot want to get out in this dreadful wet, can you?"

It was true. Elaine did not want to get out of the warm, dry coach. She did not want to set about the odious tasks of finding a place to stay, a place to advertise for a position. She did not want to face the prospect of weeks without a position, weeks' worth of interviews. And yet she must. Eventually. Her life would be changed by the absence of references, and none for the better, but she must stiffen her backbone and take her future in hand. What future? Which future? One without monsters. Was there such a place for her, such a station?

In looking at Felicity, she saw herself as a child and had no desire to leave her charge in such a desperate state. Too much did the child wring her heart. Too ill-equipped did the father seem to be able to comfort her.

Papa, she thought, as she had thought many a time since his unfortunate end, *how could you leave us in so precarious a situation? Did it never occur to you the depths to which your daughters might fall?*

Daughter to a monster. She had not known, any more than Felicity.

"Manchester it is, then." She met Wharton's satisfied nod, the sudden gleam in his deceptively beautiful eyes, with a ready, "Most kind."

"Say it often enough and I may begin to believe you." He slammed shut the door. "We shall stop in Dewsbury to eat."

Chapter 6

They crossed the River Aire, the trench for a canal's construction, then into the lonely, windswept moors for a wet hour and a half before stopping at Dewsbury. As promised, Valentine Wharton saw to their feeding. The ancient inn sat squat and strong, made of the local yellowish stone, with a peaked roof, and ceilings and doorways built in an age of shorter men. Valentine Wharton was forced to duck his head to avoid banging it on the lintel. Elaine feared for her bonnet's crown. A local haunt, not much used to strangers, heads turned as they entered. The tapman made a fuss about seeing them to a private room.

Wharton brought with him a brass-bound box from beneath the coach seat. It went unopened until the tapman tried to bring to the table a pitcher of the local ale.

"I prefer hot water," he said then, a trifle too politely, wearing the walled-off look Elaine had begun to expect of him. *A wary monster.*

The tapman's face fell.

"Come, come, sir," he cajoled. "You will be wanting a sip of our local brew. It is quite famous in this part of the country."

Mrs. Olive eyed the exchange with pursed lips and worried eyes.

Wharton placed his box in the middle of the table, clicked open the clasps, and threw back the lid. "A pot of hot water," he repeated, still polite, but with an edge to the words, as hard as the glint in his eyes.

"Just a wee dram, sir?" The tapman was persistent.

Mrs. Olive looked as if she were mightily tempted to say something, but her master was not the sort of fellow to bear interfering servants lightly. She bit her lip, and balled the corner of the tablecloth in her lap.

I remember mama holding tongue, that same fear in her eyes. The fear of father's temptation.

Felicity watched her father, as Elaine had once watched her own father, tongue caught between her teeth, tension riding her jaw. *Hoping against hope.*

Wharton's voice rose only slightly, and yet his tone and manner were not to be argued with. "I've a very good Darjeeling here, my good man, and would indulge my party in a cup."

The tension in the room dissipated like the steaming breath of the horses led past fogged windows.

"Tea! Ah!" The tapman's brows rose. "Of course, my lord. If you will."

He went away, shaking his head.

Valentine stood by a window, gazing outward, the muscles of his thighs tensed, as if he were prepared to . . . run? Do battle? Elaine could not be sure. She was sure only of Mrs. Olive warming hands by the fire with a most satisfied expression, humming a little tune under her breath.

Impatient with the wait, as only a child can be, Felicity asked Elaine, "Are you hungry? I am quite famished. Hear my stomach growl?"

"Sounds as if you've a dragon in there." She patted the child's stomach. "I am not quite so hungry as that, but I should like a hot drink."

"Papa has tea."

He glanced their way, a quick, distracted glance, the set of his shoulders changing, tension dissipating.

"And do you know how fortunate you are to be treated to such a luxury?" Elaine felt a need to stir the frozen energy of the room. She bent over the box of tea. "Do you realize how far these very special leaves have come to bring us gustatory pleasure?"

Wharton's gaze lingered. Not a monster, but a man who would drink tea rather than risk inebriation.

"Gustatory?" Felicity repeated the word with precision.

Valentine spoke. "The pleasure . . ." He stopped, brow raised.

Words died in Elaine's throat. *Yes, pleasure. A rogue would know much of pleasure. All kinds of pleasure.* Man, not monster, but still rather dangerous—a man guided, perhaps controlled, by pleasures if even half of his history was to be believed.

"It means pleasure?" Felicity pressed.

Elaine forced herself to look away from that suggestive eyebrow. She cleared her throat, licked her lips, focused her attention on her pupil. "The pleasure of taste," she clarified.

"Is that what gustatory means?" Mrs. Olive gave a chuckle. "I always thought it something rude."

And he? Does he think it rude? Think me rude? Rude and willing and interested in other pleasures? How rude and willing and interested is he?

"Tea comes from China, does it not?" Felicity asked.

"Very good. Also from Japan, and India," Elaine found safety in facts, in her role as governess.

"Papa says one must be careful to buy it from a reputable source."

"Quite right." She risked a look in papa's direction. He would seem to have lost interest in them. In her? She ought to be relieved, and yet, strangely, she was not. The emotion that flit through her, like a bird on the wing, was disappointment—a faint sense of melancholy. An impression that she, as governess, and a plain one at that, did not in any way, shape, or form, figure into Valentine Wharton's idea of pleasure.

"Why does tea have so many names, Miss Deering?"

Felicity reminded her of who she was—what she was—her place. Elaine focused her eyes on the tea, not its owner—on the fine, richly perfumed leaves carefully separated into small boxes and bags.

"Fine tea—" she closed her eyes to breathe the aroma

"—is like fine wine. So precious a commodity that under-handed merchants make a practice of drying out the used leaves for resale." She chuckled wryly. "Inferior stuff."

Again he glanced their way. This time with more focused interest.

"There are many factors in growing tea that give it its noble flavor."

"Like sun, soil and rain?" Felicity guessed.

"Precisely. Like any crop. Where you plant your seed makes a difference."

Wharton gave a snort.

Elaine immediately regretted her word choice. She had not intended to plant any sort of reprimand of his behavior in what she said. Frowning, she went on. "Tea takes on the flavor of a region."

"Rather like people," Felicity said.

Elaine nodded. "Yes. We are all shaped by place and time."

Felicity stood regarding the different tea containers. "Fascinating."

Wharton joined them, tilting his head to regard Elaine rather closely. "Almost anything is fascinating when you take a closer look."

Elaine's pulse fluttered. What did he mean to imply?

"There are lessons to be found in everything," she said quietly.

Something changed in his eyes. For the briefest moment Valentine Wharton let down a wall. He blinked, the moment gone. His lips curled sardonically. He shut her out again with a derisive, "Is there never a time when you are not the governess, Miss Deering?"

Her back stiffened. *There was a time I never dreamed of being a governess.* She shrugged, and tried not to let his barbed tone wound her. "We must each of us choose a path."

"And lessons?" He seemed to mock her, rebuilding walls.

"Paths and lessons," she said thoughtfully, considering where his had led him. "The trick is to recognize which is which."

His hand rested on one side of the tea chest, hers on the other. "And you are convinced your path must diverge from mine? From Felicity's?"

So direct that question. The look in his eyes. Not flirtation. A challenge.

She considered the path that had led her here, to a box of teas, and a tea drinking monster who might not be monster at all. "The harder lessons in my life would seem to teach me as much."

His lips thinned, but anything he might have said was interrupted by the arrival of their food. The innkeeper carried in a steaming kettle of hot water, which he used to warm, and then fill a fat, white teapot.

Valentine Wharton, true to his word, brewed a generous pot full the precious tea. The first pale amber cup full was given to Felicity, who added three lumps of sugar before lifting it to her lips with a happy sigh. Wharton ate in silence, his gaze drawn to the fire on the hearth, while Felicity chattered with Mrs. Olive. He glanced often at the child, his expression gentle, observant, vaguely puzzled, even sad, as if he studied an unknown he had little hope of understanding.

Elaine understood completely that probing, even frustrated regard. She wondered more than once if a similar expression knit her brow as she slid glances at Wharton. Once or twice he glanced at her, when she instructed Felicity on the proper usage of the lemon fork, and when she suggested to the child that it was impolite to interrupt Mrs. Olive when she was talking. Just as quickly he looked away, as if his mind had been elsewhere, as if he would return to those distant thoughts.

Elaine's attention fixed on the glittering raindrops that lingered in the dampened gold of his hair, locks almost dry where the crown of his hat had protected them. A mass of golden, unruly curl, the sort of hair that she would have thought symbolized his character perfectly until today, until he had asked for—no—insisted upon—hot water, that he might take tea rather than the local brew.

Elaine had only to look at Felicity to be reminded of what this handsome devil was capable. She forced herself to look away, to focus on the child. And yet, her thoughts would not be penned. Too often they returned to that moment, that brief and shining moment, when she had caught glimpse of the innermost man, rather than the monster she had mistakenly believed Valentine Wharton must be.

Chapter 7

That afternoon they plodded on without break in the mist-
ing rain, their progress, or Mrs. Olive's incessant snoring.
Felicity curled like a kitten in the corner of the coach, the
cradle-like rock of the vehicle lulling. Elaine found herself
inclined to drift away, to become one with the rumbling
wheels. She might have been tempted to sleep had not sight
of a horseback Valentine Wharton so completely captured
her attention.

He looks like a centaur. His horse's legs became his, the
two magically joined by a flaw in the window glass and the
rain's uneven pattern. The rippling muscles of the horse
found echo in this man's body, the swaying mane's wet slap
was mirrored by the man's dripping locks.

A fine seat. She had an excellent vantage point to observe
her benefactor's tightly muscled rump, coattails buttoned
back, united in swaying rhythm with the bay's saddled back.
A perfect match, that pounding rhythm. Elaine felt it in
the flexing muscles in her posterior as she fought to stay
upright as the carriage pitched and swayed.

How fevered I feel. How flushed. Despite the damp chill,
she loosened the buttons at her throat, reminded of Palmer,
of the reason she sat swaying in this coach today, invited

to go all the way to Wales by a rogue with a reputation of monstrous proportion.

Palmer never struck me as a dangerous creature. Poor, pitiful Lord Palmer's hot fingers groping for her buttons one evening in the schoolroom had come as a complete surprise. His voice thickly hoarse—so recently employed in the act of wishing his boys good night—had professed adoration, while she had backed away, heart pounding, eyes wide, voice caught in her throat.

He had backed her against a wall, despite protest, fear keeping her voice low, fear of waking his sons in the next room, fear of alerting Lady Palmer to her husband's iniquity. There were guests in the dining room. He had continued to advance when she could no longer back away, indeed he had used the wall to his advantage, pressing himself against her, thigh to thigh, one hand rising to cup her breast, the other covering her mouth, stifling her low-voiced cry of "No!"

There had been something of the horseman in the hard, rhythmic pressure of his hips to hers, the bruising kisses he had lavished upon her neck. She had been startled by these sudden, aggressive advances, by the unexpected flame of fear generated at the apex of her thighs.

For a moment she imagined this well-seated centaur pressing her to a wall, the rhythmic pressure of his hips to hers. Her heart raced. Her pulse throbbed. She took a deep breath, and closed eyes to sight of him, mind to thought of him and all he was known for.

Palmer's actions had spelled her ruin, the termination of their roles as employer and employed. And so she had bitten the hand with which he stifled her protest and slipped away while he cursed her impudence with a string of foul epitaphs.

He had sopped the blood from his swelling fingers with his coattail. She had spat the salt taste from her mouth, wiped his unwanted kisses from her lips, and fled downstairs to inform Lady Palmer of her intention to leave at once. She had spent her every penny in getting to Leeds, as much space as she could place between herself and Palmer.

Not so long ago. An eternity. Another life. Another person it had happened to. She had been happy to find a place at Gatehouse School for Girls—lucky they had desperate need of a governess, most fortunate they did not question the reference from Lady Palmer.

And now? *My world is shaken. My feelings shaken, my heart touched by a man who intrigues me against my best intentions. A new sort of monster, walled in, but no less dangerous. I must go. I will go, though what is to become of me without proper references I do not know.*

She looked for answers on the horizon and found only Valentine Wharton. Mrs. Olive was quite right. He rode better than anyone Elaine had ever seen astride. *How many maidservants has he ridden just as adroitly?*

It would be a mistake to go to Wales in such a man's company.

Chapter 8

They reached Manchester as daylight waned by way of the Oldham Road, driving through wet streets and dark warehouses. Felicity called out street names. Elaine spread her arms, and stretched and yawned, and wondered anew what was to become of her.

"A gloomy place, Manchester, even with the rain stopped." Mrs. Olive set aside her knitting to peer out the window. "Are you sure you wish to leave us here, Miss Deering? I cannot imagine why you should prefer this to Wales."

Felicity pouted as she traced a sudden muddy splatter at the window. "You ought not leave us," she grumbled.

Elaine made no attempt to argue. As the coach splashed to a halt in the yard of a prosperous-looking inn, her charge turned to her and asked earnestly, "Do you not like papa? Is that why you will not stay with us?"

The footmen leapt down from above, and in a scurry of activity hostlers ran from the inn to take the horses. The iron step was let down with a thump, the door flung open.

"I do not know your papa well enough either to like or dislike him." Elaine took the gloved hand that was thrust into the coach—a firm grasp. *Wharton's grasp!* She knew it with a sinking feeling the moment his fingers closed on hers, the size and shape of that hand, the very stitching of the glove, grown familiar from his handing her in.

Their gazes met as she emerged, his penetrating, as much a connection as his grip. And in his sky-blue eyes she saw hint that he had heard, his gaze, hard, none of the softening she had found earlier.

"You are very kind," she murmured.

"Am I?" His brows rose skeptically. His lips curled sardonically. His lashes veiled the blue. "I do not think you know me well enough to say so, Miss Deering."

He released his bracing hold. She took an unsteady step away, feeling light-headed—in need of sustenance. *No question he heard.*

"I beg to differ," she dared contradict his icy dismissal.

Eyes narrowed, he tipped his chin—coldly curious. "Do you?"

She nodded, took a fortifying breath, and squared her shoulders. "In handing me from the coach, which I could not safely exit without assistance, I do know well enough to deem your action a kindness."

Lord Wharton's blue eyes sparkled speculatively. "Will you accept further kindnesses from me, I wonder, Miss Deering?"

An unexpected response. Did he mean to rattle her? "That would depend entirely upon what they were."

One brow arched sardonically. "Room and board?" He helped his daughter alight. "For one night."

Elaine's pulse quickened. She considered carefully what he offered, considered carefully her response. A lot could happen in one night.

"I do not think it—"

"Appropriate?" Head cocked, he extended his hand once more into the coach in order to assist Mrs. Olive in a rather stiff-limbed descent. "Would it be appropriate to send my daughter's governess away hungry into the rain-drenched darkness, no room yet booked? I dare to venture no one would consider that a kindness."

"Come, my dear, no foolish refusals. Sup with us," Mrs. Olive coaxed, weaving her arm through Elaine's. "Felicity and I would be happy to make room for you for the night, would we not, Felicity?"

"Oh, yes, my dear Miss Deering, do not rush to go," Felicity clung to her free hand. "Papa is reading to us every night from a book of Welsh fairy tales. You must not miss the chance to hear at least one of them."

To share a room with these two? Was that what he had in mind all along? But of course. He would not dare to suggest anything untoward in front of his daughter.

I cannot refuse. My purse is not plump enough. As if to put a seal upon her decision, it began to rain again in earnest. Felicity squealed.

"Run for it, my dears," Mrs. Olive shouted.

And so they ran for the door to the inn, toward warmth and light, and the smell of good food, and the promise of a bed for the night.

Valentine Wharton had the longest stride. He reached the door first, holding it wide, rain bouncing from the brim of his hat. Felicity dashed in first, then Mrs. Olive, and finally, Elaine, who had not run so much as hastened her walk.

"I take it this means yes, Miss Deering?" Wharton followed her in, sweeping his hat from his head, leaning just outside to shake it dry.

"You are thoughtful and generous to offer me hospitality on such a dreadful day." She removed her own hat. Her drenched cloak.

The entryway to the inn was a narrow one. It forced them into rather intimate proximity as he shrugged his way out of his dripping overcoat. *Close. Too close. Palmer would have tried to brush against me.*

"Is it possible you might still experience a change of heart, Miss Deering?" Valentine Wharton's brows arched playfully. He seemed to laugh inwardly as he hung his coat on a peg, then reached for hers.

She spoke quietly. *The child must not hear.* "It would not do to raise Felicity's hopes." The feeling of intimacy was enhanced by her whisper.

Elaine thought of Palmer. His eyes would have raked over her as she removed articles of clothing. Valentine Wharton's glances were keen, even unsettlingly delving at times, and yet his cool, shuttered gaze remained distant— all emotion hidden other than a jaded contempt for the world.

He is not a man of covert glances and suggestive leers. Only his language is, on occasion, suggestive. Provocative. Open to misinterpretation. And he would have me misinterpret. It is to his advantage to keep his opponent off balance. Like swordplay, her every conversation with him. Barbed. Sword blade keen. His wit piercing.

"It would not be a kindness to falsely raise my daughter's hopes," he agreed with a trace of sarcasm. "She has too often been disappointed."

He stepped past her without so much as the brush of a sleeve, that he might help Felicity and Mrs. Olive from their coats—the perfect gentleman.

Elaine could not help wondering, *Do I misjudge this man as much as I misinterpret him?*

Chapter 9

Val set aside the book of fairy tales and removed the freshly pressed coat donned for dinner. A quiet affair, the evening meal, predictable but welcome. Nothing like a wet day's ride to stimulate his appetite. They had been served a very good leek soup, a well seasoned leg of lamb, and roasted potatoes, with a bread pudding to finish off the meal. He had refused the recommended wine and the port, rum, brandy, and ale that were offered in its stead. He had done his best not to think of the spirit's bloom of welcome warmth on a chill, wet evening such as this.

He had turned instead to his lifeline, his fresh source of belly-warming liquids—his box of teas. It was the only time she looked up from her plate, Miss Deering—when he reached for the tea. Quiet, keep-to-herself-and-her-own-private-thoughts Miss Deering had kept her head down when he said "No, thank you," and "No," and again, "No, thank you" to all offer of spirits, but up her head bobbed when he said quietly, "I would like more hot water."

Their eyes had met. She had looked at him with something akin to approval. Oddly pleasing, that this wary creature should approve.

What would he do without his little brown leaves, in their

brass bound caddy? He had grown fond of the ritual steeping of their riches. Rather like his former ritual making rum punch. One must request a tea pot, of course, not a punch bowl, and the musical clink of china rather than crystal.

He loved opening the shining brass clasps on his inlaid wooden box, the whiff of tea leaves, the curved neck of the squat, round-bellied pots, the heating of the china, hot water steaming, swirling with the dark mysteries of the leaves. He had grown to appreciate the anticipatory wait as the water darkened, the perfume of tea and freshly cut lemons rising along with the steam, the distraction of preparation, of allowing the leaves to settle, the strainer to catch stray leaves, a welcome distraction as those around him were entertained by the music of corks popping and the clink of bottle or decanter to glass.

Her eyes were the color of steeped tea. Dark and liquid, a promise of steaming heat. Their depths pinned him with measuring looks, assessing and reassessing his every move. *I read the truth in those tea-leaf eyes.* He could read her stillness, her silence, as clearly as if she had spoken. He had surprised her with tea and hot water. It pleased him to be unpredictable.

Why should her opinion matter? He rid himself of the confinement of his neckcloth, unbuttoned his waistcoat, and rolled up his shirtsleeves. He thought of Palmer. A story there, and not a happy ending.

He flipped through the book of fairy tales, searching. The nightly reading was his favorite time of day, a relaxed moment with Felicity, an opportunity to form fresh father-daughter bonds. The habit had begun while his leg healed and Felicity recovered from the fever that had almost been the death of both of them. Reading of princesses and magical slippers and trolls who guarded bridges or granted wishes had given them something to talk about.

A tap sounded upon his door. He opened it, book in hand, to find Miss Deering, pale hands demurely clasped.

"Felicity is ready"—in a glance she took in his casual state of undress, eyes quickly downcast—"for her bedtime story."

"And you?" He tucked the book under his arm.

She peeped uncertainly through the door at him.

Come in, come in, said the spider to the . . .

He chuckled, thrust aside the thought, and took up two candleholders and a glass covered lamp. "Are you ready for a good bedtime story, Miss Deering?" He knew his question, his tone, made her uncomfortable. The devil in him wished to tease her, to test the level of the discomfort that made her long to seek employment elsewhere. *She fears I might be the man gossip makes of me. That I weave a web of deceit to ensnare her. Like Palmer.*

He handed her the lamp, pushed past her into the hallway, and shut the door on the room that made her uncomfortable. His room.

She watched uncertainly. *See how she strangles the neck of the lamp.*

"Anxious?" he asked, his emphasis such that she might interpret the word in several different ways.

A trace of offended defiance lit her eyes. "No, sir."

She lies. She is anxious, even afraid of me, of the position I offer, of this summons from my bedchamber, of how close I stand. She kept looking at his arms, as if bared skin were dangerous enough to keep her poised to run.

"Are you sure?" he prodded with a trace of sarcasm. "You look rather anxious."

She shook her head, eyes downcast.

"I had hoped you might be anxious."

That won him a frown. How forbidding the ordinarily demure sweetness of that face when she frowned.

"I love a good story, myself."

"Story? Oh! Story. I did not think . . ."

"But of course you did—think," he said. "It is why I wish to hire you—for that thinking mind of yours."

She looked at him, earnestly trying to understand when he deliberately meant to confuse.

He stopped outside the doorway to his daughter's room, hand on the latch. "There are dragons, spells that must be broken, princesses in need of rescuing, all sorts of intriguing dangers. But only in storybooks. I vow, I cast no spells. You need not fear me, nor the taking of this position."

She wet her lips with the nervous dart of her tongue. "No, sir?"

"And yet you do."

She glanced up, said nothing. Fear peered out at him

from the dark drink of her eyes. The lamplight wavered, the wick burning low. He reached out to adjust its height.

She seemed bent on the same objective. In a small movement, a casual twitch, she froze, inching her hand away from his.

"You did nothing to tempt him, did you?"

She blinked, as if he had slapped her across the face with the question. The oil in the lamp swayed. "Palmer?" Light flared briefly in her eyes as the wick burned brighter. "No. Nothing." Heat in her response. Anger.

"Then you've no reason to be anxious." He flung open the door.

She followed him into his daughter's room. *He deliberately confuses. And I am intrigued.*

The room boasted a crackling fire, a window that looked down over a busy street, and a rather large curtained-off dressing room. The furnishings consisted of two walnut-framed beds and a tall clothespress, the beds at cross-purposes, creating an L against two of the walls. Felicity was tucked into the larger of the two. She had insisted that Elaine must share it with her rather than make a pallet upon the floor. Mrs. Olive sat upon the other.

Valentine Wharton sank onto the bed his daughter occupied.

She seemed used to this arrangement. She made room for him, and once he was settled, lamps and candles positioned just so for the best available reading light, the book opened, the right page found, she leaned closer. His lordship tilted the book that she might better see the painted illustrations.

Elaine went to the windowseat. It seemed inappropriate to sit too close to Valentine Wharton while he focused on his daughter.

Wharton looked up from the page. For a single heartbeat his eyes locked with hers, well-shaped brows lifting, as if he found something amusing in the distance she placed between them. *As if he knows my fear. As if he revels in it.*

Felicity called out in wheedling tones, "Come sit with us, my Deering. Oops!" Her hands flew to her mouth to stifle laughter. "I mean . . ."

Valentine could not contain his own laughter. Blue eyes

sparkled. Dimples carved his cheeks. His amusement contagious, Felicity could not contain her giggles. Their laughter was echoed by Mrs. Olive's plaintive cry of, "What did she say? Pray tell, what is so funny?"

Elaine smiled. *I am not made of stone.*

Felicity stopped giggling. "I called poor Miss Deering, *my* Deering," she explained to Mrs. Olive before rushing to profess, "I meant no disrespect, Miss Deering."

"Of course you would not," Elaine said quietly.

"What's that?" Mrs. Olive sounded affronted. "Did you call her a coarse widnot?"

That set Felicity to giggling again, course widnot that she was.

Her father smiled, and turning to Mrs. Olive, said quite distinctly, "Of crows she widnot."

Even Mrs. Olive laughed heartily at that. And Elaine in her windowseat could not resist joining in. How good it felt to laugh. How unexpected to sit in a bedchamber with Wharton's merry gaze meeting hers as they chuckled and chortled and made themselves silly.

Felicity patted the counterpane beside her as she came out of a giggling fit. "Come, Miss Deering," she coaxed.

Elaine shook her head. "I prefer to sit here if you do not mind."

Valentine gave his daughter's shoulder a squeeze. "You must allow Miss Deering freedom to choose for herself where she would sit, Felicity, and as much as we found amusement in your temporary lapse of memory, I would prefer that you addressed your governess by her correct name in future."

"Yes, Papa." Felicity nodded, head down, laughter stilled, shoulders bowed. With the faintest reprimand he managed to cow her completely. *What a pity.*

Valentine eyed his daughter over the edge of the book, as if he would say something, and yet he seemed unable to find the words. He rubbed at his brow before settling the book firmly in his lap. "There once was a village in Wales, the villagers of which lived their every day and night in mortal fear."

A quick glance at Elaine, no more than a flicker of eye contact—long enough for Felicity to ask, "What did they fear?"

"The Widnot," he said.

Felicity pounced on the book. "You made that up."

"Right there." He pointed, a teasing light in his eyes.

"What's a Widnot?" She did not sound convinced, and yet there was laughter in her voice. A good sign.

Valentine cupped the top of his daughter's head in the well of his hand, a gesture so gentle it tugged at Elaine's heartstrings, the more so because the child did not appear entirely comfortable with her father's touch.

"You are not afraid, are you, that I would read to you of Widnots?"

Felicity shrugged, and peered at the pages of the book, as if he held secrets from her there. "Of crows I widnot," she said.

He chuckled. "The Widnot held the villagers prisoners in their homes with nerve-rending screams. Those who dared go out were never seen or heard from again, swept up in the talons of the great scaled beast."

"A dragon?" She guessed.

"Yes, a dragon. Shall I continue? Or will such a tale keep you awake?" He turned pages as if to search out a less frightening story.

Felicity stayed his hand. "I shall not be afraid tonight."

"How can you be sure?" he asked.

"Miss Deering will be in the bed with me."

"Ah." His lips quirked. "How fortunate you are."

"A fortune?" Mrs. Olive asked, hand to ear. "Did you say something about a fortune? Is it a story about lost treasure, then?"

Valentine exchanged an amused glance with Elaine.

"Felicity's fortune, lost to me," he said. "What say you, Mrs. Olive? Shall I find all three of you huddled together for safety in the morning if I read this dragon's tale?"

Mrs. Olive made an offended huffing noise. "I think not, sir. It is not the dragon's tail one must fear, but his teeth, and fiery breath."

"Shall we all of us sleep in one bed tonight for safety's sake?" he asked his daughter. "I might be frightened myself if I keep on reading."

Felicity giggled and fell back against her pillows. "No, Papa. We would not fit. Besides, it would not be proper."

"I should think not," Mrs. Olive said starchily.

"Surely dragons are not the best of bedtime reading, my lord," Elaine dared to suggest.

"Oh no, Miss Deering!" Felicity hopped out of the bed to comfort her. "Do not be afraid," she soothed, spreading her arms wide for a hug. "Dragons are only make-believe."

"So your father claims." Elaine embraced her warmly, remembering poor Felicity had no mother to fling arms about her.

She looked up to find the father watching them in that instant with longing, a yearning meant for his daughter, and yet the affection in his eyes rocked Elaine. *Too intimate his glance—too warm—too needy.* She did not know what to do with such a look. Her own father had never, to her knowledge, regarded her so.

Felicity had no notion her father examined her so intently. She was playing with a lock of Elaine's hair, curling the straight, dark strand about her little finger.

"I am not afraid, so you must not be either," the child said firmly.

"Why is that, when a whole village lives in fear?"

"Because, silly." She shook the lock from her finger, smoothing it. "There is always a brave knight, or a prince, who slays the dragon."

"That's right." Mrs. Olive nodded.

Elaine felt compelled to ask. "Never a woman?"

"I do not know." Felicity looked to her father for answers.

His lips quirked. "I heard tale once of a woman brave enough."

"A princess?" Felicity wanted to know.

Wharton shook his head. "No. A brave governess."

Felicity glanced from Elaine to her father and back again. "A governess?" she asked in disbelief. "Like Miss Deering?"

"Very much like our dear Miss Deering," her father said smoothly.

Mrs. Olive, brows raised, regarded Elaine as well. "Really?"

A smile tugged the corners of his lips. "She smote him in the wing."

"What, pray tell, became of the dragon?" Mrs. Olive laced the question with sarcasm.

"Oh, he roared a bit. But in the end he limped away and was never heard from again."

Elaine had to smile at that. She knew just the dragon he meant.

"Let us hope so anyway," she murmured.

Chapter 10

The story finished, Val tucked Felicity into bed, kissed her on the forehead, pinched out candles, and gathered up the book and a lamp to light his way. Stopping in the doorway, he bid them goodnight.

"Good night!" Felicity called sleepily from the depths of her pillows.

"Good night," Mrs. Olive sounded almost as tired.

Val glanced at Miss Deering, brows raised. "Sleep well, ladies."

"Sweet dreams, Lord Widnot." Her voice was gentle.

As if she knows my dreams are anything but sweet. Returning to his own bedchamber, he stripped off his clothing, wondering, *What sweetens the dreams of a governess?*

It had been a good day, despite the rain, despite Miss Deering's reluctance to work for him—an inconvenience—no more than an inconvenience. *I have known bad days.* This was not one by any stretch of the imagination.

It had been a good evening, Felicity and Mrs. Olive spellbound by the story, Miss Deering watchful, as was her way—the cat in the corner. *Might she go with us to Wales after all? This shy, watchful creature who has captured my daughter's heart far better than I? Dear Miss Deering?* He

would have to chase down a governess in Chester if he
could not convince her to stay. He had little hope of finding
anyone who would qualify for the post in St. David, or
anywhere else along the way, for that matter.

*She wore a look in her eyes this evening, my dear Deering.
Tucked in the windowseat, trying not to laugh. A look to
give me hope.*

If she was set on leaving him he had best prepare. There
was an advertisement to write. He sat at his portable secre-
tary to jot something down before he snuffed the candle,
before he removed his shirt and breeches. He thought of
Palmer. The rogue.

*I was once a drunken rogue. A dragon to be feared.
Lord Widnot.*

He wondered, as he undressed, if Penny could ever forgive him completely. He could not help but think of her at
this hour of the night, of the dream he had so long held of
her love. *Her lovemaking.* He laughed, the sound bitter.
*She never made love to me. I was too drunk to know it
was Eve.*

Ironic, really, this fixation with his touch-me-not. Doubly
ironic that he should attempt to employ another touch-me-
not—Miss Deering—who wanted no more to do with him
than Penny had in the end.

Women liked him, generally speaking. A certain stamp
of woman. Camp followers, whores, lightskirts. Felicity's
mother, Eve. She had relished his sarcastic wit, his irrever-
ent, neck-or-nothing style. He had won his share of tender
moments, heated kisses, passionate declarations, temporary
unions, fevered, futureless couplings.

He had no idea how to go about it, really, the business
of wooing a decent woman, of committing himself to a lasting love, marriage. His parents had a lasting marriage, and
yet they appeared to him to be mild-mannered examples
of tepid companionability. He could not imagine them fer-
vid in their affections, fevered in their lovemaking.

*I am nothing like them. Too little passion, and I have too
much of it.*

He snuffed the light, crawled between cold sheets, and
stared into the sudden unfamiliar blackness of the room's
corners, seeing a flash of faces, the lasses he had taken to
bed with him. He could hear the whisperings of their

voices—professions of ardor, of love. His not among them. He had wooed them but never claimed to love them.

The loneliest time of day, bedtime. Always had been. *Will it always be so?* Surely not, if he took a wife. A tricky business, to find a suitable wife. His father had wagged a finger. His mother had shaken her head, hands up, as if in defeat. "Decent women have been warned against you, my son, against your wild ways."

He had shrugged, said something flip and caustic, not knowing how to ask for help. How to tell them he felt the bumbling fool amongst decent women, destined to say and do the wrong thing. Decent women were reduced to babbling idiots by his sharp-tongued attempts at conversation; others simply avoided him. Those who did not braved an introduction in hopes of future acquisitions. They did not interest him; none had interested him but Penny, so kind to Felicity, so good with animals. She had embodied all that he was not—Lord Widnot—a man of scaly reputation. Even when he had been convinced Felicity was hers, when he was certain he had fathered her, Penny had been to him inviolate, with an innocence he did not know how to reclaim. The heroine out of a fairy tale.

Fool! What a fool I have been. Will there ever come a day, a woman I can respect who will find enough to respect in me? To love me? To wed a wastrel, a scoundrel, a once drunken fool?

He closed his eyes, closed his mind to the voices from his past that too harshly reminded him of his own failings. Still wondering, he fell asleep to dream of Miss Deering, the doe-eyed Deering on the run, and he with a pack of hounds that looked like dog-size dragons, after her.

Mrs. Olive snored, which kept Elaine tossing and turning in the bed beside a completely motionless Felicity, her mind on the question of her future. *No references! What is to become of me without a decent reference?* The possibilities seemed limited, and hopelessly dreary. No one of standing would take a governess without references. Must she turn to a different source of income? *Shall I write to Anne?* Her sister might be able to find her a position as companion to a lady of means.

She came to no clear answer before she drifted off. There

were so many good reasons to leave Wharton's party, chief among them all she had heard of his past. And yet some part of her kept coming up with reasons to stay—Felicity's plaintive voice sounding in her mind, Mrs. Olive's cheerful coaxing, Wharton's dry, disinterested sarcasm.

He is not what I had expected—not a wild, womanizing drinker. Tea. He wants tea, and cold rides in the rain, and bedtime stories of dragons and princes! She could not decide if he breathed fire or wisdom when he spoke to her, when her heart lurched at mere sight of his handsome, knowing face. *Can I be objective? Even sensible, serving such a man?*

It had been easy to resist Palmer. The beast. But how would she react if this beauty of a man turned his attentions her way? *Can I resist such temptation?* Would she?

Elaine rose to the first graying of dawn with a feeling of exhaustion when Mrs. Olive cheerfully prodded her shoulder. "Come, my dear. The master likes an early start."

Early start, indeed. The sun had yet to fully illuminate the sky. Felicity still slept the deep, impenetrable sleep of youth. Elaine stood at the window of the little room, brushing out her hair in the pale morning light as she stared down at the bustling street, her mind just as busy.

Manchester was known for weavers and spinners. There would be merchants here, country squires, a nobleman or two. She could find employment if she decided not to go into the wilds of Wales with Wharton. She wanted to laugh. The whole idea was too alliterative by far.

"What think you of the master?" Mrs. Olive asked.

Elaine set aside the comb. *Think of him? He is handsome. An enigma. I do not trust him.* She could not admit as much to the man's housekeeper. She parted a lock of hair into three sections from the crown of her head. "I have yet to form an opinion."

"You see him in better times, you do. I will say that. Tell me, do you know if you mean to come with us, Miss Deering, to Chester?" Mrs. Olive sponged her face and upper arms from one of the basins, groping for the linen Elaine placed to hand. "Or do you bid us farewell after breakfast?"

Elaine spread her hands and shrugged.

The older woman dabbed moisture from her face and

smoothed her fly-away hair. "Ask for a sign, my dear." She went to work on the arrangement of her lace cap. "I asked for a sign when I questioned whether I should come back to him."

"You left?"

"Oh, aye." The old woman glanced at the sleeping child, keeping her voice low and confidential. "The master was deep in his cups. Had cast off his friends, and sent the child away to boarding school, where she contracted an illness and must be sent home again, and all the while he was drinking himself into an early grave."

Here it is, just as I suspected.

Mrs. Olive stepped closer to whisper, " 'E shouted and raved when 'e was drunk. Not a pretty sight."

Father. Stumbling in late at night, brandy on his breath, hat and neckcloth askew, casting up accounts in the garden, on the stairs. Not a pretty sight.

"His parents were repulsed by his behavior. They'd no idea how to tame him. So, they took off for a tour of Europe. Left his lordship to sink or swim on his own, and he was sinking, my dear. I'd no wish to be around, you will understand. It was a dreadful business. Only Yarrow, that's the butler, and a few of the maids stuck with him through the worst of it."

Worst, indeed! Here are my greatest fears confirmed. Wharton is all that I have heard of him and more! He is, God forbid, my father all over again.

Shaken, she asked, "What sign did you get?"

"Hmm?" Mrs. Olive cupped her hand to her ear.

"How did you know it was right to go back to him?"

"Well, I heard he went nigh mad with worry over the child, didn't I? Betsy, the upstairs maid, told me how it was he had called upon Miss Foster, of all people, to sit with poor Felicity through the fever."

"Penny Foster? Felicity has mentioned her."

"Well, when I heard that *she* went to him, of all people, poor child, that *she* could forgive him after all that he had done, well, how could I do any less once he got shot and came off of the liquor?"

"Shot?"

"Oh, aye. Cupid shot him. In the leg." She lowered her voice. "To stop him, you see."

"Stop what?"

"Why, suicide, love. 'E was on his way up the mountain with poor fevered Felicity, ready to throw himself off a cliff. Thought she was dead, you see. Thought he had killed her, getting drunk while she was ill."

"No!"

"Oh, aye. Truth be told. God bless Master Cupid and Miss Penny for stopping 'im."

"Was he in love with her? This Penny Foster?"

"Aye, love. A canny one you are to ask. 'E still is, you see, if I read the signs right. But that is another story and another time to tell it. The wee one stirs." She whisked herself away, through the curtain, toward the bed, where she said, without taking pause for breath, "And how are you this fine morning, Miss Felicity? Ready to rise and shine?"

Elaine stood at the mirror, the braided tail of her hair grasped in her hand, the braided tale of Wharton's past harder to grasp. *Valentine almost killed Felicity? He had been drunk when she was ill? Oh, Papa, how can men so forget themselves?*

She watched the dear child stretch and yawn in the bed. She wondered about this woman, Penny, whom Wharton still pined for. What had Valentine done, that she must forgive him for?

Will I ever forgive Papa? Neatly rolling the end of the braid into a knot at the nape of her neck, she pinned it into place. *I cannot do it again. I cannot place myself in such a man's care.*

Felicity's touch startled her, the child's hand tucking into hers. "Your hair is very pretty that way." Felicity stared up at her, her eyes very wide, very blue. Her father's eyes. "Will you dress mine in the same fashion?"

"If you like," Elaine said. Her hands delved the soft, wildness of Felicity's curls. *Wrapped around her finger. I am wrapped around her finger.*

They went down to breakfast together, Felicity's hand in hers, their hair identically plaited, and in the mirror on the landing it was not Valentine Wharton's child she saw smiling back at her, but the mirror image of herself at a much younger age.

I cannot leave her, any more than I would abandon myself.

* * *

They were met in the private breakfast room by a booted and spurred Valentine, coffee cup in hand. *He does not look like a drunkard.* Elaine tried to imagine this handsome, well-built young man with speech and gaze and gait affected, to imagine this snide, self-confident creature ready to take his own life for his illegitimate daughter's sake. *His eyes are bright. His gaze intent and clear. How do I look to those eyes?*

"A word, Miss Deering," he said when she would have turned to the sideboard to fill her plate alongside Felicity and Mrs. Olive.

He went to the table, pulled out her chair, sat himself beside her.

Elaine tensed. *What is this?*

No reason to fear. It was only to push a packet of paperwork in her direction that he sat so close. The packet was sealed, the wax bearing the imprint of his signet ring. She looked up, puzzled.

He shrugged and leaned back, saying, "I've no wish to hasten your parting from us, Miss Deering, nor to encourage it, but if you are to leave today I wanted you to have a proper recommendation to take with you."

A recommendation! He means to give me a recommendation! Her heart sang. Her blood raced. She stared at the packet that bore his seal, in thrilled disbelief. *But he barely knows me.*

"Read it, if you wish," he suggested, handing over his butter knife, handle first.

She slid the knife neatly under the seal, the bulk of the wax left intact. An added cachet to present a recommendation bearing a nobleman's seal.

Unsure what to expect, she unfolded the page. His handwriting was bold, well-formed, and even. And in that hand he had written fine words: that she was "well-informed in all subjects", that she was "neat and tidy of appearance", that she taught deportment as well as the use of five languages, that she had "protected his child from the bullying of rougher students", and that in a time when he had been "unable to care for his offspring, indeed incapable of the task" he had been secure in the knowledge that his daughter was "safe in Miss Deering's capable hands."

A glowing recommendation! This once drunken rogue gives me a glowing recommendation, and I have done nothing but think ill of him. I am ashamed.

Tears sprang to her eyes, her future secured with no more than a few words on a piece of paper, and the imprint of a signet ring. She must not allow the tears to fall, to mar that perfect page, that blessed ink. She sniffed, and dabbed at her eyes with her handkerchief, and carefully folded the page into its original square. He stopped her thanks with a wave of his hand and a sarcastic, "So kind, I know."

"Yes," she said unevenly. "So very kind."

He leaned forward again. This time she did not flinch.

"And yet there is a price," he said.

Her brows rose. Would he ruin the gesture?

He pinned her with sky-blue eyes, spread his hands, and said in an awkward rush, as if unaccustomed to asking favors, "I am hoping that in your gratitude you will agree to stay with us until we reach Chester. It is the last place before we enter the wilds of Wales in which I think I might be able to contract another governess to take your place, and I should prefer to look there rather than here in Manchester."

Elaine nodded, tucked the precious gift of his personal recommendation into the deep pocket of her gown, and said quietly, "You have done me so many kindnesses, how could I say no?"

"You've only to open your mouth and utter the word," he said sardonically.

She looked him in the eyes. "I know very well how to say no."

He seemed for a moment left speechless by her bold regard. Then he nodded. "And so you do, for I have witnessed it, O mighty dragon slayer. Forgive me. I ought not to scold. Rather, I should thank you kindly,"—his eyes twinkled mischievously—"and encourage you to eat a hearty breakfast, and compliment you on the arrangement of"—he glanced at her hair—"my daughter's hair. It is very pretty braided thus."

Clever. He is a very clever man. Kind and clever. He words everything just so, bending me to his will, and I cannot take offense, even at his compliments.

Chapter 11

The streets of Northwich were lined with ancient, timbered houses. There they stopped to change horses and to eat. They did not linger. Clouded skies grew menacing. Just beyond the village of Hartford, before they had sighted the crossroad to Tarporley, great, fat drops of rain pelted the windows, just a few at first, and then a steady thump at the top and sides of the carriage, like insistent, drumming fingers.

"Rain again!" Mrs. Olive said in disgust. "I begin to believe we shall never see the sun. Poor master! Poor lads! Never a full day dry."

"Was that thunder?" Jumpy as a cat, Felicity peered out at the rain.

Elaine knew how unnerved Felicity became in storms. Valentine Wharton might relish this sort of weather. Not so, his daughter.

"It was raining that night," Mrs. Olive whispered to Elaine. *That night Cupid shot Valentine. The night a fevered Felicity had come close to dying.*

Elaine had surmised something unsettling was connected to stormy weather. At school, she had taken to sitting with Felicity on lightning-laced nights, least her cries wake the other girls. On the worst nights, when thunder boomed, shaking the very walls, Felicity had trembled and wept. Elaine had sung songs to her, and cradled her in her arms, and wondered what nameless terror Felicity refused to speak of. She suggested that they must all sing a song now, rather than allow her charge to sit wide-eyed on the seat beside her, flinching with every distant boom, every distant flash.

Felicity refused, pressing face and hands to the window as the rain pelted down harder than before. "Tell Papa he must come in." So plaintive was her tone, so agitated the rocking body, that Elaine slid down the window at once, calling, "Sir, the child needs you."

He took one wild, wet look at his daughter's face and called to the coachman, "Hold!"

His mount given over to one of the footmen, he dashed inside, rocking the coach, stirring them to make room. Mrs. Olive tucked away her knitting. The slate Elaine and Felicity had been spelling words upon found a home in the door pouch. The three females bunched their skirts out of the way of the sudden dripping bulk of Valentine Wharton.

Droplets splashed everywhere, from the opened door, from his hair, from coat lapel and capes. His boots shed wetness upon the floor boards, dampening skirt hems. He swept off his hat and poured a small river from its brim. The wings of his overcoat brought the weather with him. He slid the coat from his shoulders and held out the sleeve ends to Elaine, as if it were customary for a governess to undress him without so much as his asking assistance.

Because it was the sensible thing to do, the dripping sleeves would soak her skirt otherwise, Elaine obliged him, equally wordless.

The sleeve was cold. The soaked gloves she brushed against warm. He stripped them from his hands, slung them over the edge of the doorpouch to dry, and ran his fingers like a rake through sodden hair, sweeping it sleekly away from his brow, from the blazing blue of his eyes. A trifle overwhelmed by his sudden flurry of purpose and presence, a trifle overawed by the power of his gaze, Elaine sat back as far as she could, hands folded in her lap. She diverted her gaze from the intensity of blue eyes and dripping hair by looking down at gleaming boots, at the puddles gathering beneath his heels, but found her gaze drifting upward, along the soaked seam of his pant leg, deep blue, the muscles straining against wet fabric. The muscles of an outdoors man.

She glanced up. He watched her, an amused tilt to his lips. She looked away at once, cheeks fired. Felicity leaned into the damp shelter of her father's arm. "I am glad you decided to come in out of the rain."

For the briefest instant their eyes met again, as the child attempted to snuggle closer. "You must not lean on me, love. I am soaking wet."

At once the child's face took on a wounded look, as if he went out of his way to hurt her. *How tender she is. How much she strives for his approval.*

Elaine handed Valentine Wharton her lap blanket. He took it with a grateful nod, and using it first to dry his hands and face and hair, to blot his legs and wet boots, placed it at last in the hollow of his arms, and beckoned to his daughter. "Come. Now I am dry."

But Felicity had perched herself on the seat between Elaine and Mrs. Olive. She shook her head, lower lip outthrust.

"Go on now," Mrs. Olive prodded. "Go to your father. Don't be a goose."

Felicity shook her head the harder.

Valentine frowned, so forbidding the look, Felicity cowered, burying her head in Elaine's lap.

"Come, come, little one. Chin up," she coaxed gently. To no avail.

Wharton's mouth pinched tight. He wore for a moment a defeated expression.

"Let us sing a song." Elaine suggested briskly. The suggestion hung tremblingly upon the air. It seemed an idea destined for failure.

"A song?" Valentine's brows rose.

"Surely there is a song we all know."

Elaine felt the chill of the missing blanket, shivered with the sudden nearby crack of another flash of lightning. The horses whinnied. The coach trembled with the boom of thunder that followed. Felicity let out a muffled screech, fingers clutching, head burrowing under Elaine's arm.

"A lullaby?" Valentine Wharton asked evenly, and without awaiting their approval, this generally snide and sarcastic young man broke into slightly off-key song without the slightest sign of embarrassment.

"Sleep, my love, and peace attend thee, all through the night."

Chapter 12

"It is not night, Papa." Felicity sat up to object.

Thunder rumbled. The child cowered.

"I know, my love," Val said gently, "but we shall pretend. Simply close your eyes and imagine yourself swaying in a great cradle."

Lightning flashed. She closed her eyes, shook her head, opened them again. "I am not a baby, Papa," she protested. "I shall be ten in four months' time, in case you had forgotten."

Mrs. Olive made a little noise of objection. Miss Deering leaned close to whisper a reprimand. Felicity ducked her head with a stricken look. Val hated to see it, hated to think his daughter feared him, or his opinion of her, as she feared storms.

"I have not forgotten how old you are, Felicity," he said, his attention unwavering. *I have not forgotten why you fear storms.* "All too soon you will be a young lady chasing away a bevy of suitors."

Her eyes brightened. She did not flinch when thunder rumbled again. "A bevy, Papa? Do you think so?"

"I am sure of it," he said. "But for now I should like to

pretend you are my baby girl and sing you a lullaby." He held his arms wide.

Felicity pushed away from the haven of her Deering's arms, shifting sides of the coach, so that she curled up in his arms, asking, endearingly, "Sing another verse, Papa. I am sorry to have interrupted."

He met approval in Miss Deering's eyes as he sang several verses, cuddling his daughter. Mrs. Olive felt emboldened enough to join in. Soon the carriage swelled with their combined voices.

Felicity fell asleep, her head nestled in the hollow of his shoulder, the rocking motion of the carriage and the good cheer of song lulling all of them, Mrs. Olive's eyes closing, Miss Deering's lashes fluttering now and again, no matter how much she tried to hold them high.

Val did not want to fall into jouncing, cramped, uncomfortable dozing himself, and so he shifted his arm beneath the borrowed lap blanket, that the weight of Felicity's head might not send it to sleep, and asked his daughter's dark-eyed governess, "Are you cold?"

She sat directly opposite him. He had not missed the hunched position of her shoulders, the way she rubbed her hands together. He knew she was cold and asked out of courtesy—out of a need to know how forthcoming she would be with him.

She started to shake her head.

He eyed her through lowered lids. "Do not say no when you mean yes, my Deering."

Her lashes fluttered down again, in surprise, not weariness. *My Deering! She was not his. What possessed him to say such a thing?*

"I do apologize," he said abruptly.

At the same time she blurted, "I am a little chilled."

They eyed one another uneasily, and then he made it worse by suggesting, "You are welcome to warm yourself with my overcoat."

Her eyes flew wide, focusing on the coat flung across his knees.

"It is not so wet as it was. And quite warm."

"Have you not need of it, yourself, sir? Your leg—" she hesitated, gaze falling, "I mean—your clothing is wet."

"I appreciate your noticing," he said in jest, provoking another startled look from long-lashed eyes. "But I will survive. Take it. Please, I beg of you. Unless, of course, you wish to share the warmth."

She eyed the overcoat with alarm. Indeed he made the suggestion in jest, knowing she must refuse so unorthodox an arrangement. *It amuses me to test the depths of her prudery.*

"I could not, sir."

Of course, she could not.

"It is large enough to drape both our knees. An unusual suggestion, I know, but sensible. Must I wake the child to retrieve your lap blanket?"

"No."

"Shall I prod Mrs. Olive to share hers?"

She turned to consider Mrs. Olive, whose head had fallen back upon the seat. Her mouth gaped on a whistling intake of sleepy breathing.

He smiled, and she, seeing the smile, must smile as well.

Her gaze fell. "No, thank you. I would not bring discomfort to anyone. It is why I said nothing."

"Oh, but your body cries out." *She is too easy to provoke. The alarmed look returns.* "You shiver," he clarified. "Come, do not be silly. I cannot sit watching a woman suffer when there is so easy a solution."

IIc meant to hand her the coat, to cease his teasing, but she stopped him in reaching for the coatsleeve, her grasp halting, tentative, fear in her eyes.

"It will not molest you," he said impatiently.

Her gaze flew up to meet his, shocked. A terror he could not mock looked out at him from the deep dark wells of her eyes. *Damn Palmer. What did the bloody twit do to her?*

"No, of course not," she agreed. *Any young female who valued her employment must agree.*

"That is what you were thinking, was it not?"

She blinked, shook her head.

"Do not say no when you mean yes, my Deering," he said brusquely, his tone mocking, bruised by her willingness to think the worst of him.

Her chin fell. Her gaze. Her lips were pursed. She let go her hold on the overcoat.

"You ought not call me that."

True. I ought not. Funny how it persists in slipping out of my mouth that way. "Quite improper, I am sure," he said. "Now tell me about Palmer."

That earned him a direct look. She shivered.

Is it cold or Palmer that troubles you, my Deering? "Had his way with you, did he?"

So intently she regarded him, as if with sharpest gaze she might discern all that lay in his heart, the core of his intentions.

"No, he did not!" she protested with quiet heat.

Oho! Methinks the lady doth protest too vehemently. He arched an eyebrow, unused to so delving a gaze, so ardent a denial—intrigued by it. "No? Tried to have his way, then?"

She nodded.

"You managed to stop him?" he drawled. "The scar on his dragon's wing?"

She nodded.

"Hit him, did you?"

"Bit him. Hard enough to draw blood," she murmured, her regard no less focused, no less wary.

He laughed, pleased to see she looked tempted to break into a smile. *So, Palmer tried to palm her, did he?* He thought of Penny, of the way she had once looked at him— love in her eyes—trust. It added fuel to the fire of his temper.

"Likely no more than he deserved!"

Felicity stirred, her head turning against his shoulder, a mewling noise issuing from her throat, as her fingers curled against his lapel.

"She suffers nightmares," he said.

"I know," Miss Deering said quietly.

Of course she knows. How many times has she been awakened by my daughter's cries?

"She told you why?" he asked brusquely.

"No, sir. Only cried out for her papa."

"And for Penny?" He knew all too well the sound of those cries.

"Yes."

"She raised her."

"So she said."

He settled his daughter more comfortably against his shoulder, settled his own temper, with a flick of the wrist rearranged his coat, flung the tail-end of the garment across the skittish little governess's lap.

She smoothed the weighty, lined fabric across her lap, not refusing, as he had thought she might. He eyed the hills and valleys her knees and his knees made, warmed by the sight, by her acceptance of his warmth. And then he looked away, watching the rain-drenched countryside rumble by, wondering what life might have been like had it been Penny Foster's knees opportunity warmed. He imagined what it might have been like to be married, to have the little one just born his own rather than Cupid's.

"She married my best friend," he said.

She watched him from the far side of the coach.

Dear Miss Deering. Not Penny. It will never be Penny. He gave his head a shake.

"Ah!"

She tried to sit still, to sit straight, despite the pitch and yaw of the coach, his coat tugged between them, connecting them, one side still damp from the rain, the lining warm with his body's heat. She was uncomfortable with that connection. Her whole body spoke of that discomfort.

"You probably know the whole of it," he said bitterly.

"The whole of your life? Your daughter's? I hardly think so."

"My shame?"

She blinked, confused.

He glanced at Felicity, at Mrs. Olive, to be sure both slept. "Come, come, Miss Deering. You know my daughter's circumstances, her history?" *That I left a poor girl pregnant? That I credited the wrong woman with the child's birth? She knows, I can see it in her eyes.*

Miss Deering's gaze slid often to the child as she spoke, her concern that they might be overheard equal to his own. "I know that she was illegitimately conceived."

So harsh those words, even when whispered.

"That her mother died in childbirth." *Eve. Poor Eve.*

"That you were unaware of her existence until your return from France, and that she was well cared for by Penny Foster."

He exhaled heavily. "And thus you know the whole of it, just as I said."

"I think not."

No?

"I also know that you took her in when many a gentleman of your position and status might have denied her very existence. I know that you see to it she is well educated, and that you seem very fond of her—indeed, that you may have risked your own life, and reputation, in providing for her."

He said nothing. There seemed nothing to say, only a moment of unspoken communication as she looked him in the eyes, gaze steady.

"She fears me."

"Felicity?"

He nodded.

She shrugged. "She has yet to learn to know you."

The coach lurched through a rut in the road, throwing their knees together, no avoiding it, and she did try to avoid it, her legs, her body held stiffly away from his beneath the swaying lap blanket of his coat. Sleeves trailed about his thighs. The furred collar rested soft as a lap dog beneath his hands, and he found himself not at all averse to bumping knees with this dark-eyed governess who saw far more than he had expected.

"I beg your pardon," she gasped.

Their eyes met, her dark, fearful gaze sliding away.

"You've no reason to beg me for anything," he said.

She made no reply.

"No reason to fear."

He could see her reflection, the pale, peaked forehead, the dark wells of her eyes, watching, judging. She had judged him in absentia for many months. For as long as Felicity had been in her care.

He laughed, a dry humorless noise that fogged the window, eliminating for the moment that pensive reflection. "No need to bite," he promised. "No fire left in this old dragon."

He was happy to see hint of a smile touch her lips, and in his belly, embers stirred, an unexpected heat.

That he attempted to put her fears to rest surprised Elaine. That he noticed her concerns at all was queer enough. That he was savvy enough to discern the reason for her uneasiness was startling. That he cared to make the attempt to calm her was nothing short of a source of wonder. In its own way, an additional concern. *I am used to fading into the background, the focus of none but my pupils' attentions. Valentine Wharton does not seem content to allow me to so fade—just as Palmer was not content. It worries me. I must not allow him to catch me unaware—alone—vulnerable. I will not allow it. Never again.*

She closed her eyes and feigned sleep, but could not allow herself to doze on the way to Chester, through the rain, not while he was in the coach, not while his coat graced both their knees, his legs swaying against her gown, brushing and swaying with the rocking of the coach no matter where she tried to direct her own limbs. The roads were not so well paved here as they had been in Leeds.

He did not doze; neither did he choose to talk. His prerogative. *Not my place to start a conversation. I would have no idea what to say to him.*

He simply turned his head to the window and watched the countryside slip by, and now and then glanced down at the child with a softening of his features, and rearranged the arm that cradled her head.

Once he looked Elaine's way, a quick glance that passed over her in the manner to which she had grown accustomed— as if she were not really there. She took some comfort in that, and at the same time felt a pang of regret, for when he had talked to her, when he had asked her about Palmer, he had looked at her as if he saw her, really saw her, as if her answers mattered. It had made her blood race, and her fear rise, and she had felt very alive in that moment, very aware.

But now his head, the fair curls drying—angelic curls—and he no angel—no saint in this Valentine—turned away. His piercing, blue-eyed gaze remained fixed on the landscape, and she faded into her familiar sort of oblivion, watching him, weary of the rocking. She came to life in a knifeblade-sharp awareness whenever the coach rocked and once again their knees banged, his boot tops brushing the fabric of her skirt.

What thoughts provoke this deep breath? One might almost call it a sigh. The heat of it momentarily fogs the view. He seems, in the very sound of that exhalation, in the unrelenting concentration of his gaze, unhappy.

She did not know what to make of him—she didn't.

What she did know was that he knew she both feared and respected him, and that the combination of emotion, like the uncontrollable banging of their limbs, left her feeling rattled from the roots of her hair to the tips of her toes.

Chapter 13

The coach stood waiting for the Whartons outside one of the mullion-windowed shops that made up the heart of Chester's commerce. Valentine and Felicity were buying tea.

Mrs. Olive sat knitting, while Elaine made every effort to take interest in a book. But the words swam on the page. The sentences made no sense. Her gaze kept drifting to the doorway. *Whose coach will I sit in next week, or the week after that? And when I am Mrs. Olive's age, whose coach will I sit in then?*

With a sigh she marked her place and patted the comforting bulge of paperwork in her pocket. Wharton's unexpected gift. She need not fear too much her future with such a letter to recommend her.

Across from her, the clicking knitting needles stopped. "That gentleman in the rain, at the school."

Does she mean Palmer?

"A former employer?" The old lady tugged at a ball of yarn.

"Yes."

"Wanted you back, did he?" The needles resumed their

work. In and out, in and out, dark gray yarn weaving itself into light.

"Yes, he wanted me."

"And yet you did not go with him." She tugged at the truth as gently as the wool.

"No."

"Was he cruel? Did he beat you, my dear?" In and out, in and out, she would knit the truth together, the light and dark of Elaine's past.

"He did not beat me."

"Was he then a drinker with bad temper?" Click, click, click. She came to the end of her skein.

Elaine shook her head.

"Aha." Mrs. Olive bent to pluck up fresh yarn and with the skill of much practice, started fresh thread. "Tried to have at you, did he?"

Elaine sat silent, humiliated, unable to so much as nod.

"It is a common problem when one is young and pretty," Mrs. Olive said matter-of-factly, as if that should prove a comfort.

Elaine regarded her reflection in the window of the coach. Not pretty. She had never considered herself pretty. Her features were too ordinary. Too serious. It was the reason her mother had suggested she consider taking a position as a governess.

"My sisters inherited all the looks of the family," she said.

"Did they now?" Mrs. Olive glanced up, as if to study Elaine's face thoroughly for the first time.

"Two of them have found husbands."

The older woman smiled, and pushed her stitches further down the needle. "And none to offer for you but a married man?" She tsk-tsked, head shaking, and smoothed the wool that draped her knee. "No need to blush, dear. Men will not trouble you so much when youth's bloom fades."

So pale her cheeks in the windowpane. *Has my bloom already faded?*

"And do you mean to stay with us, my dear? You need not fear the master would do anything untoward."

"I am glad to hear it. But . . ." Elaine sighed, and pleated the fabric of her skirt with nervous hand. "It is not that."

"What, then? Pray tell me. Perhaps I can set your mind at ease."

The truth was best. "My father was a drinker."

"Aha. The master's history with spirits has you worried?" Mrs. Olive looped yarn about her finger. The click of the needles commenced with renewed fury. "And have I discouraged you?" she fretted. "I have, have I not? In telling tales, blabbermouth that I am."

Elaine watched the busy harvesting of twisted wool. She envied Mrs. Olive her ceaseless productivity, never a wasted moment. "I knew," she said, "before you said a word. There were others before you to tell tales of the notorious Valentine Wharton. It always figured into my reluctance to accept his offer."

Mrs. Olive shook her head and tsk-tsked under her breath. "And yet, not a drop has he touched in the longest while. It is everywhere to tempt him, at every inn, and posting house, and dinner with friends or family. You see his fixation with tea."

"My father swore he would never touch the spirits again, that he would not be tempted by cards."

"Broken promises?"

She nodded.

"Poor dear."

"Poor father. It ruined him—health and wealth. He was doubly cursed. Left us in straitened circumstances at his death. We had no true idea of the extent of his debts, you see. Numerous debts. It is the reason I was forced—" she stopped, frowning, "the reason I chose to become a governess, and my younger sister a lady's companion, and my two elder sisters have married not out of love but necessity."

"Honorable choices. Is it many siblings you have?"

"Five."

"Oh dear, I have dropped a stitch." Mrs. Olive unraveled a row to repair her error. "And how many are brothers to see you are cared for?"

"All girls."

The needles talked while the two fell silent.

"We six have always been very close and can rely upon one another in the direst of circumstances."

"How fortunate. Then you've nothing to worry you?" She did not sound convinced.

"I have been blessed with education enough to support myself."

"I know what you are going through." Mrs. Olive smoothed her errant yarn. "As a young woman I was widowed, my husband killed in the navy." Such sadness in her eyes. Such loss.

"I am sorry to hear it."

"I thought I would never recover. Could not imagine myself happy in anyone else's company. I counted it a blessing we had no children."

"Why?"

"Why, without encumbrances I was free to take up service."

A blessing? She counts that a blessing?

"Mine has been for the most part a happy life, a comfortable one. I wish you the luck I have had in finding positions where your services are respected, needed, and well paid for. I think you would be hard-pressed to find a better master than his lordship."

"Yes, but . . ."

"Mind you, I understand your hesitation, but you must not allow fear to rule you. Master Wharton is the best of men sober. His parents are wonderful, quiet people, and you love the child. You cannot be certain you will find anything better, and most likely will land in the middle of something very much worse. Trust me in this. I have had a great many years to see that every employer has his weaknesses, every mistress her faults, and as for children—well—you might end up in a position where you are expected to teach a score of rambunctious little monsters, who evidence not the slightest lick of respect or affection for you."

A bleak picture. But no more time for discussing it. The bell jingled on the shop's door and out stepped dear Felicity, a bundle in her arms. Valentine held the door for her, another parcel in hand.

Felicity ran to the coach, and when the footman jumped down to open the door for her and helped her with the step, she would not relinquish her package. "It is for Miss Deering," she insisted.

"And had you luck in finding some tea?" Mrs. Olive called out to her.

"Oh, yes," she said. "All sorts of tea, and this for Miss Deering."

"What's this?" Elaine asked, taking the parcel thrust into her hands.

"She insisted you must have it." Wharton leaned in the door.

"So that you may remember us when you go away," Felicity said.

"Open it," Mrs. Olive encouraged.

Elaine attempted to do just that, but the twine that tied the parcel thwarted her shaking fingers.

"Allow me." Wharton sank into the seat across from her and snapped the twine in gloved hands, as if it were nothing. With the twine something inside of Elaine snapped and fell away.

As the coach was set in motion, as masses of paper packing unraveled, Felicity, unable to contain herself, said, "It is the most clever little teapot, Miss Deering."

Elaine lifted the teapot, a short, squat, brilliantly colored pot of a shape more Oriental than English.

"A dragon, do you see? A Chinese dragon."

It winds about the pot—and you, dearest child, wind just as tightly about my heart.

"Such a bright color it is," Mrs. Olive said. "But I do not see a dragon."

"Here. These are the eyes, and here the mouth."

"Do you see it now?"

"Aha. A bit of a puzzle. All pattern. The whole pot covered. It does not look at all like any dragon I have seen before."

Indeed it did not look like an English dragon, too stylized, all triangles and circles, glossy eyes rings of color on color, its wrinkled snout doglike, and from its mouth the spout poured red and gold fire. The same stylized red and gold flames coiled inside the set of four cups, and on the outside, stylized clouds billowed.

"Do you like it? Papa agreed that you could not help but think of us every time you used such a thing."

How archly Valentine Wharton observed her reaction. "Not afraid of this dragon, are you Miss Deering?" he drawled.

Afraid I am captured entirely. "No, sir," she said quietly. "No fire in this creature without hot water in his belly." She turned the pot, the porcelain so cool she wished she might press it to the heat in her cheeks. "A magnificent dragon. A kind and thoughtful gift. Unforgettable."

"You will not forget me?" Felicity asked with a child's urgency.

She cupped the child's cheek, far warmer than the teapot, far dearer. "How could I ever forget you, Felicity? Impossible, my dear."

How pleased she seemed to hear it. How difficult it would be to find another position where her pupil tried so hard to please, where her employer noticed she existed.

Wharton cleared his throat. "We mean to walk the walls of Chester, Miss Deering, and Felicity wondered—"

"Yes, will you walk with us?" Felicity asked anxiously. "Please? Mrs. Olive does not care for such activity."

Mrs. Olive nodded. "Too hard on these old joints to be climbing stairs, my dear, much less walls."

"Please, Miss Deering. Papa tells me they've a great wall in China, a huge wall that stretches across the country, like Hadrian's wall in Scotland, which I told him of, for he would know what you taught me."

"Would he?" she asked quietly, and for a fleeting moment she allowed her gaze to turn in his direction, to meet the distant sky blue.

"Why does man feel compelled to build so many great walls?" Mrs. Olive wondered aloud. "Keeping people out. Keeping people in. Seems a great bother."

His lordship said softly, "We all build walls, Mrs. Olive."

"If only to establish boundaries," Elaine added quietly. Valentine Wharton was watching her. *Too many walls? Or not enough?*

"You will join us?" he asked, as he shook out the paper he had purchased, along with his tea. And on the page there were rows of black boxed advertisements for the hiring of staff. "Or do you prefer to spend your time studying these?"

Elaine stared at the advertisements a moment. Dreams, hopes, walled up in black ink. Unknown monsters?

"I should like to join you," she said.

"How far will you go, Miss Deering?" Valentine drawled.

"They stretch entirely around the city," Mrs. Olive warned her.

"All the way to China?" Felicity asked with a laugh.

Elaine gave one of the child's fair curls a tweak. "Not quite so far, but perhaps all the way to Wales?"

"My dear!" Mrs. Olive's knitting fell, forgotten. "Do you mean it?"

"Hoorah!" Felicity crowed. "Papa! Miss Deering means to stay!"

"Indeed," Valentine said, as he folded the paper, tucked it away, and looked at her with blue eyes not quite so distant as before. "I don't suppose we shall be needing this, then, shall we?"

Chapter 14

Val led the way to the top of the city walls, by way of the recently built Northgate. A plain classical arch, it lifted them above the crack of the whip and the rattle of coach-wheels, above the bustle of the Pied Bull's coal-blackened brick and pale quoining. One could see the arched windows and ribbed spires of Chester Cathedral, the clock tower above the town hall. The fullness of spilled ale and tobacco smoke wafted from the open doorway of the Blue Bell. He had glanced into the fermented gloom, turned his back on temptation, once again said no.

Felicity ran ahead, Miss Deering following, her skirt brushing his boot tops. *I need a drink. A woman.* He looked away from the sway of hips, the sway of dark skirts.

To his right, far below, glittered the narrow swordblade blue of the canal, overshadowed by the wall, boats and barges lined up, waiting, wood creaking on water, ropes slapping. Voices echoed as the great wooden doors to the locks creaked wide, water sluicing. Another world. The air smelled damp, of wet stone, mud, and lapping river. *I am a man on a wall looking down. Removed. Distant. So small my shadow on the water.*

Ahead of him his daughter scampered, her voice like

birdsong, her delight evident in peering down first on one side of the wall and then the other. Between them, Miss Deering. Black dress, black bonnet. Blackbird, wings folded. Not a crow. She had not the voice of a crow. *Bird in hand?*

She told Felicity why a city should require walls that one might walk—the Romans, the Roundheads—explaining how standing above one's enemy placed one at an advantage. *An advantage to have her, to know she goes with us to Wales.*

Beyond the canal stretched fields—empty fields. *As I am empty. Lonely.* Beyond the fields, the Welsh hills. Not so far now.

"Imagine men on horseback, lances held high," she said. "Imagine tournaments of mail-clad knights, standards fluttering in the breeze."

He could see it, just as she described—not so long ago. *Broomstick for a horse. Mop handle for a sword. I rode off on a dream and woke up at Waterloo. How does my daughter envision herself? What childish dreams does she dream?*

He turned to gaze at the young lady who had decided he was not the dragon everyone painted him—at least enough so that she stayed with Felicity. *What dreams does a governess dream?*

She spoke to his daughter, taught her something in every sentence, as if it were the easiest thing in the world, the two of them chattering, smiling, happy, his daughter asking question after question. Miss Deering answered patiently, seriously, as if the answers mattered, as if his child mattered—dear Deering.

Ahead of them rose a round tower, part of the wall, the top crenelated with stony teeth. Felicity ran in through an open archway, the tower's throat. Miss Deering turned to look over her shoulder, and from her lips her breath drifted white. *Dragon's breath.* Their gazes met, in her eyes a question.

"Let her go," he said.

"She loves ruins," she said fondly, waiting for him to catch up to her.

"That explains it then."

"What?"

"How she could love a ruin like me."

She walked beside him in pent silence. "She loses herself in the past. Do you, my lord?"

He was momentarily taken aback. "A good question. But tell me, Miss Deering, do your thoughts move behind or ahead of you?"

Her brow puckered. "I do not follow."

"That's good, as I would not lead."

Her eyes narrowed against the sun—or was it his teasing ways?

He relented. "You consider a future with us."

"Yes. Would you now object to it?"

"Not at all, and yet your hesitation cannot be deemed flattering."

Her gaze fell. "It is not my duty to flatter or fawn."

"True enough, my Deering," he drawled. "But are you sure we are your cup of tea?"

Her lips curved, almost a smile, an expression that hinted of more, of unspoken layers of meaning. A ghost of mischief wafted across her features, thin as the heat that wafted white from her lips. "How could I leave, my lord, when you would give me Darjeeling in a dragon teapot?"

He smiled. How indeed. In witnessing that drift of emotion, feeling stirred. *I know now why Palmer wanted her.* Like the breath of the dragon, the knowing warmed him.

Chapter 15

Valentine Wharton's gaze sent a chill down Elaine's back whenever he looked at her, a strange biting chill that, quite perversely, turned her insides liquid and warm. It made her long to say yes to him, no matter the question. Thus Felicity's mother must have felt, fallen prey to this heaven of blue eyes and quirking lip.

"Pemberton's Parlor," he said. "That's what they call this tower."

From above them Felicity waved, hands urgent, as if she would lift them. "Come up. Come up," she called.

"Coming," they responded in perfect unison, intimacy in the exact timing of their mutual response. Valentine Wharton laughed, his laughter completely devastating, all flashing white teeth and a sound of boyish mischief. Elaine smiled self-consciously and looked away, toward the tower's dark entrance.

"Who is Pemberton? And why a parlor?"

He laughed again.

He captivates me. Does he know? Has he any idea how much he moves me with his humor, his laughter?

His voice echoed as they stepped through the archway. "Originally the tower was so large it straddled the wall, and anyone who passed this way must walk through it. Goblin's Tower they called it."

"Oh?" His arm formed an arch as he held the door, and she must step beneath it to enter. *Is he Goblin Tower? Or Pembleton Parlor?*

"Goblin was taller, and much more imposing." He seemed to read her mind, to find her amusing.

They stood almost face to face. "You know this story—how?"

His smile widened, teeth flashing, his expression as impishly youthful as the sound of his laughter. The door, released, allowed darkness to close in on them.

"My father told me. His father told him."

"I see." She climbed, listening for the sounds of his following, imagining the lad this man had been. She could hear the change in his breathing as he climbed.

"Pemberton was a mayor who could not afford to rebuild the tower to its former glory, and so the Cestrians named this paltry little replacement his parlor in jest."

"And was he amused?"

He laughed, his voice echoing in the stairwell, the noise surrounding her, making her knees go weak.

"I've no idea," he said. "I only know that three generations of Whartons found it funny."

"Four," she said, and pointed.

At the top of the stairs Felicity stood laughing, arms akimbo.

And so we find towers to talk about, my daughter and I. Miss Deering's doing—she makes it so easy.

She stepped back from them when they reached the top, allowed him and his daughter an illusion of space, of privacy.

"What is the name of the next tower?" Felicity asked.

"Bonewaldesthorne's," he said, surprised he remembered, surprised to hear his father's voice in his memory. They had chuckled at the name. "A fairy book sort of name. A troll's name."

Felicity nodded, pleased he should say so. "Or a wizard."

"Yes, a wizard." They stood a moment in companionable silence.

Unwilling to allow their conversation to die, he asked,

"Would it surprise you to hear this tower once stood at river's edge?"

"Really?" She stared over the edge of the wall at the tower's foot, and then toward the river, grown distant.

"The river shied away. A second tower had to be built." He pointed down the curtain wall that connected the two.

"Why did the river move?" she wanted to know.

"Perhaps it grew bored with one bed and chose to sleep elsewhere."

She laughed.

He glanced in Miss Deering's direction. The governess gave no sign of having heard his remark. *Perhaps best. It was, on second thought, too risqué a remark for a young girl's ears.*

"I know the real reason the river moved," his daughter said confidently, unaware either of his regret or any need for it.

"Do you?"

"Miss Deering taught me. You see, the river stirs the mud, which it can carry when it runs, and which it drops where it grows tired."

He laughed. "And so it was weary rather than bored, was it?"

"Silt. It is called silt." She looked pleased to know the answer.

"Very good," he said, the praise meant for Miss Deering as much as for his daughter. "And now I am grown tired and would silt." He perched on the wall that looked down toward the river.

Miss Deering laughed, a choked-off, stifled laugh, as if she were afraid he would disapprove of the noise. Silted up, that laugh. *She has been listening all along, pretending not to hear.* He wanted to urge her to let her laughter flow, let it babble like the river as the locks were opened. He refrained, cautious where Miss Deering was concerned.

Must not alarm the rabbit. Must not allow her to suspect I am drawn to her. She will hop away. He focused on Felicity, slid wayward glances at the governess. He must remember she was only the governess.

A bad habit, to long for a rabbit—forbidden game. He wanted to laugh.

"Who's in the mood for a cup of tea?" he asked, and

was met with enthusiasm from both of the damsels at the top of what was left of Goblin Tower.

Darjeeling in a dragon teapot. He could not repress a smile.

Chapter 16

He avoided them on the following day, or so it seemed to Elaine. As if he had allowed himself to get too close, and now must withdraw. *Perhaps I imagine it. It is his habit to ride horseback rather than in the coach.*

And yet he seemed averse to look in their direction, riding with a fierce intensity, he and the horse breathing plumes of white when they stopped to eat a bite in Wrexham beneath the glory of the church's fine, soaring, pinnacled steeple. He made little conversation, even less eye contact. A curious creature. *He lives in a tea cup. And as much as it confuses me, it confuses his daughter more.*

Elaine set to work with a slate and a row of sums, and turned the maths into a game using the numbers of hills before them, and in them a certain number of quarries and mines, and into those mines a certain number of colliers must climb. In Wrexham they counted smoking chimneys and brickworkers and tilemakers, and before the sun began to wane Felicity claimed the sums rather simple to figure, rather than the insurmountable obstacles she had earlier declared them.

As they topped a hill Wharton called a halt in a spot where the road looked down upon the silver ribbon of a river in a valley where the pale drum towers of a castle encircled a boxy courtyard, a lovely prospect.

"We will be putting up for the night at the home of old family friends," he called from horseback, the bay gone golden in the light of a setting sun.

"Friends, Papa? Who?"

"The Biddington sisters. The eldest, Charlotte, has a son named Robert who is close to your age."

"Do you see the castle, Papa?" Felicity pointed out of the window.

Taller than the trees that backed its haunches, the castle's crenelated towers caught the light of the setting sun, the stone bleached bone colored, the series of six squat towers accentuated, tall walls boxing them. An emerald green slope of sheep-dotted pasturage led to a grove of young elm, and beyond the park and gardens that hugged the house, a wooded area. Like a lace apron on an overbearing stone fortress, a magnificent, gleaming, white wrought-iron gateway beckoned.

"That is Caxton, where the Biddingtons live."

Felicity's eyes went round. "We shall spend the night there?"

"Indeed. If they will have us."

"Really, Papa? Are your friends princesses?"

"No, my dear. Sisters to a baronet, heiresses to a great fortune."

Marital prospects, Elaine thought, and for the first time that day understood why Valentine Wharton did not so much as glance her way.

The carriage scattered sheep and dusted the oak and elm flanking the road. An avenue of lime led to the white gates. Exquisitely ornate cast iron dogs sat atop tall metal columns. The gates themselves were a gleaming white froth of metal vinework, flowers, and birds. A coat of arms crowned the arch opening onto groomed lawns, graveled walks, rows of trees—evidence of a fortune housed here, an age old fortune, wealth and prosperity on a scale Elaine had never before had the privilege of observing so closely.

Past a bowling green they rattled, neat kitchen gardens boxed by yew, a sunken deer fence. The remains of what had been a moat led them into a pointed archway that pierced the north curtain wall beneath the slitted eye of an ancient lancet window. Within the castle's encircling stone arms they rolled, into the manicured green of a vast courtyard.

The inner walls of the castle were draped in honeysuckle vines. Windows gleamed with dying sunlight. Arches at one end of the quadrangle offered cover to a walkway. A blue-faced, diamond-shaped clock high on one of the towers marked the exact time of their arrival. An inscription chiseled in stone over a smaller doorway read

THIS   :   NEW   :   BVILDING   :
AND : THE : TOVER : WAS : BVILT :
ALL   :   IN   :   ONE   :   YEARE   :   BY   :
THOMAS   BIDDINGTON   KNIGHT
1636

Neat in matching uniforms, crisp white aprons and collars, a long line of servants awaited them in front of a columned, porticoed doorway. The footmen and Mrs. Olive were led away at once, in the direction of the servants' quarters, across the echoing length of cobbles that edged the courtyard. Valentine Wharton was directed past the gauntlet of servants.

Elaine hesitated by the coach, uncertain of her direction. *The servants' entrance—Will I ever grow accustomed to it?* Felicity clung to her fingers with the urgency of fear. "You will stay with me?" she begged.

Elaine gazed down at the neat part in the child's hair. *Caught between worlds, both of us. Poor child.* Taking a deep breath, she drew her charge into step behind Wharton, past the row of curtsy-bobbing, forelock-pulling servants. *The illegitimate child and the governess. Who are we to be bowed to? The fallen in birth and means. And yet, we will not sink to the servants' entrance. Not unless he orders me to it.*

The Biddington sisters greeted Valentine with warm affection: touching his arm, kissing his cheek, looking upon him with unquestionable delight. Three slender sylphs in flowing gowns, their hair was fine and curling, ashen brown, their eyes the same bewitching blue gray, and their arms long, slender, and grasping.

With cool, distanced curiosity, they regarded his daughter and her governess, their warmth reserved for the world and hierarchy they understood. Their voices remained cultured and cordial, but it was with a visible change in demeanor they regarded walking evidence of how the boundaries of that world might be breached.

"This is your recently discovered child, is it not?" one sister asked.

Felicity squeezed Elaine's hand a little tighter.

Valentine turned, with a fleeting look of shocked surprise, as if he had not considered how Felicity might be received. The emotion was quickly veiled. He spoke with deceptive ease, as if to make introductions was nothing out of the ordinary, as if Felicity were welcomed wherever he went. "My daughter, Felicity. And her governess, Miss Deering."

"You keep a governess?" Surprise in the question, their very hair seemed to twitch and stir in unspoken agitation. "Indulgent papa."

Overindulgent, the woman's tone seemed to imply.

"Indeed, a most fortunate little girl." Soft, well-groomed hands held Felicity at arm's length for inspection.

Felicity kept her head high, and yet she shrank back against Elaine's skirt.

"What a pretty thing."

"Blessed with her father's eyes." *Cursed with her mother's shame.*

The thought hung unspoken. An awkward little silence bloomed, and then, curls bouncing, their heads seemingly alive with snakes instead of hair, they led the way through an echoing entryway lined with columns, the Portland stone floors dotted with black marble diamonds. The sisters spoke all at once, polite attempts to fill the silence, to banish all awkwardness.

A three-headed Gorgon of babble.

Hot water was called for, the order resounding in the stairwell.

"You will want to freshen yourselves."

"Perhaps a change of clothes."

"You will want food to take the edge off your appetite."

"And a glass of wine?"

Accomplished hostesses, they would make their guest comfortable, leading him up the grand modern cantilevered staircase topped by enormous green marble columns and decorated with gilded swags and a painted frieze of roundels in the ceiling. Chinese porcelain flanked a carved lion and a unicorn. A case clock chimed on the landing.

"We've a bottle or two of the burgundy that pleased you so much."

"I shall just ring the bell."

"Summon my footman." Valentine Wharton charmed them with his heart-stopping smile. "I would share a cup of a wonderfully rich Assam Souchong I stumbled upon at a surprising little shop in Chester."

Again the silence. *They are surprised.*

"How lovely," they clamored, their cheer too marked.

"I understand tea is fast becoming the vogue in London."

"Perhaps the child would like some milk and poppy seed cakes."

"What did you say her name was?"

"Felicity."

"Yes. Would she like to play with a lad her age?"

"It is all right that the child should play with Robert, is it not?"

"But of course." The eldest forced a smile. "I am sure dear Robert would welcome the company. I believe he is in the Old Maid's Tower."

"The governess must be shown the way." *Shown the way, out of the way. Into the old maid's tower.*

Faces from the past lined the walls, richly dressed, lace at their throats, faces that spoke of wealth, prosperity, and power. Faces that found them wanting—the illegitimate child and the governess.

Elaine stiffened her spine. *I know my place, my station.*

She beckoned Felicity. Together they turned to follow the maid who answered the bell's summons as though afraid to speak or look upon her mistresses. She bowed her head and turned her face to the wall as directions were given, and then her soundless black slippers scampered up the stairs ahead of them with unseemly haste, as if in flight, as if in fear—or perhaps, in all fairness, as if she simply had a great deal of work to do.

Chapter 17

The lad, Robert, had two great armies of carved ivory and ebony wood chess pieces disposed in fighting position across hills, and valleys of green baize. "You will not touch them, if you please," he said, "for I have been very careful in their arrangement, and I am not at all certain that a girl would know how to go about playing at sieges and battles."

Felicity, too shy to protest and unused to the company of little boys, hung back wordlessly.

Elaine eyed the two of them a moment before she asked, "Have you paper and paints? Watercolors? We shall entertain ourselves that way, and you may continue your battles uninterrupted."

The nanny, an older woman with little real control over her charge, thought that a splendid idea and went at once to fetch the paints.

Settled at a table, brushes in hand, Felicity continued to eye the lad with unabashed curiosity as he made explosive noises and mimicked the sound of trumpet calls and the anguished cries of the injured and dying.

With little hope of distracting Felicity entirely, Elaine suggested, "Perhaps we could paint bits of landscape for our kind host's battlefield."

Felicity, who eyed their "kind host" without the slightest evidence of appreciation, brightened. "Do you mean groves of trees, or a lake?"

"Precisely. We might do walls, and haystacks and barns or cottages, even a castle if you are feeling ambitious, and we shall cut them out and devise a way to make the pictures stand up."

Elaine did not mention that she and her sisters had built just such a landscape for their dolls when she was a girl, nor that they had been far more enthusiastic playmates than the lad who glanced their way only occasionally. In watching the plight of a child trying to insert herself where she was not really wanted, for the first time she fully appreciated her good fortune in having been blessed with loving sisters.

"That sounds splendid," Felicity said. "That way the wounded will have cover to retreat to."

"Care to join us?" Elaine asked the boy, who edged toward them, his battle sounds fallen away.

"What do you know about retreats, and taking cover?"

"My father is a marksman," Felicity informed him with the same belligerence that had faced down Miss Bundy's posture perfecter.

"Really? What color is his uniform?" He sounded unconvinced.

"Bottle green. With a black velvet collar trimmed in black braid."

"The Experimentals!" He was awed, and Elaine, who knew little of her employer's history, found herself listening intently as the lad sat down and took up a paintbrush and did his best to impress them with his knowledge of regiment and rank, battlefield victories and failures.

Thus they got along for the better part of an hour. A landscape of painted trees and a stone barn took shape, and a lake shone blue between two hills of green baize, and the children laughed and chattered and got along rather famously despite their stand-offish beginning.

"Where did your father fight?" the lad asked as he put the finishing touches on what appeared to be the ruin of an old castle.

"Vimiero, Vigo, Waterloo," Valentine Wharton's voice startled them from the doorway. He lounged against the doorframe, looking very much as if he had been there for some time. *How long has he stood listening?*

The children abandoned their paintbrushes and ran to him. The lad asked, "Did you shoot many men, sir?"

Felicity echoed the intriguing question. "Did you, Papa?"

As curious as she was to hear the answer herself, Elaine felt it an inappropriate topic for children. She opened her mouth to say as much, but Wharton did not hesitate in his response.

"Regrettably so," he murmured. "It is what one does in battle. But I will tell you the very worst thing one does in battle if you will show me what you are doing."

The worst thing in battle?

He glanced at Elaine, as if he could feel the heat of her stare. As the children led him in, his lips twisted in a teasing smile. He winked, as if he knew her fears and would allay them with his customary charm.

Elaine watched him with all the brooding attention of a protective hen over a clutch of eggs, and now and then he shot another look her way and smiled a teasing smile.

The children were pleased to show him their landscape with such a provocative promise to motivate them, pleased with his every sign of interest as he drew them out in detailing how they had managed to make the pictures stand on wooden legs, admiring the little island on their painted lake.

All the while Elaine imagined the worst things soldiers did, the worst picture he might paint for tender young minds.

"You must tell us the worst thing one does in battle, my lord," Robert reminded him.

Felicity went very still. Elaine felt her jaw tighten.

He picked up a black knight and said, "The worst . . . undoubtedly the worst thing about battle is the loss . . ."

Loss of limbs? Loss of life? Loss of human decency?

"Of all one leaves behind." His gaze met hers, a playful, teasing look. *And yet sad. How have I missed this profound depth of sadness in him?*

"You see . . ." He cupped his daughter's chin in the palm of his hand—such a gentle touch. "I might have seen my daughter born and known her mother had died had I not been with Moore in Copenhagen."

How intently Felicity listened to him, how unblinking her regard.

Elaine loosed pent breath in a sigh.

"I might have celebrated her first birthday or seen her first steps, but for the fact that I was on my way from Sweden to Spain."

Great tears welled in the child's eyes. Her father handed her his handkerchief, a snow-white flag of truce between them. His regret was genuine. Moisture gleamed unspilled in his eyes as his daughter's tears flowed even more freely.

"I might have heard her speak her first words, indeed read her first letters, but for the fact that I was following Wellington into Belgium."

Felicity fell into his arms, weeping upon his shoulder. He held her close, patting her back, murmuring in her ear. *He wins my heart, along with his daughter's.*

Elaine coaxed the lad into a conversation about his ancestors' roles in distant battles, that Felicity might recover herself without an audience. When father and daughter had time enough for the wiping away of all trace of tears, the two joined them.

"Enough of battles, lad," Valentine said. "Tell Felicity and Miss Deering what the Biddington and Myddulph mottoes are, for I think them fine words, well worth remembering."

Robert Biddington Myddulph drew himself up proudly. "Do you know Latin?" he asked Felicity.

Felicity looked at Elaine uncertainly. "Only a very little," she said. "Miss Deering has only just begun to teach me."

"Can you translate *In veritate triumpho*?"

Felicity's brow puckered. "Something about triumph."

Very good, Elaine thought, and waited for Valentine to say something—to notice the child who so desperately wished to win his approval. And when he made no move to do so, she said the words for him. "Very good, Felicity."

Her praise was lost as the boy Robert spoke with an attitude of superiority, "I triumph in the truth."

"Wonderful words," Wharton said, with a smile for the boy. "And the other?"

Can you not see the look of longing in your daughter's eyes? Elaine wanted to shout. *You must recognize her intelligence as much as her grief.*

"*Sublimiora petamus.*" Hands on hips, the boy uttered the phrase like a challenge.

Felicity threw a desperate look in her direction. "I don't . . ."

"*Petamus* is to seek," she said. "Now, can you guess what *Sublimiora* means if you take the first half of the word?"

"Is it something like sublime?" Felicity asked.

"And what does sublime mean?" her father asked, head cocked.

"The exalted," Felicity said.

Valentine shot a look at Elaine, surprised his child should know. "Very good," he said, the praise meant for both of them.

"Seek the sublime." Felicity blushed with pleasure, and Elaine felt the same bloom of pride her student experienced, for there was a hint of the sublime in this moment of truth and growing understanding between father and daughter.

A bittersweet moment, for it occurred to her that such moments of pride in her student, in her teaching, might be all of the sublime that was left to her.

And in watching Wharton as he left them to return to the world that had once been hers, a world that no longer welcomed her, Elaine's heart ached all the more as she thought of her father and mourned what might have been.

Chapter 18

It is time to take a wife. Time to beget an heir. Valentine sat amidst the Biddington sisters as the first course was carried in on silver trays and knew it was true. He must look for a suitable match. Someone of good reputation and excellent family, like these excellent sisters. Someone attractive enough to grace his table, like Penny. He could not long for her forever. Indeed he had not thought of her for several days.

Curious.

He had not thought the trip could distract him so completely. He had Miss Deering to thank for that. Too much time worrying over the governess had left him little opportunity to dwell on the past.

Penny. He could not clearly conjure her face to memory.

It is best that I forget. Someone else must insist hot tea arrive at his elbow throughout the meal, rather than the butler with his wine carafe. He shook his head, held a hand over his glass, and considered something other than the spirits' mellow wash down his throat.

Kisses. He would think of kisses. The sweet taste of a woman's willing mouth. He looked at the eldest Miss Biddington. Not that mouth. No, another mouth, another smile. He would never forget the reluctant bloom of Penny's all too infrequent smiles. Like Miss Deering. The quirk of her lips never meant to be alluring, and yet he could not stop his eyes from fixing on the plump plush of her lower lip. An honest mouth. A generous mouth.

He thought of Palmer. Was this how his inappropriate desires had started? Over dinner, as he watched another woman's lips? Miss Deering tucked away upstairs, with the children—gone but not forgotten. He must not think of her, vowed to himself he would not think of her—and then, of course, could think of nothing and no one else.

He would look for a woman of interesting conversation, keen wit, a more than adequate intellect. *Miss Deering.* He shook his head. *The boy. It is the lad makes me think this thing.* Such pride the ladies take in knowing he carries on the name. Did his own mother once hold such hope for the future? Nothing but chaos and shame had he left in his wake. Even Felicity—dearest child, dearest motherless child.

It is time to take a wife. One who understands. One who can love my ill-begotten child. One who holds hope for her future.

And from into this self-directive again rose thought of Miss Deering, wise, understanding Miss Deering, who loved his daughter almost as much as he.

Elaine sat in the housekeeper's parlor at a small drum table before the fire, a privilege Mrs. Olive made sure to thank the housekeeper of Caxton for not once but many times.

"But of course," Mrs. Corwen said with a laugh. "You did not think I would relegate you to the heat and noise of the kitchen, did you?"

"Very kind of you to welcome us to your comfortable parlor."

Laughter and the clink of crystal and china sounded from the formal dining room, just below, an arena Elaine had once thought to have dominion over.

How little thought I gave then to where the housekeeper ate.

She knew better now the descending order of privilege and authority that had once ruled in her father's house, much as it did in this castle. Gardeners ate in the potting shed, from buckets they carried away from the kitchen after the kitchen staff ate in the kitchen, but only after the house staff had been served in the great hall at a long wooden table, seated in descending order of power and importance. And this service was commenced only after the house-keeper had been taken a tray in her own private parlor, said tray not to arrive before the sweet and cheese course had been delivered to the master or mistress and their guests in the formal dining room.

And visiting governesses?

Governesses did not belong in the kitchen any more than they belonged in the formal dining room. Elaine was to have been served a tray in her room—a lonely prospect—but when Mrs. Olive was asked if she cared to join the housekeeper of Caxton in her private parlor by the same maidservant who delivered the tray, Elaine asked, "May I join you?"

The maidservant looked at her as if she considered the request quite odd.

Mrs. Olive, eyebrows raised, had asked, "Are you quite sure you wish to join us, my dear?"

Stepping down. It is seen as a step down to make such a request. Relinquishing power. And yet what power have I?

"I do not care to eat alone," she said. She did not tell them she had only picked at the tray they had given her earlier in the day, the soup gone stone cold by the time it was carried up from the kitchen.

Dear Mrs. Olive looked as if she sympathized with her plight. "Do you think Mrs. Corwen would mind terribly?" she asked the maidservant.

"I shall just go and ask, shall I?"

Elaine's tray of food was congealing by the time she returned, but it did not matter.

"Mrs. Corwen would be quite pleased to have you," the maidservant bobbed a curtsey. "She is in a bit of a fluster making sure the parlor is tidy, Miss, so we shall walk slow, if you don't mind, so as not to arrive before she is satisfied."

"Oh dear," Elaine said. "I'd no intention of making her go to any trouble."

"No trouble, miss. She called Tibbs and Gibson to do the dusting."

Elaine closed her eyes a moment in chagrin, realizing how she had upset the natural order of things. Now two of the maids had been called away from their duties.

In the end, though Mrs. Corwen's room was tidied to perfection, and the trays of food delivered and arranged just so for them to begin their meal, she did not get to eat after all. Just as Mrs. Corwen finished saying a blessing over food fast reaching room temperature, a rap sounded upon her door. The underbutler interrupted to say, "Miss Deering is required in the saloon, Mrs. Corwen."

"Is Miss Felicity ready to be sent away to bed, then?" Elaine rose from the brief comfort of her chair and turned her back on a much desired plate of roast beef, potatoes, and peas.

"I do not know, but you are to come at once, if you please."

And so she was led away, without a bite of dinner, to the saloon, where she was not, after all, required to take Felicity to bed. The final course of brandied pudding had yet to be served, and the children had been promised the treat. Valentine Wharton was in the midst of declining his portion of the dessert when she entered.

"Miss Deering!" He seemed pleased to see her. "Felicity has just been telling these ladies that you are proficient at playing the harpsichord. They are most anxious to know if you would mind playing for us."

Of course she could not refuse him, her employer, and never had Elaine been more conscious of the fact.

The harpsichord occupied one end of the saloon, a room that despite enormous echoing grandeur entangled its occupants in a reaching, curling, artfully repetitive pattern of trailing vinework. The ceiling was a golden bower of intricately plastered and carved timbered boxes, row upon deep row of them, edged in overlapping esses of fine gold scrollwork. A deep blue ground and more fine, vinelike gold elegantly framed cameo paintings of mythological characters, a false heaven of them.

The walls, deep buff with gold-trimmed, white wainscoting, came alive with a vivid forest of tapestries and twisted, gold-framed rows of pale-complected ancestors. Gold vine sconces twinkled with candles, the moving light giving the faces in each portrait a sense of movement, as though they turned to watch her pass along the vine-laced Aubusson rug, blue flowers and green leaves on a green ground. Gilt-wood pier tables where coffee and cakes were being served on inlaid vinework satinwood drew her eyes only momentarily. It was the harpsichord that dominated the room, a beautiful, golden, gleaming masterpiece of inlaid walnut.

It was the most beautiful instrument Elaine had ever seen. Without a note played it seemed to sing. Exquisitely fine inlaid wood trailed pale golden vines and birds and fan-shaped shells below and above the starkly black and white keyboard. More vines trailed from inside the instrument, the length of the tightly stretched harpstrings, around the strut that held open the case.

The maker's name was entwined, and the date, 1742. Elaine felt as if the tendrils must wind themselves about her fingers, her arms, her waist as she sat to play a prelude by Bach, one of Corelli's concertos, then Mozart. The sounds she coaxed from vibrating strings became part of the background while the pudding was served, conversation continuing, the music but one more beautiful element in a room filled with beauties designed for the satisfaction and entertainment of those who could afford the very best.

Her stomach growled as the pudding was put to flame, cut, and eaten, coffee and tea served in transparently thin porcelain along with equally thin and brittle conversation. The plates and silverware were cleared, and still she played, her fingers, like the vinework, clinging to the harpsichord, become a part of it. As the diners rose from the table she played, haunting and sweet, a song of unrequited love that spoke of the loneliness squeezing at her heart.

"Who, I wonder, was the delightful Lady Greensleeves to cast off her love discourteously?" her hostess murmured.

Elaine looked up from the keys, the sudden movement dizzying her, or was it finding Valentine Wharton's gaze fixed upon her, that made her swoon? The pale golden curls of his forelock overshadowed an unexpected sadness in his captivating blue eyes, as if the instrument she played was his heart. His sadness had nothing to do with her, she was quite certain, a sadness unnoticed by the women who sought to entertain him with polite conversation.

They wondered in bright, unaware voices if Valentine would not care to dance. Elaine wondered hungrily if she might beg a cup of tea and a biscuit.

Valentine Wharton blinked, straightened his shoulders, gave a brisk nod. He danced with fine precision, but he did not look as if he enjoyed himself, any more than she enjoyed the unladylike gnaw of hunger.

Bemused by his expression, Elaine became the background again, an impetus to moving feet, nothing more. She played and played, song after song as they pranced and pirouetted until she began to feel light-headed, the sensation most disturbing, the music blurring before her eyes. She missed a note, could not find the right keys. When she tried to stand, the room spun into darkness.

Chapter 19

Val reacted at once, ignoring his partner's surprise at mis-played notes, at dance steps gone awry. He rushed to catch Elaine as she fell. Into his outstretched arms she slid, as if her bones were turned to water, as if she belonged there.

"Smelling salts!" He lifted her in his arms, thistledown of a woman, the warm weight of her no trouble in his arms, no trouble at all, and he was beside himself with worry—with alarm. Was she ill? Had she been ill all along and he too blind to see, to notice? Too caught up in the past to properly observe what was right under his nose?

Not smelling salts but a burning feather the butler brought at once, efficient man, while his mistress latched onto Val's arm and wondered, "Is she ill, my lord? Given to fits of fainting? Is there danger of contagion?"

Val could not respond in any way but to say, "She is only newly come into my employ," while his heart raced with concern, for Elaine Deering had come to mean more to him in the few days they had been together than he might have expected—and yet he knew so little of her.

His dancing partner, completely ineffectual in assisting with the crisis, felt compelled to say, "How curious that she who has been sitting should faint away while those of

us who have been whirling about the room and are quite
light-headed with dancing, should be nice as ninepence."

He ignored her.

"Are you ill, Miss Deering?" he leaned close to ask. Her
lashes fluttered. She sighed and opened her eyes. "Shall I
send for a physician?"

She shook her head weakly, seemed to immediately regret
having done so, a pained expression crossing her features.

"No physician. It is nothing. Only that I have not eaten.
It leaves me light-headed."

Not eaten? She had played music for them for hours on
an empty stomach?

"Why did you not eat?" Anger rose in him that she
foolishly brought this upon herself, not eating.

"No time," she said, and pressed a hand to her forehead
as if it ached. "I was asked to come immediately."

Of course. No time. They had called for her in the very
moment when the servants were sitting down to dinner.

"Send to the kitchen at once for broth, toast, tea." He
ordered the butler. "Have it delivered immediately to Miss
Deering's room."

"Yes, sir. And will you require a footman to carry her
up?"

"I shall carry her myself," he said, and lifted her without
any other word of warning, to the dismay of all concerned.

"Valentine!" the Biddingtons sounded appalled.

The governess herself protested. "Please put me down. I
am sure I can walk." She made weak struggle in his arms.

"And I am damned certain that you would topple over
the moment I set you down," he scolded, unswayed by any
of their opinions. "Do not make this any more difficult
than need be, Miss Deering. I shall just carry her to her
room," he informed the others. "Felicity will open doors
for me."

"Yes, Papa." She rushed ahead of them, pleased to be
involved, her eyes round with concern.

His hostesses nodded open-mouthed.

"Arms about my neck, Miss Deering," he instructed.

"But I do not think—"

"Do not think, Miss Deering; only know that it will be
easier for me."

"Yes, sir." She obliged him, the soft roundness of her

breast pressed to his chest, arms sliding about his neck, her breath quick and warm against his chin. The ribs of her stays, at odds with his own ribs, prompted thoughts of unlacing such an obstruction—dangerous thought with her face so close to his, the almond-scented soap smell of her hair teasing his nostrils.

She would not look at him. Her lashes fluttered downward, dark against the milky pale of her skin, milk staining strawberry as he shifted her in his arms and tightened his hold—and thought of drinking her in.

"That's more like it," he said briskly, as if he were completely unaffected by her proximity. He could not allow her to know he wanted to kiss her. Too selfish a desire. Inappropriate, she would have said. Highly inappropriate. And yet, he could not stop looking at the satin smoothness of her lower lip, could not ignore the pull of her clean, soapy smell and the seductive weight of her body against his.

"Do you faint often without food, Miss Deering?"

She nodded, a quick bob of her head. He reveled in the warm roundness of her rump against his stomach. He must remind himself that she was ill. He must not take advantage. She was his daughter's governess. She had been taken advantage of by her last employer, and she had left him. As she would leave him. *As Penny left me.*

"You need not worry," she said. "I am generally very careful."

"Of course you are," he murmured, and at last she looked up at him, a quick, startled meeting of their eyes, not careful at all, her mouth so very close to his he thought of nothing so much as passionately kissing her as her breath warmed his cheek. It had been too long since he had kissed any woman, indeed wanted any woman but Penny.

As quickly as she had looked at him, he looked away and thought of Felicity, illegitimately born of just such thoughts turned to action.

His daughter held the door wide to her own room, saying, "It is too far to climb the stairs, Papa. Is she all right?"

"Miss Deering is faint with hunger. Given a bit of food she will be well again." He steeled himself with fresh resolve in stepping into his daughter's bedchamber, a woman in his arms.

"I am hungry, my dear. That's all." She echoed his words, voice trembling, vibrating against his chest, her uncertainty vibrating all the way through him.

A dragon's appetite stirs in me, and not for food.

"Light-headed," she said, as he leaned down to deposit her on the counterpane, feeling light-headed himself as he released his hold on her.

"Like when I spin and spin with my arms out, and then I fall down and the whole world is spinning?" Felicity's voice seemed to come from a distance for in that moment Miss Deering looked into his eyes, candlelight caught, a sparkling flare of light in the depths of that visual exchange that fizzled through him like a Roman candle against the darkest night sky. *As I am spinning now, her body the fulcrum, the heat of the dragon in her eyes, the scent of her desire rising to consume me.*

Her mouth was moving, the dark lashes fluttering down to hide what he had discovered in her eyes, in the musky scent of her.

"Very much the same, my dear," she said.

Like our desires, he thought as he fell back as one stunned. He made a concerted effort not to glance in her direction again, not to respond to the dizzying tune of her voice, the dizzying loss of the heat of her body. He made every effort not to think of how completely light-headed he wished to render her with kisses and the roving passage of his hands. *Palmer all over again. Damn Palmer! Damn my own inappropriate desires. I want a wife, not simply a lover, do I not? A mother for Felicity.*

He needed the governess to be a governess. No more. No less. For the sake of his daughter he dared not risk losing this fine and beloved influence in his daughter's life so soon after convincing her to go with them to St. David. For the sake of his soul he dared not lose himself to the searing heat of the dragon of desire.

Chapter 20

Elaine missed the strength of his arms, their warmth, the scent of him. His soap, his cologne, grew faint. She shivered.

"Papa has sent for something to eat." Felicity plopped herself down on the edge of the bed even as her father withdrew.

"Are you thirsty?" he asked, and not waiting for her answer he directed his daughter to fetch a glass of water.

"I do apologize," she said, feeling very awkward sitting on the edge of her bed with a gentleman in the room. Especially this gentleman, who was by all reports no gentleman at all. *And yet—and yet—he is all that is gentlemanly to me.*

"And what would you apologize for, Miss Deering?" He took up what would seem to be his favorite position, leaning nonchalantly against the doorjamb. *To keep his distance. Though there is nothing distant in his eyes.*

"I apologize for creating a scene." She took comfort in decorum, finding safety in it. Unable to voice her deepest reasons for contrition. *For inappropriate thoughts. For wishing. For feeling. For dreaming fairy tale dreams.* "I apologize for not eating as soon as the tray was brought."

"And why did you not?"

"Silly, really." She shook her head, voice dropping. "I—I did not wish to eat alone."

His brows rose, as if he had never considered that she ate alone.

And now she tripped over her words, fearful he might think too much of her mention of loneliness, that he might misinterpret her meaning. "There were always so many of us at table—at home, at the girl's school."

Felicity, who slid under his arm, glass of water in hand, said, "One could not feel lonely with so many people to talk to. Not for long."

For a moment he stared at her, as if seeing her, really seeing the ache of her loneliness, for the first time.

A savory smell announced the arrival of the promised broth. He fell back from the door to allow Mrs. Olive entrance as she cooed, "Here is a bite to eat my dear. And faint with hunger you must be by now. Did no one think to feed you?"

A last look in her direction again, a quick look, no emotion perceptible in that look, and Valentine Wharton was gone. Her knight in armor—gone, no more dragons to slay.

Felicity ran to stop him. "No story tonight, Papa?"

Elaine could hear the thin reed of her voice over the clatter of crockery and silverware, as the tray was arranged on her lap. She saw him shake his head but did not catch his remark.

Elaine silently rejoiced to see how close the child stood to her father. Her charge began to feel more comfortable in his company.

Again he shook his head, and she could not make out the low rumble of his voice until her own name caught her ear, and in his turning a little more in her direction she heard him say, "Miss Deering must have time to repair. Now, go and keep her company."

How kind he is! How unexpectedly considerate!

On the following day, Miss Deering assured Val that she was perfectly able to continue in their travels.

"I would not in any way cause delay," she assured him over breakfast.

Val tipped his head to regard her, his neat, tidy, dark-feathered bird of a governess. Her cheeks were no more wan than usual, but then, it occurred to him that the black she wore completely overpowered any pale color her cheeks might possess.

I've no intention of testing your stamina, my dear Deering.

"Of course you would not," he said. "But you see, it is not really your doing that we are delayed. A dressmaker arrives at Caxton today, from Chester. She comes highly recommended, and it has been brought to my attention that Felicity is fast outgrowing everything in her traveling trunks."

"Indeed, she is."

"I did not think you would argue the point. I am told that you and Mrs. Olive have let out hems and seams as far as they may be taken."

"Yes, we did."

"You need not have troubled yourselves. I have every intention of seeing my daughter adequately clad."

Her chin dropped a notch. "Yes, sir."

"Too brusque." His father's voice in his head offered reprimand. *"You wound all that is tender, Val."*

He softened his tone. "You will bring her along to the sewing room when she is summoned?"

"As you wish."

"I trust you will not find it too fatiguing to give the woman your measurements as well?"

"My measurements?"

Fear in her eyes. I have grown accustomed to its absence. "I mean to see you newly clothed, Miss Deering."

How severe the set of her mouth. She means to argue against it. I knew she would. She thinks of Palmer again, and I would not have that. That is not why I would see her better clothed. Is it? "I outfit all of my servants in fresh livery when they enter my employ, Miss Deering."

"I am not a servant, sir, and it is customary for a governess to provide her own clothing."

Ah, she would have him believe it pride then, not fear? Pride was easily addressed, perhaps even undressed. "Turn back your cuffs, Miss Deering."

She stood a moment, unmoving, before she thrust out her hands and did as he asked.

He knew they were worn. He had noticed her wrists, that

she tried to hide her cuffs' frayed condition with discreetly stitched lines of black, grosgrain ribbon. He took her hands in his, hands that trembled a little at his touch, that telling sign rocking him with sudden surging desire, a roaring heat that flamed low in his groin.

He took a deep breath, turning those delicate hands, delicate wrists, examining more closely her handiwork, not so much because he required a closer look, but because he wished to hold onto the feeling inside himself, to feel the flutter of her pulse. "Tidily done. A fine, even stitch. I see you've a mind for economizing." He released her, the tension between them palpable. "But worn, nonetheless."

She nodded. Head bowed, tucking her frayed cuffs behind her back. "Yes, sir."

It had not been his intention to shame her, nor to in any way belittle her. And yet he knew that the reason she could not meet his eyes had less to do with the energy that coursed between them at his touch, and more to do with what he said. He went on, his tone very gentle, "You will understand that just as I would not have Felicity appear ill-clad, neither would I have it appear that I have in any way cut corners in seeing to her care, clothing, or education."

"No, sir."

"I know it is the fashion for governesses, ladies' maids, and companions to receive their mistresses' castoffs."

Elaine Deering looked up at him, her backbone, her shoulders very straight. "I apologize if I have in any way brought disgrace to your household."

"Disgrace! You are a complete and utter disgrace!" One of his father's favored complaints, and he would in no way echo the insult that still pinched him raw.

"Nonsense," he barked. He closed his eyes, inwardly stilling his father's unhappy voice, stilling his own impatience. "You are, Miss Deering," he said carefully, gentling his voice, his tone, "unfailingly neat and tidy in your appearance. A picture of calm, grace, and manners. I can only hope my daughter takes note in learning how a lady should present herself. I have no quarrel with your taste or decorum, but as there is no mistress of my house to endow you with unwanted clothing, I mean to see you clad in the same manner and frequency as the rest of my staff. And in a color other than black, if you please."

She is not pleased. The tabby with back arched.

"Black is most practical, sir. It wears longer than any other color."

"But entirely tedious, Miss Deering. Funereal. I think too much of mourning."

She glanced down self-consciously at the black of the gown he had begun to detest sight of. She wore a stricken look in saying, "I am very sorry. What color then, would you choose for me?"

So quietly she asked. Too quietly. *She does not consider my offer a kindness.* Stifling impatience he said, "Your choice. I entrust the cut and color of three dresses to your own discretion."

"Three, sir? Surely one is enough."

"We go to the seaside, Miss Deering."

Her brows rose, as though she had no idea as to his meaning.

"Sand. Salt. Sun. All unforgiving to fabric, Miss Deering. You will require at least three changes of clothing in order to maintain your customary tidiness."

She bent her head to him, as any servant would. With the gesture the gulf between them widened, a development he had neither anticipated nor desired.

Dress fittings accomplished, the dresses to be sent by post as soon as they were finished, Elaine saw nothing more of her employer that day. She was not asked to dine in the housekeeper's parlor. No request was made for her to play the harpsichord.

When music rose from the drawing room it was one of the Biddington sisters who entertained Valentine Wharton.

Elaine felt bruised and forgotten, inadequate, unwanted, her poor mended dress too shabby for such a house, such a company of ladies.

She must remember her place. She, the ill-clad governess who must be fitted for dresses rather than disgrace a gentleman among his peers. *How embarrassing, degrading, to be clothed by a gentleman of Valentine Wharton's stamp. Surely it smacks of impropriety?*

And yet, Mrs. Olive saw nothing unusual in it. The dressmaker did not so much as raise an eyebrow. And so, she sat in the muted wash of the music, her food growing cold, and imagined how different her evening might have been had her father not lost a fortune at cards.

And in imagining thus, a future that might have been, Elaine was moved to rise from the deflated upholstery of the cast-off chair that graced her temporary room, a chair that befitted her station and the transitory nature of her position.

By the meager light of a single flickering lamp, she curtseyed to an imaginary partner and waltzed about the tiny room that had been assigned to her, in imaginary finery. She danced until the music stopped and she must open her eyes to cold reality, and an even colder night, as she stripped off her dreary, wholly unworthy, oft-mended black dress without benefit of hot water or a fire and jumped betwixt much mended linens without the luxury of warming pan or hot-water bottle.

Chapter 21

At dawn, dressed again in offensive black, fingers shaking with the cold, Elaine plunged her hands into the welcome warmth of funereal black gloves, her breath rising white in the foxed reflection she met in the mirror, and went down to breakfast. There they were met with a great deal of early morning fussing and feeding as their hostesses complained that they should neither leave so early, nor so hastily, on empty stomachs.

They mean to snare him. Elaine observed how intently they watched her employer as he voiced appreciation for their expansive hospitality. When he mounted his horse, he bent to smile at the youngest of the Biddington sisters, Deliah. She stood for some time speaking to him and stepped back from the stirrup she clung to with obvious reluctance. *His future, waving handerchief.*

If not this wealthy heiress, he would find someone like her to fall in love with, to marry. Elaine found herself melancholy in acknowledging the truth, hopeless of her own bleak prospects where love and marriage were concerned. The mourning black of her clothing seemed all too appropriate this morning. Who did governesses marry? Clergymen, or butchers, or bakers, or bankers? Not a handsome gentleman who stood to inherit title and fortune. Certainly not this handsome gentleman. That dream was best forgotten.

Like dreams, they put Caxton behind them and headed deeper into Wales, green hills rising up to swallow them, the roads narrower, less cared for, the horses laboring, and yet she found herself content to be once again in the warm confines of the coach, rocking and jolting onward, ever onward, the sight of Valentine Wharton horseback, powerful thighs gripping the bay's back, far preferable to another day in the Old Maids' Tower of Castle Caxton.

It was pretty country, remote and wild, thinly populated but for the green valleys in the midst of soaring cliffs and rocky rises. Purling streams ran in rivulets across the roads and beside them, water that ran and skipped and foamed. There was beauty here, unlike the beauties of England, similar and yet separate, as her own life had grown similar but separate from childish expectation. There was beauty in that, too.

They stopped in the pretty town of Llangollen to buy provisions for a picnic. The lilting Welsh tongue that was spoken by the innkeeper who served them proved completely unintelligible to all but Valentine. In his seeing completely to their needs there was something just as foreign, just as unsettling. Elaine felt dependent. Too dependent. *His direction. His largesse. His sense of propriety. His shadow.* Every time Valentine looked her way Elaine felt as if the sun shone, as if she were more brightly illuminated, and when he looked away she fell into darkness.

They went on through the sunlit valley, across an ancient stone bridge spanning the River Dee, past a ruined castle on a limestone cliff. By way of the signage along the road Elaine gained some sense of the language. Felicity concentrated on her sums, Mrs. Olive on her knitting.

The chuckling Dee ran between steep roadside cliffs, thick woods and corn fields hemming them in, as her life was now hemmed in.

"I am curious; why do we go by way of these steep back roads in Wales rather than by better-paved, and far less strenuous, English ones?" she asked Mrs. Olive as they jounced across a pock-marked bridge.

"We would not gain a view of Snowdon by English

roads." Indeed at that moment, in the distance, they gained a fine view.

Nose pressed to the window, Felicity said, "Papa wanted me to see Wales. When he was a child his father brought him for a summer."

Elaine clapped her teeth together involuntarily as they passed over yet another pothole. *He does this for the child's sake!* Wharton proved as surprising as the landscape. They passed a stone—big as a whale—big as a ship. Another bridge sounded beneath the horses' hooves, and beneath them the earth fell away, into a gorge where water tumbled milk white.

They rolled through the little market town of Corwen, fish in the streets, the smell of fish in the air—salmon, grayling and trout—and all the while Elaine thought of her own father when she was a child—a man so steeped in drink and debt he had, more often than not, been unable to utter the names of his daughters with either accuracy or the slightest hint of kindness in his voice, much less plan for them a trip to Wales.

They spread a picnic in the shady foothills of the Berwyn Mountains, and when Wharton stood some distance from them, staring at the view while he ate a meat pie and an apple with the hand to mouth economy of a man used to dining where he stood, Elaine drew upon a broader history to tell Felicity of Owen Glendower, a hero of the fifteenth century who had led a rebellion against England's king from these hillsides. She thought such a topic might interest a gentleman who had led men into battle, but he seemed not to hear them, ignored them in fact.

As she spoke she tried to still the rebellious state of a heart and mind that seemed bent on mourning, today, all that she had once taken for granted about her future. Caxton Castle stirred these feelings. In its wake she felt as inconsequential as painted pasteboard.

Felicity's attention to the tale of Glendower reminded Elaine of her place, her strengths. Knowledge. Guidance. History. She had these to offer. The child drank it in even as she moved about, gathering leaves and wildflowers, blossoms twirling in her hands, questions spilling from her lips like the petals that fell at her feet.

Wharton roused from his reverie at precisely the moment

Elaine began to think the child's unending curiosity grew a trifle tiresome. He stilled her bright-eyed overabundance of energy saying, "In silence you may find more answers than in questions, Felicity. Do not, I beg of you, become the tiresome sort of female who enjoys above all else the sound of her own voice."

Elaine thought at once of the sisters of Caxton castle. Their ceaseless prattle had stirred a longing within her for silence. And yet it pained her to see the child wounded, afraid to speak.

Indeed, Lord Wharton seemed at once to regret his sudden outburst. "Come," he said to his crestfallen child, and held out his hand.

When she hesitated, Elaine nodded reassuringly. "Go on, dear."

"I am sorry, Papa," the child said, her voice gone high-pitched and nervous. "I did not mean to annoy . . ."

He shushed her, saying, "Now, close your eyes and listen."

In closing her own eyes, Elaine found herself listening, she knew not what for.

"What do you hear?" he asked, voice gentle, a murmur on the wind.

My heart. I hear my heart. So loudly it beats. To his voice it quickens.

"The wind, the trees," Felicity said, her voice a thin piping, "the river, a kestrel keening."

"What else?" he asked, encouraging. "Listen carefully."

Again they fell still to listen.

"The horses champing. The rattle of their harness. Your breathing."

"Something else."

A long silence stretched while they all listened, and then in frustration the child said, "Nothing. What else?"

"Can you not hear your own heart?" he asked softly.

Elaine's eyes flew open. *Her thoughts! Did he hear her very thoughts?*

His daughter was nodding, curls bobbing.

"The rhythm of your own pulse as it rushes through your veins, like the wind through the trees, like the water on the rocks?" All his focus was on his daughter.

Elaine watched him with fresh eyes, fresh appreciation, as he bent to the child's ear. "Listen!"

"I hear," Felicity said.

"A good thing to stop and listen to the sound of one's own living, now and again, in places of profound stillness such as this. Yes?" He swept his arms wide to encompass the hills.

His words tugged at Elaine's heart, touched her soul.

"Yes, Papa," Felicity agreed.

Elaine was very quiet for the remainder of their picnic.

"What a kindness, my dear," she said, as she and Felicity repacked the hamper, "that your father speaks to you so, that he would share with you the workings of his mind."

"Your father did not speak to you of such things?" Felicity slipped her hand into Elaine's.

Elaine shook her head. "I do not think my father understood the power and beauty of silence." She turned to find Valentine Wharton listening, though he pretended not to.

"Feeling melancholy?" he asked later, as she briskly shook crumbs from a tablecloth.

"Melancholy? Do I appear melancholy?" Snap went the tablecloth.

"Yes, in fact you do." He caught hold of the flown end of the cloth, helping her to fold it, taking it from her when their hands met for a single, scintillating moment.

She pulled back as if burned. He pretended not to notice, the cloth making a neat square in his hands. "Is it the mountains?"

"Why should mountains make me melancholy?" she asked sharply, immediately regretting her tone.

He stared out across the countryside, at earth that flowed away from them like a giant's rumpled tablecloth. "I think it is the size," he said. "It is the same in the Pyrenees. Somehow mountains, the unmoving immensity of them, helped me to place myself in perspective to the battlefield, to the dragons of war."

"Dragons?"

"Taking lives. Watching friends maimed or killed."

She flinched, surprised that he would admit as much to her, a trifle shocked that the taking of lives might ever be placed in any perspective other than that of horror.

"It is that way as well, in Cumbria, where I hale from," he said. "One finds oneself in such scenery." *How faraway the look in his eyes. How sad. What part of himself had he so lost that it needed finding in mountains?*

Elaine shivered as he stepped away from her, toward the hills.

Felicity interrupted her reverie, tugging at her arm, insisting, "Come. We must put more of the road behind us."

"Why is that?" she asked as she followed the child back to the coach.

"The lake of beauty."

Her father spoke. "We shall make it by nightfall. Never fear."

"It is a magic lake, isn't it papa? Tell Miss Deering. Please, Papa."

"When we get to Bala," he promised, handing her into the coach, hand out again for Elaine.

A magic lake? A palace? Another fairy tale, as make-believe as the effect his touch had on her hand as she stepped inside, as wonderfully touching as the moment in which he had bent to his daughter's ear and bade her listen to her own heart. She did not want that tingling flash of feeling to end, the firm promise of his touch. And yet she must let go, must remind herself of the mountains, of truth's perspective—of dragons.

Life is not a fairy story. The maiden in distress does not always get her knight in shining armor. Magic lives in a child's head, not in lakes or a gentleman's fleeting grasp.

Chapter 22

Val guided the horse onward, beside the frothing race of the Dee, taking the south fork, the road that led to Glany-rafon. As he rode, he thought of the silence of the fells in Cumbria—of the silence on the battlefields in Belgium in the moment before guns roared.

Bala nestled at the north end of the long and narrow Llyn Tegid, the Beautiful Lake, a magical sight gleaming in the golden light of a setting sun. He found himself eager for the motion of the horse beneath him to cease, the chill of the air to be warmed by a blazing fire, a hot cup of tea, the soft promise of a well-aired bed, a woman's touch.

He found himself thinking of Miss Deering's hands: fine boned, firm grasped, skin soft, nails trimmed. He thought of the look in her eyes as he clasped her hand. Such a depth of seriousness, of searching desire to understand the inner workings of his mind. So watchful she always seemed, wary. Quiet. Depths to her quietness. Like the mountains, unmoving and strong. Beautiful. Elemental.

He thought of the graceful turn of her wrist as she plucked magic from a harpsichord while other women danced, until she was faint with the playing, with hunger. He thought of the warm weight of her in his arms, the soft yield of her breast against his. He had not failed to mark her hand's trembling when he had lowered her into bed. He lingered on the idea of lowering her onto a bed again, of provoking a far more passionate trembling.

He pictured the modest fall of her lashes against alabaster cheek, the strawberry blushes whenever his gaze lingered. *Has she alabaster breasts and strawberry nipples? Almond-scented kisses? A beautiful lake in the milky valley of her thighs?*

He stifled the thoughts, his rising desire, reminding himself that he had vowed not to make a mess of life again. Not like he had with Penny. No. He must remember that dearest Miss Deering created a bridge of words between him and his daughter. She found goodness in him, and kindness. She would find neither if he, a man of worldly cravings, proved successful in tempting desires Palmer had failed to reach.

The sky, the still mirrored surface of the lake, the mountain doubled, turned on its head in rippled silken reflection, was awash with color as he handed a road-rumpled Mrs. Olive out of the carriage, then lifted his dozing daughter from arms in which he perversely imagined his own head pillowed.

Dear Miss Deering had no awareness of his thoughts. Her sun-touched face glowed with childlike wonder as she took in the view. "Beautiful!" she whispered.

Oh God! he thought. *She is beautiful in this light.* He faced the lake, lowered his nose to nuzzle the soap-clean warmth of his daughter's curls. "Beautiful," he murmured.

The echo of land and sky was stunning, the weight of the child beautiful in his arms. The warmth of her breath against his neck brought such peace to his heart, such a feeling of purpose, and contentment. He remembered being held thus in his father's arms, the heat of breath, of body, lulling him to sleep. Beautiful.

"Valentine. Valentine. Wake up, my son. You must see the sun on the lake." He had roused himself, met with a brilliant panorama of coral-, sapphire-, and bronze-haloed mountains mirrored on a similar stillness of lake.

"Did the sun drown?" he had asked his father sleepily. His father had laughed. Beneath his little boy legs, his father's chest and belly had rocked with laughter.

Miss Deering turned, hints of the sunset's sheen reflected in the pearly translucence of her brow, in the soft curve of his daughter's cheek.

"It looks as if the sun is swallowed up by the lake," she said.

So gently she touched upon his childhood. So gently the sun and all its reflected shades of saffron and salmon and blue added color to the moment, to the memory, to the satin curve of her cheek. He had to ask, "Does the sun drown, do you think, or is the water set ablaze?"

Miss Deering's bird-wing-brows rose, as if she found something remarkable in the question.

"Do I surprise you, Miss Deering?" He breathed the question through his daughter's curls, holding his own sunshine. "Do you think me a gentleman who glories only in ballrooms and battlefields?"

"I do not know what to think of you, sir."

"Good. I like to keep people a bit off balance."

She had nothing to say to that, merely looked at him.

"My father brought me to Llyn Tegid when I was a lad," he said, quietly, unwilling for her interest to wane, unwilling to wake the child.

She waited, this quiet tabby cat of a governess. Waited rather than prodding him to explain. So different from the Biddington sisters. So peaceful to stand watching a brazen sunset with such a demure woman.

She is the lake. Will I drown in her? Or set her ablaze?

"Were you close to your father?" he asked.

Mrs. Olive seemed to appear out of nowhere in that moment, bustlingly efficient. "Shall I see her tucked safely into bed, sir?"

"Please do." He transferred the child into the housekeeper's welcoming arms, catching the look that passed between housekeeper and governess. *What's this? What have I touched upon, all unknowing? This look of understanding from the housekeeper? This fleeting expression of gratitude from the dark-eyed tabby cat?*

When Miss Deering might have followed Mrs. Olive indoors he stepped toward the bronzed glitter of the lake and said, voice mild, "Would you avoid me, Miss Deering? Or is it my question?"

She did not answer at once. He had not thought she

would. Before she spoke, before she could offer him platitudes and escape into the inn, he walked into the golden light, into the freshening breeze, casting a long shadow, knowing that because he employed her, she must follow.

Chapter 23

Elaine drew her cloak close about her shoulders, shivered with the chill of the oncoming night, with the potential lurking in the darkness, and followed Valentine Wharton toward Lynn Tegid's gilded sheen.

I must answer, she thought, but knew not what to say— how to begin. Her jaw felt frozen, the same rigidness possessing her limbs in following this man into the deepening shadows, a tension filling her body with every step they placed between the golden glow of lamplight from the inn and the mystery of the lake.

His voice wafted over his shoulder, his tone gentle, the words unexpected. "You do not think very highly of me as a father, do you?"

She stopped, stunned. She had not been thinking of him as a father at all in that moment, to own truth. Not here, as night crept up on them. How to reply to such an accusation?

No anger in his gentled voice. "I cannot blame you, really." Like the lapping of the lake against the pebbled shoreline. "I have done little enough with my life to give anyone a glowing impression of me, and yet, neither am I the man my own history paints."

His silhouette cut darkly the water's liquid gold—the lines of him enticing—curling hair, broad shoulders, muscled calf and thigh.

A bird flew above him, a black vee against the brightness, loosing a jittering call as it settled in the arms of a tree. The call was answered by a chorus of twittering, a flutter of wings, a subtle rearrangement in roosting birds' hierarchy. Like her heart that sudden flight, her fluttering pulse awaiting his every word and gesture, her mind considering what it would be like to settle in a very different pair of arms.

She caught up to him, untangled her tongue, and forced the truth from constricted throat. "Sir. You mistake my impression of you."

"Do I?" He turned to look at her a moment, features stark in the flood of golden light. So very handsome, chiseled. Beyond her mortal touch. She was but a governess, and he—

"It troubles me"—he bent to pick up a stone, the tension that eddied between them like the rippled lake when he threw the stone—"that my daughter fears me, that she finds little to say to me."

"She is . . ." *Mortal. Like me.*

"Easily wounded?" he asked, and turned to look her way.

"Yes." *Walking wounded. The child forgotten. As I was forgotten by a father who drank, who forgot my very existence, my future.* What to say to this father who did not forget? Who looked at her in such a way she would not have him look away?

The voice of the lake soothed her, the gentle movement of the water, the settling calls of the birds, the fact that he kept his distance and spoke of his daughter's needs.

"Give her time," she suggested, "and the right questions. You will draw her out. She wants to talk to you."

"Did your father know the right questions to ask?"

She remained silent a moment, remembering, sadness stealing over her like the night's shadow. "We rarely spoke."

"Is that so?" Interest in his response, in the arrested arc of his arm. The stone in his hand was temporarily stayed from its watery end.

I did not mean to rouse this interest. This keen look in his eyes. Did I?

"A foolish man, then?"

How to get out of this conversation? Too keen this interest, these delving looks, this quickening within. "On occasion all men are foolish."

"And women?" His voice lowered, lent deeper meaning to the question, his tone almost seductive.

"Doubly so." *Am I foolish now to revel in his interest, in the sunset cerulean of his eyes?*

"What stimulated your father's foolishness, that he would not recognize his daughter's longing?"

She swallowed hard, a frisson of expectation accompanying his words. Did he know he stimulated longings as he stood there? As they opened hearts and souls in the glimmering light of dusk? She did not want to tell him her father's foolishness, did not want to look into the knowing blue of sunstruck eyes. He recognized her thoughts and feelings far better than her father ever had. In that way he became dangerous.

"Come, come. A simple question surely, Miss Deering."

She shook her head, dared a quick glance at him, as the light faded, the gleam in his eyes doused along with the sun. "You will not like the answer."

"How so?"

"He was foolish," she blurted, "in the same manner you once were."

"A rogue?" So swift the question, his tone defensive. Gravel scraped harshly beneath his boot. She found herself surprised he no longer considered the description apt.

"Women were not Father's downfall."

He stared at her a moment, lips pursed—thinking, tossing the stone from hand to hand. The pink wash of color in the sky softened the harder edges of his features even as shadows gathered in the hollows of cheek and brow. She could see by the movement of his eyes the moment in which the answer came to him. He flung the stone.

"A drinker, then."

She nodded.

He leaned forward with an expression of disbelief, of regret as gray and overshadowing as the coming night. "Was he really?"

She nodded, said softly, the words flowing like water, "A profound and angry drinker. It destroyed his good temper, his marriage, his sense of purpose, his love of friends and family. And when there was nothing left of fortune or future to lay waste to, it destroyed his will to go on."

He met this revelatory outpouring of words with a moment's shocked silence. Even the birds ceased their chatter. Only the voice of the lake gathered and ebbed between them like the last of the light. Fingers of darkness threatened to steal his face from view.

I should not have told him, not thus. Too harsh the words, too bald.

"I am sorry," he said, earnest weight to the words. She did not want him sorry, did not want pity, but she was wrong in jumping to that conclusion. He said, "I have been operating under a misconception."

Misconception?

He moved closer. "I thought you hesitated for other reasons." He closed the distance between them with a fluid grace, nothing awkward in his movements as he loomed closer. So dark his eyes now, deeply shadowed, wells of knowing. As if he saw her, really saw her, even in the gloom. As if he knew far more than she wished him to know in that enveloping darkness as the mountains closed in on them, encroaching upon the silvered light sparkling upon the dark silk of the lake.

"In coming to Wales," he said.

Out of the gloom rose the specter of Palmer—closing in like the darkness, like the mountains, like her fear.

Her heart thudded hard. She clenched her hands at her sides, prepared to fend Wharton off.

"Am I very much like him?" he asked, no more than a silhouette now against the lake's pewter gleam.

Her head jerked, her breath caught on her surprise. *Did he mean her father? Or Palmer?* It did not matter, really, the answer was the same either way. "No. Not in the least."

A shadow among the shadows now, his features were swallowed by the night. His voice, teasing, seductive, all too dangerous, spoke from the gathering gloom.

"But then you have never seen me at my worst."

She rubbed her hands together. Nervous. Cold. "No. Nor

never hope to, Mr. Wharton. I should have to leave you
under such circumstances."

"A dire threat indeed." He sounded amused.

She hung her head, stung.

Better able to see than she—his back to the reflection of
the lake, her face fully to it—he reached out from the darkness to cup her chin in kid-gloved hand, the sudden soft
friction of his fingers a pleasantly sensual shock. Elaine
opened her eyes wider, pulling in a sudden breath, and with
it the leathery scent of him. She struggled to catch a
glimpse of him, struggled with the sudden rush of desire
that spread from the point of her chin where his touch,
gloved though it was, warmed her flesh.

"Come, come, Miss Deering," he murmured. "No downcast looks."

She listened for the hint of seduction one might find in
almost everything he said. The fascinating silken undertone
of his voice. Soft, like his touch, gloved like his hand, and
yet heat pulsed in his every word.

"I've no desire to lose you. I give you no good reason
to leave my service, do I?"

She took a deep steadying breath, squared her shoulders,
lifted her chin, away from his hand, the heat—the lure of
both. So stiff her voice sounded in response. "Not yet, sir."

She turned to go.

"Thank you," he said, his voice so very gentle she must
stop and turn.

*How warm my cheeks. How loud my heartbeat. His touch,
like a candle's, burns.*

The darkness could not claim him entirely. She caught
the gleam of his eyes, the pale edge of his neckcloth against
the dark wedge of the mountains. "What would you thank
me for, sir?"

"For answering difficult questions forthrightly. For
allowing me a glimpse into my daughter's mind."

"Yes, sir." She took a step away from him, away from
the lure of his voice, his gratitude, her desire for more
of both.

"And now, before you slip away, Miss Deering." His
voice reached out to stay her. "I would—"

"Yes, sir?" she whispered, afraid if she spoke any louder

her voice might give her away, afraid he must hear in it her desire to stay with him here in the darkness, lulled by the magic of the night air and the voice of the waves upon the shore. Afraid he would feel the building heat within, a desire that seemed born of the darkness—and the memory of his touch upon her chin.

"I would tell you the tale of the lake."

"Yes sir."

"Legend has it, you see, that there is a palace under the waters of Llyn Tegid."

"A palace?"

The lake hushed against the bank, hushed the secrets he would reveal. He closed the distance between them again to whisper, "A hidden treasure, Miss Deering, in the lake's dark, watery depths."

He stood too close in the darkness, his whispered tone provocative.

And yet the feeling, the throbbing heat he roused within her was strange treasure. A treasure she could not refuse. Her own golden palace. A hidden lake of burgeoning desire. The breeze off the water moved like cool fingers through her hair, cooling her chin where he had cupped her face in gloved palm. She ached with a startlingly strong need for him to touch her again. She pictured for a moment his taking her in his arms, as Palmer had. Pressing his body to hers, his lips to hers, a liquid lake in mouths met.

"Intriguing idea, is it not?"

She blinked, shook her head to clear it. He meant the drowned palace. The palace was an intriguing idea, not these wild, wanton thoughts. *I must drown these feelings, this shocking need. Bury them deep.*

"The idea of anything precious lost forever is undeniably intriguing." She could hear wistfulness, an undisguised trace of sadness in her voice. She hoped it was lost in the darkness, in the unending wash of the waves, like the palace in the lake, like the possibility that this man of all men might ever have occasion to honorably quench the knifelike flame of her desire.

What madness was this, born of moonlight and fairy tales? She contemplated trifling with a known rogue, an admitted rogue! A dangerous undertaking—the height of foolishness. There were no fairy tale palaces for a plain governess who allowed her virtue to be compromised.

"Good night, sir," she said, as she turned her back on him. "I thank you for sharing the tale."

And from the darkness, his voice drifted, so gentle she could not be sure she heard correctly.

"Good night, my Deering."

Chapter 24

Val arranged for a boat the following day.

"A boat, sir? Whatever would you be needing a boat for?" Mrs. Olive was not at all pleased.

"Why to see the lake, of course, and perhaps to fish."

Just like when I was a boy.

"Fish? The child will not be wanting to fish. It's a daughter you have, Master Wharton. Not a son."

"She might like to fish," Miss Deering ventured quietly.

"Do you like to fish?" he asked, ignoring Mrs. Olive's wrinkled nose.

"As it happens, my sisters and I are quite the anglers. Of the six of us only Florence did not care to fish."

Six! Six sisters? So much I do not know of Miss Deering.

"Sensible girl." Mrs. Olive was unusually opposed to the excursion. "You will not catch me fishing. Nasty, smelly things, fish. No, I shall keep my feet firmly on terra firma, if you please," she said, demonstrating the only Latin she knew. And then she muttered, "I thought we were in a hurry to get to St. David."

"The horses needed a rest," Val said, "as do we all."

Six! Has she brothers in addition?

"Do you not long to be quit of the coach and rattling along over uneven roads for another day?"

Six dowries. Six husbands to be found. No wonder she wound up a governess.

"A day on the lake sounds splendid," Felicity rushed to agree.

Six dear Deerings! How did a father manage?

"You are welcome to take the day and do as you will, Mrs. Olive," Val said, his thoughts distracted.

Mrs. Olive brightened. "Do you mean it, sir?"

How did the mother manage, her husband a drinker, a wastrel?

"Yes, uh, yes, of course. We leave you to your own devices, the lads as well, unless they wish to come."

The footmen were more than happy to go fishing, but the coachman shook his head and said he would prefer to walk about a bit. And as the old codger was rather smitten with Mrs. Olive, Val was none too surprised to hear it.

It proved a perfect day for boating. The fish did not seem to be biting, or did not care for the bait at any rate, but no one seemed to mind. The sky was clear and blue, the mountains casting their reflections the length of the lake, as if into a mirror.

Felicity could not bring herself to hook a worm without squealing, but she managed to convince the footmen to replenish her bait whenever required, and so they were all quite happy to laze about with their poles, soaking up the sunshine and listening to the lap of the water and the creak of the boat, the breeze like a gentle hand to push them along.

There came a point when Felicity was thus entertained, and the footmen intent on replenishing their lines, that Val sat himself down next to dear Miss Deering, the neck of her stiflingly high-necked dress intriguingly unhooked, as she lifted her face to the breeze, eyes closed, an uncharacteristically relaxed expression softening her features.

She opened her eyes at once at the creak of the wooden bench, her hand moving at once to refasten the errant hooks. He watched with some amusement as her fingers strove to clasp them without success, the hooks being very tiny ones.

"A perfect day, is it not?" he asked.

"A lovely day," she agreed, still fussing, the hooks uncooperative.

He pretended not to notice.

He drank in a deep contented breath, surreptitiously eyeing her throat, the slender grace of her wrists. "Just like when I was a lad."

"When you first learned of the palace in the lake?" she asked.

"Yes. A rather remarkable trip."

"In what way remarkable?"

"My father had shown little interest in me until that time." He leaned back, lounging comfortably, deeply interested in the way the sun touched her hair, striking light in the darkness.

Does she look more like her father or her mother? He took a deep breath, savoring the freshness of the breeze, the faint hint of almond soap, remembering.

"A magical summer it was. It lives perfect and golden in my memory. Like the sunset last night."

She surprised him in saying, "And now you would give a wonderful golden moment of a summer to Felicity."

He nodded.

The hooks proved problematic. Her hands fascinated him, the shell pink tips of her fingers. He rather enjoyed watching her struggle, and yet he asked, "Might I be of assistance?"

Her eyes went very wide. "That would not be . . ."

"Appropriate?" he teased. "Doubtless not. You ought not to have unfastened them to begin with."

She blinked at him with an expression of such consternation he must laugh and say, "Leave them be, Miss Deering. This is not a day for high-necked black dresses that stifle one unnecessarily. I would not have you fainting again. There are none here who matter who will care that your hooks have come undone." *None but me.*

She looked toward the shore, hands stilling at her throat.

He turned to see what drew her eye.

There, waiting for them at the dock, stood a man he knew at once to be Cupid, and a woman, skirt kicking in the breeze, her hand raised to hold fast a straw hat, to shield the eyes of a swaddled babe in her arms.

His heart lurched.

"Penny!" Felicity cried out in delight.

From his lips came soft echo to his daughter's cry.

"Penny!"

Chapter 25

Elaine found the golden moment on the lake turned to brass as the boat returned to the pier.

"Penny!" Felicity cried, leaping from the boat.

Valentine Wharton's relaxed pose underwent drastic transformation, his body suddenly tensed in every muscle, like an arrow in a drawn bow, his body shouting what his mouth could not. *Penny!*

The Shelbournes were on the way to Shrewsbury, a visit to Penny's aunt, who must see the new baby. They had told Val's mother they might chance upon him in Bala, promised to bring him news—grave news, if the look in the tall, dark-haired gentleman's eyes gave clue—Cupid—this was certainly Cupid, but Valentine Wharton did not see the gravity in the gentleman's eyes, his gaze fixed almost exclusively on the woman, the woman in turn focused rather exclusively on Felicity, who ran from the boat into her arms with a cry of such gladness it warmed the heart.

"My dear," she said, "how you have grown! Grown beautiful."

Such tenderness in her eyes, in her voice. Valentine Wharton straightened in hearing it. He seemed to go all hard as he stepped from the boat, his chin, the posture of his back and shoulders, the manner in which he thrust out his hand to the gentleman, saying, "Cupid. Last man on earth I expected to see here."

"Val." The young man would not let go his hand. "Val, I've news."

At last Penny Shelbourne looked at him, over the top of Felicity's head. In her eyes a great sadness brimmed. "Val," she said.

Elaine stepped from the boat as she said it, her footing swaying, rocking, uncertain beneath her feet, as uncertain as the quaver in Penny Shelbourne's voice.

"What is it?" Valentine demanded. "What is amiss?"

Solid ground. Elaine's feet found solid ground at last, and still she felt the sway of the boat in her limbs, the lift of the deck beneath her feet. An illusion. An unsettling illusion.

"Your father, Val . . ." His friend let the words hang unfinished.

Val froze. She had never seen him stand so still. His jaw seemed set in stone.

The young woman's pained look increased. She shot a look at her husband, the look of a woman at a loss seeking support where she knew herself most likely to find it. Then she looked again at Val, and there was love in her eyes, and sympathy, "His heart, Val," she said.

It was hard to gage how the truth hit him. He made no movement to reveal as much. Indeed, his face remained stonelike—emotionless. Then, without word or gesture or glance again at his visitors, he strode away from the circle of eyes that watched too keenly his reaction to this dreadful revelation.

Penny made a move, as if to go after him, but her husband, quite sensibly, caught hold of her hand and drew her to him, Felicity as well, and said, quietly, "He needs to be alone, my loves."

Both heads nodded. Penny shifted the babe in her arms, wiped a tear from her eye, for the first time glanced blankly at Elaine. Then gathering Felicity closer, she turned into her husband's shoulder to let the tears flow, murmuring indistinctly, "Poor Val."

"We dealt him a bad blow," he agreed.

Felicity, who watched the whole with great uncertainty, chin tipped high, her hand creeping into Elaine's, asked in a whisper, "What has happened?"

Elaine knelt to look her in the eyes, to brace her shoulders, to murmur gently, "Your father's father, Lord Wharton, my dear. His heart has stopped."

"Dead?" she asked with a child's bluntness, her gaze rising to meet Penny's, to gain confirmation.

"Yes," Penny said quietly.

"And Father? Has he gone to cry where I cannot see?" She asked it of Penny, as though she would know the answer better than anyone.

"I should think perhaps he has." So serious her expression, so sad her eyes. The child stood on tiptoe to look upon the sleeping baby.

Elaine felt his eyes upon her, then, the one they called Cupid, measuring her, measuring the child's reaction.

"Introduce me, my dear," he touched Felicity's shoulder, a loving, fatherly gesture, her fingers smoothing back wind-tousled hair.

A distraction, the suggestion. A wise move.

"Is this the new governess we have heard so much about?"

Heard? What have they heard?

Felicity made shaky introductions, her efforts interrupted by Mrs. Olive, who came red-eyed to meet them from the inn, tears springing fresh when she heard that the new Lord Wharton had gone for a walk, and that none knew when he might return.

Felicity flung herself at Penny Shelbourne's skirts weeping then, and the woman guided her away, that the child might feel some sense of privacy, Cupid lifting the sleeping baby from her arms.

"Isn't it a pity about the poor man's father?" Mrs. Olive whispered to Elaine as they stood waiting at a discreet distance, part of this, and yet, for the moment, unnecessary. "More's the pity they never really had a meeting of the minds about poor Felicity. Mild-mannered and sweet-tempered as he was, Valentine's father was undeniably stiff-necked. He considered it quite inappropriate to keep the child housed at the Manor. Convinced his son to send her away to boarding school, he did. Never acknowledged her connection to him when they were in the house together. I know for a fact she goes unmentioned in the will."

Elaine frowned, touched by this added layer to poor Felicity's plight. "How unfortunate."

"Yes, doubly so when I know my master—ah, my lord, asked his father again, right before we left, if he might not bring the child home with him on his return."

"And what did his father say?"

"Not while he was still lord and master of the manor. And Valentine snapped back at him that the day would soon come when that would no longer be reason to stop him."

"Oh dear!"

"Aye, regretting such words today, I'm thinking."

Elaine blinked back the sudden tears. She remembered the last words she had said to her own father. Unforgettable words, unforgivable. Words she wished unsaid.

"The baby is wet," Shelbourne murmured to his wife.

"I shall just go and change him." She reached for him at once. "Do you mean to chase after Val?"

"Yes. Ought to see how he bears up."

Elaine knelt to offer Felicity a fresh handkerchief. "Come, come, my dear. It is quite all right to cry when one has good reason. Now blow your nose."

"Let me take the wee one," Mrs. Olive insisted. "I have yet to see the lad in his entirety, you know."

"And a marvel of perfection he is," Penny boasted with understandable pride as she carefully handed over her precious charge. "You must come and ogle his exquisitely formed fingers and toes, Felicity. They bring back such pleasant memories of when you were given into my care." She put her arms around Felicity's shoulders. "Perhaps you will tell me about school?"

Felicity enthusiastically agreed, ready to be led away.

As easily, as swiftly as that their shared past made Elaine quite suddenly an outsider, unneeded, invisible, left standing by the lake, the wind running its fingers through her hair.

Used to being relegated to the background in Lord Palmer's household, Elaine found herself placed once more in that position by strangers from Valentine Wharton's past, by the death of a man she would never have the privilege of meeting, whose passing now made Valentine Lord.

Her discomfort was, she decided, after a few moments of unexpectedly biting melancholy, a selfish waste of time. It was not often she was left alone with her thoughts—and in such a perfect place for thinking. And on this day, of all days, she must cherish the opportunity for quiet, for contemplation. She went walking, choosing a path that led her in the opposite direction from that the others had taken.

The lake spoke to her as she walked, its voice soothing, peaceful, its whisperings of life, not death. It seemed logical to assume that the trip to Wales must be cut short, that the new Baron, the Right Honorable Lord Wharton would wish to return to Cumbria to assist in the settling of his father's estate.

This might be her last opportunity to treasure the lake.

The town of Bala was quiet under the afternoon sun, the stillness gently broken by the sound of singing, a choir practicing beneath the high steeple of Bala's ivy draped church. Peace and a feeling of well-being might be found in those voices, a sense echoed by the call of birds that flitted above her head from the trees as she passed. A wagtail flashed yellow and black, its flight wavering, then a magpie, starkly black and white, in a swift flutter of wings that ended in a long glide to a tree were a jay gave a hoarse call. A woodpecker rattled and tapped.

Parallel to the lake she went, along one of only two long streets, the soft sounds of the lake against the shore as comforting as bird call. To the northernmost end of town she strolled, thinking of her father—of the day he had died, a day without birdsong, without the sunlit comfort of a lake. It had rained that day—the day truth unfolded and her future was made clear to her.

Her feet led her to Tomen Bala, a grass-covered mound as tall as a three-story house, the path very steep, difficult to climb without tripping over one's skirt, and yet she managed, in need of exertion, something to ease a heart's aching.

Tomen Bala, she had been told by the innkeeper, was supposed to be a beacon hill, or perhaps the grave mound of an ancient, beloved king.

Death—there is no getting away from it.

She was breathing hard by the time she reached the top of the mound, where she looked out across the lake and thought of the palace buried beneath the waters. A romantic notion, like the future she had once taken for granted. Like a fairy tale.

The top of the mound, almost twice as wide as it was tall, offered a spectacular view. Below spread the lake, sparkling in sunlight, the water rippled—scales from a dragon's back—surrounded by the three cloud-kissing mountains, Arennig Fawr, Aran Benllyn, and Aran Fawddwy. Lilting names on the tongue, a mad scramble of consonants on the page, an undulating mirror of rock and heather, shrubbery and sky against the lake, an oddly exhilarating optical illusion. She tried to puzzle out where their boat had drifted that afternoon, and recaptured some of the peace they had found in the view, in the caress of the breeze on her cheek, in the whisper of the lake, in the heat of the sun on her shoulders.

"This is not a day for high-necked black dresses." She could hear Valentine Wharton's voice as clearly in her mind as if he stood beside her. She could see the blue of the lake reflected in the blue of his eyes as he watched her hands. She undid the hooks at her throat and breathed deep.

There was welcome shade beneath the one tree that grew atop Tomen Bala, a good-size alder, its bark scored with the names and initials of those who wished to mark their climb, or link their name with another's.

Would I link my name with that of a heartbroken man? Am I in love? Foolishly, hopelessly in love? Love brought Valentine Wharton here with his daughter, a memory of the love of the father before him who had brought his own wild child into the rugged hills of Wales, a place of beauty, a place of reflection, and at its heart the peaceful blue of the lake.

Elaine sat in the grass and considered her feelings for Valentine, for his motherless daughter. The shadow of the mountains claimed the spot where she sat, chilling her, so that she drew her black cape closer, tied her bonnet more securely under her chin, and rehooked the high neck of her dress.

The sky went a deeper azure. The sun slid lower, casting the hillsides in a haze of gold and lengthening shadows, and still she sat, motionless, thinking—of their knees beneath the cover of his coat, of the grip of his arms when he had carried her to her bedroom at Caxton, of the caress of his voice in the darkness, lakeside. She had to admit herself a woman smitten, a woman troubled by pangs of jealousy that Wharton was a man clearly in love, not with her, but with the woman who had come such a long way out of her way to tell him of his father's demise, his best friend's wife—Penny Shelbourne.

Heart aching, Elaine leaned back in the long grass, hiding her thoughts there, and stared at the blue of the sky rather than confront the color of her feelings.

Chapter 26

A voice sounded from the pathway, rousing Elaine from an unplanned doze to sight of a sky gone deep turquoise, the shadows wrong, too long, the grass, the lake tinged with gold.

The voice was Penny Shelbourne's. She said something about the view to be had from such a vantage point.

Elaine's first instinct was to jump up and say how do you do, and indeed the view is quite spectacular, but when she opened her mouth what came out was a breath catching, "Ow!"

Her right leg had gone to sleep. Her left foot had no feeling whatsoever until she moved it, a wooden limb. A pang shot the length of both legs when she moved them, all pins and needles. *How long did I sleep?*

And then her whole body sank lower in the shadows that wrapped her. Valentine Wharton topped the lip of Tomen Bala—Lord Wharton. No mistaking his silhouette against the sinking sun, golden hair gleaming, his shoulders, his torso, his horseman's thighs grown familiar—even beloved. Elaine had to admit she loved him, this titled, privileged gentleman, that she felt jealousy in watching him extend a helping hand to another woman.

So close they stood for a moment, he and Penny Shelbourne. Closer, surely, than was entirely necessary? Closer than Elaine liked to see.

The mountain's shadow reached for her, the ground gone cold and damp. Elaine's hands trembled. Her legs tingled with a thousand pins and needles. A shiver ran the length of her spine as Valentine Wharton said, "I am glad to have this moment alone, Penny, just we two. Many is the time I have longed for it, and we were always interrupted."

Dear God! Elaine closed her eyes. Did he mean to make love to a married woman? His best friend's wife? Was Valentine Wharton all and more than she had ever imagined?

She wished she might stop up her ears and fly away from Tomen Bala. What to do now? She could not interrupt in the very moment when he complained against it. She gave her leg an irritable shake and bit her lip in order not to cry out. She could not stand up in this moment without falling down, but neither could she simply sit wordless. They must eventually realize she lurked in the shadows, a snake in the grass.

Open your mouth, Elaine! Stand up, and shake out your cloak, and then shake out your legs. And then what? Hobble past them without falling down?

Was it possible? Could it be done? No. Her vocal cords were as paralyzed as her legs, for in that moment Val—her beautiful Val—took Penny's hand in his.

Elaine could not look away. Nor could she speak. Her jaw froze, her breath trapped. Her heart still went on beating, its steady thump sounded in her ears. The same pulse throbbed in her wrist, her fingertips. These hands he had touched. Her fingers had tingled then as much as her toes did now. Did he render her numb as well as mute? No. Every nerve ending seemed awakened to a new and tingling awareness, as if she had never before understood the sensitivity of her own flesh.

Did Valentine Wharton stir the same tingling awareness in Penny Shelbourne? It pained Elaine to think it must be so.

"I have been beastly to you," he said, voice low, apologetic.

Beastly? In what way beastly?

"I cannot blame it all on the spirits, though they may

have misled me. Not a day has passed that I do not regret having so abused you."

Abused her? What has he done to this woman? Do I really want to know?

"Can you—will you—forgive me?"

Elaine buried her face in the sweet smelling grass, ashamed. This apology was not meant for her ears. To continue listening was unpardonable, and yet there was no getting up now—not now—no explaining why she had not announced her presence earlier.

Penny Shelbourne removed her hand from his. Elaine risked a glance as the silence between them lengthened. Did she mean to refuse him? Surely no woman could refuse such a moving plea.

He seemed to hold his breath. God knew Elaine held hers.

Penny said at last. "I am glad of your apology, Val. I agree, we must put the past behind us. Felicity and Alex love us both too much for us not to be good friends. But as for forgiving you—"

He tensed. The line of his back tensed, as if he braced for a blow. Elaine tensed as well, a tension born of sympathy and the well-deserved worry that she must eventually be found.

"I forgave you long ago," Penny Shelbourne said.

Elaine wanted to loose a heavy sigh of relief but dared not risk making a noise. Val's shoulders visibly relaxed.

She paced away from him, this woman he had once loved. "How could I not forgive the wild young man who has become such a loving father to Felicity? She does well with you, Val. You should be proud."

He turned to face the lake. "Give all thanks to Miss Deering. She molds Felicity into a model young lady, not I."

Elaine almost choked to hear such an admission. She buried her face in grass again—a mistake—it tickled her nose. She came very close to sneezing. Not true, Elaine thought, and yet his praise pleased her—it renewed her intention to stop this despicable eavesdropping. Model young lady, indeed! She focused on flexing her toes, on moving her great, gallumphing, wooden-block feet. She must not listen to another word. She must slither down the side of Tomen Bala without their ever knowing she was there. Without a sound. A daunting task, but she would do it—she would—as soon as she could move limbs without crying out involuntarily.

"You underestimate your impact, Valentine Wharton," Penny said, "on all the women in your life. You always have." She laughed. "I am sorry to have underestimated this governess of yours."

Elaine froze. This she must hear.

"I know not to rely on gossip for the true accounting of a woman," Penny said.

Memory stirred—something Felicity had said. Penny Foster had borne the brunt of a great deal of malicious gossip on the child's behalf. She had allowed an entire village to mistakenly believe Felicity was her illegitimate daughter, rather than the local strumpet's baseborn brat. But what had gossip to do with her, the true accounting of her?

"How wrongly everyone misjudged you, Penny Foster." Valentine Wharton's voice softened, went husky. "I misjudged you."

How warm his tone. Unexpectedly gentle. Intimate. *Pins and needles in my heart.*

"Penny Shelbourne now," she corrected him.

"I have not forgotten."

Wistful. He sounded wistful. Elaine closed her eyes to that, an echoing emotion in her own heart. This had nothing to do with her.

"You will always be Penny Foster to me."

"Town touch-me-not?"

He barked out a laugh. "Cupid told you?"

"He did."

Old memories. Mutual memories. Nothing to do with her. She really ought to be crawling down Tomen Bala now. Hands and knees. At least far enough that she might stand and not be seen by them.

"I ought not to have called you that," he was saying. "It was cruel."

Penny responded with affection in her voice. Forgiveness. "I will always be grateful to you, Val."

"Grateful? How so?"

"For bringing your friend Cupid home to Appleby."

He did not sound as happy as she. "A great many things might have been different had I not."

"Yes. We would not have met. I might not now be a mother."

"Or married," said he, and Elaine chose that moment to shift her position with a wince, with a sudden rattle of unsettled stone.

"Or married," Penny agreed. "I was well on my way to becoming the village spinster."

Elaine stopped, grass-scented hand to mouth, pain shooting through her legs. She must wait another moment, then try again.

"I was in love with you, did you know?" He paced the perimeter of Tomen Bala, treading closer as he said it, his words loud and clear.

Oh God! Elaine flexed her toes and flexed her legs, forcing the burn, the pain. She did not want to hear this. How it pained her to hear this.

Penny seemed to think he spoke in jest. "In love with me? You demonstrated an odd way of professing your affections, Val."

His laugh was harsh, his voice tight with pain. "The spirits did my talking. They have, I'm sure you've noticed, singularly foul mouths."

Elaine stifled a laugh, her hands flying from her ears to her mouth. She devoutly hoped neither of them heard her sudden breathy exhalation. Strange how one might wish to laugh and cry simultaneously.

"You are now a sober man."

"I drink tea." His pacing brought him closer. "Can you picture it?"

Elaine could picture him no other way.

"You will do differently next time."

"Next time?" His voice sounded as if it came from directly overhead.

Elaine fell still, afraid he must hear the slightest of moves, afraid she must sneeze.

"Next time you fall in love. You will, you know. A Valentine cannot go unloved through life, brokenhearted. It goes against grain."

Elaine held her breath, awaiting his answer, afraid he must see her.

He laughed. A pained sound, no mirth in it. Lord, he

sounded as if he stood directly above her. "You think a broken heart easily mended?" he asked gruffly.

Sadness washed over her, as gentle as the sound of the lake below.

"Mine was broken, Val," Penny reminded him, "and now is mended."

He whirled and paced away, his voice grown more distant, his tone ironic, even bitter. "And I did the breaking, didn't I?"

"You did."

"Not a kindness."

Elaine lifted her head. She could just make him out in the twilight.

"You may find this strange," he drawled, his distant, uncaring manner recovered. "But there are those who persist in finding me kind, despite all my failings."

Elaine caught her breath.

Penny spoke carefully, her voice grown distant. "I have always seen the potential for kindness in you, Val."

He laughed brusquely, the noise a dismissal of her claim. "When?"

"Dearest Val." She sounded in no mood to grow maudlin, her voice hard to make out, as if she had begun to climb down Tomen Bala. "I shall always fondly remember the lad who kissed me first."

With that she was gone, into a darkness that left only the scent of her perfume to linger and the memory of her words.

Elaine remained very still in the grass where she lay, deeply moved by their exchange, waiting for Valentine Wharton to tire of the view, to follow his childhood friend. She could not relax until he was gone, could not rid herself entirely of the pins and needles until she relaxed.

It was with utter surprise and disbelief that she heard him say, "And what of your first kiss, Miss Deering? Will you remember it fondly?"

She lay face down in the grass a moment, too stunned to move, breath held. Had he really known she was there the whole time?"

"Come, come. Don't be shy," he coaxed from the growing gloom above her. "You cannot think I would not see you."

Chapter 27

Val studied the slope below, sure he had seen the pale moon of her face illuminated by the last saffron and salmon rays of the sun, the shape of her cloak a shadow among the shadows. There, he could make out the peak of her bonnet, the black splay of wool against the grass. His imagination did not run away with him. The all too proper and appropriate Miss Elaine Deering sat up with a most unladylike moan.

"I am sorry not to have revealed my presence earlier, my lord." Her voice floated up, irresolute, uncertain. "I ought to have said something."

"Yes," he agreed. "You bloody well ought to have."

"I had no intention of eavesdropping, my lord."

My lord. Not sir, as she had once called him, but his father's title with all its connotations of responsibility, and maturity.

"Really?" he drawled. The word could not be more caustic, burning with well-deserved scorn, the emotion not only meant for her but for himself, that he should step into his father's shoes.

"It was Ow! OW! Ow! impossible to extricate myself, Ow! from where I was sitting without . . ."

The heat of his anger cooled in an instant. "Are you injured?" He vaulted through long shadows down the gloom-touched side of Tomen Bala to stand over her, breathing hard. Had she fallen? Perhaps been lying here unconscious? Why did she not get up?

She muttered meekly, "Injured. Not at all. Ow! Ow!"

"And yet you would seem to be in pain."

He knelt beside her in grass gone indigo, the scent of it, the scent of her rising to meet him. He closed his eyes, the better to drink it in. Sweet almond. Grassy almond. She always smelled of almond—marzipan—his favorite sweet. He opened his eyes with a mind to taste such a sweet, wondering what her lips tasted of—her mouth—a skulker's lips—his for the taking here in the growing darkness where she had dared to lurk—listening.

She waggled her feet back and forth rather furiously beneath the dark folds of gown and cloak—a most curious and amusing amount of fabric twitching drawing his attention to her nether regions.

"Ow. It is only that my feet have gone completely numb."

"Fell asleep, did you? Or does crouching in the dark listening to other people's conversations have a tendency to cut off one's circulation?"

She sighed heavily, said unhappily, "Yours did not seem a conversation that ought to be interrupted, my lord."

"Ah! So it was a kindness not to announce your presence?"

"No more a kindness than eavesdropping, my lord." She bowed her head, her bonnet hiding guilt-laden features. "I am terribly sorry"—she sighed again—"for such an impertinence."

Hand outstretched, he asked brusquely, "May I assist you in rising?"

She did not immediately grasp his fingers. "Most kind of you, my lord. But if you will just give me a moment. The feeling only now begins to return to my toes. I fear I would collapse if I tried to stand."

He laughed. It really was a laughable situation, dreadful as it was to think she had heard far more than he should have liked her to. "I would be happy to catch you," he drawled, deliberately suggestive.

The bonnet tilted back. Her face caught the last of the day's light, pale pink, pearl-like. "Quite unnecessary, I assure you."

"Oh, but it might prove amusing," he teased, knowing his tone unsettled her, perhaps as much as he had been unsettled to find her here.

"My limbs are rather more painful than amusing at the moment." She stretched out her right leg and waggled toes again, revealing a rather provocative view of her ankle.

"Off with your shoes," he ordered.

"My lord?"

"Come, come. It is a matter of circulation, Miss Deering. Your shoes most likely contribute to the problem." He reached for her heel.

She struggled to pull away, wincing.

"It would not be—"

"Appropriate?" He laughed, and capturing her heel loosed the laces of her walking shoe, tipping out a rather shapely foot cased in worsted wool. "How appropriate was it of you to sit here without a word?"

"It wasn't. And again I do apologize."

As inappropriate as his reaching for her other shoe, well-preserved leather, much polished, worn down at the heels. A most serviceable specimen, entirely appropriate footwear for a governess. Entirely inappropriate that he should loose the laces and slide it from her foot.

"You do not think I mean to take advantage, do you, Miss Deering? Or perhaps I have revenge in mind, and would bare your legs for your most improper silence while I bared my heart to the woman I once loved?"

Her bonnet shook a no, and yet she watched him uneasily, suspicious. He touched on truth with his taunts.

She ought to be suspicious of any man who would cradle the all too intimate warmth of her stockinged foot in the palm of his hand. Of course he did not tell her as much. He lied, as he applied pressure to her heel.

"It would be a great unkindness in you to think I take advantage, when my only aim is to restore proper circulation to your sleeping limb."

With the same assuredness with which he chastised her, he rested a much-darned, wool stockinged heel upon his thigh, and kneaded at her muscle as if it were bread dough.

She flinched, cried out, "Pins and needles. Oh, pins and needles!"

"I know, I know," he soothed, thinking she deserved as much, her punishment for listening to his heartbreak. "My batman used to do this to my feet of an evening, after I had spent all day in the saddle. Right here." He pressed the arch of her foot, remembering the shooting pain, the heat scorching all the way up his leg to his groin. "It used to hurt the most right where the metal stirrup bit into my boot. That spot carried the weight of my entire body most of the day."

She could not stop a moan escaping her lips, could not avoid arching her foot against his thigh.

He pressed his lips together, trying not to evidence satisfaction as his hands moved higher, beneath the mended edge of her skirt, smoothing rumpled wool, kneading ankle, and calf.

Dear Miss Deering's breath caught more than once in her throat as he worked, as muscle and nerve melted to his touch. He would lay odds she had never before been touched thus, that her legs were no longer in the least bit numb. He would lay odds he would touch much more before he was done with her.

"The stocking ought to come off as well," he suggested. How far might luck be pushed? "No need to be shy. I can see little in this light."

Indeed the sun's rose and gold had almost completely faded from the sky, so that they peered at one another in a growing darkness, the edges of everything gone soft, his anger, her resistance, the rumpled edge of her petticoat, the white fabric catching and holding the light.

He delved deeper its hidden mysteries. No need to see. The feel of her was enough, the high, sensitive arches of her feet, the tight round apples of her calves. He imagined undoing stocking tapes with the same deftness he had slipped off her shoes, a deftness born of practice, the heat of his fingers, his palm, against bare skin.

"My lord. I do not think—" Her breath caught as he delved a particularly sensitive spot.

"Do not think," he said. "Do not object. Simply answer the question you have been so neatly avoiding, Miss Deering."

Lost in his touch, she repeated faintly, "Question, my lord?"

"Your first kiss?"

She stiffened, might have pulled away, but he drew her foot deeper into the snare of his hands, hard against a flexed thigh. "Was it dreadful?"

"I do try to forget it, my lord." Her voice was brittle, the tension in her foot more resistant than before.

"But kisses are meant to be memorable." Like the feel of her beneath his hands, the growing heat. He longed for more, for the taste of almonds—sweet marzipan kisses— for the heat of flesh against flesh. "Why forget a kiss?" His hands stilled a moment. "Was it Palmer?"

She nodded, head down, bonnet in the way. He almost reached for the ribbon—to undo it, as he had undone her laces, as he meant to undo her stocking tapes. Palmer stopped him. Damn the man.

"A most unpleasant experience," she said. "A kiss under protest."

He sighed, closing his eyes to the dark lure of desire, his mind to the reckless need that drove him to imprudent behavior—Palmer's wantonness. He reached for her shoe, held it as a cobbler might, that she might slide her foot back into it, that she might put leather and laces between them. "No one before Palmer?" He tied the shoe snug. The dragon within thrashed and raged.

"No." How pitiful that single syllable.

"No mistletoe kisses?" He reached for the other shoe. Resolute. Resigned.

"No, my lord." She grew impatient with him. "With so many sisters there were other lips to compete for the lads' attentions."

Six sisters. I remember. "But this is a tragedy, Miss Deering." He cradled her heel a moment longer, her heat in the palm of his hand, her shoe waiting, tongue lolling. Desire seared through him, ached heavy in his groin, throbbed with the beat of his heart. Like the burning need for drink, she raged through him. Innocence in the palm of his hand. First kisses. How he longed to educate this governess in the arts of lovemaking. And yet, she would leave him, as she had left Palmer.

Inappropriate—his thoughts, his desire, his intentions.

Like Palmer, and he would not be anything like the man. Never again. He drew a deep, fortifying breath as he drew the shoe snug about her foot and gave it a tidy bow, tying up his need, his desire. He stood, to give himself distance, to give himself air, to stop himself from taking her into his arms.

She took a deep breath, looked up at him, from beneath the lip of the confounded bonnet. "Surely tragedy is too strong a word, my lord."

No, he thought, *not too strong. Not strong enough.*

"Perhaps, had you been better kissed you would better understand my opinion." He extended his hand to her while the idea hung between them, seemed to vibrate from the tips of his fingers, an invitation.

She stared a moment at his hand. As governess, an employee beholden to his generosity, giving in to desire, to kisses, would change everything—from this day forward. He knew that. She knew it, too.

"Perhaps one day I shall better understand." She put her hand in his, a gentle clasp, her eyes downcast, allowing him to assist her in rising. He waited for her gaze to rise as well. He meant to kiss her if she looked up. He would take it as a signal if desire spoke to him in her eyes, in a look.

She did not look up. When he did not immediately relinquish his hold, hoping that at last she must look up, if only in question, she surprised him, saying very gently, "I have yet to offer you my deepest condolences on the death of your father, my lord."

In this mention of his father he felt the weight of responsibility. He released his hold on her. It pained him to let her go, to release the potential of arms and lips—sweet comfort on a day he much needed it.

"You would have liked him. I am sure he would have liked you."

He focused on the path that led away from this burial ground of kings, beacon hill where lovers carved their names, a place where he had almost made a fool of himself for the second time that evening.

He did not expect the question she posed, as she slid down the path after him, indeed her voice in the darkness quite took his breath away.

"Might I ask your intentions, my lord?"

Chapter 28

"Intentions?" he drawled sarcastically, as if she asked something completely untoward—or suggestive. "You assume too much in asking."

Elaine stopped, stunned. He had been so kind in his ministrations to her, and all the time she had worried, prepared herself for inappropriate advances—like Palmer. She was sure, in such a compromised situation, he would attempt to take advantage—like Palmer, and yet not like Palmer. She had halfway hoped for kisses from this man, never from Palmer.

But he had refrained, been all that was gentlemanly and restrained, despite the tension that hummed between them, beneath his hands, beneath her skirt, not the rogue he was painted to be—not interested perhaps, as she was sure he would be, must be, should be—but in no way cruel or sarcastic until now. Why now?

May I ask your intentions, my lord?

Of all the words she might have chosen, these were certainly open to misinterpretation in such a moment, hard on the heels of his hands—Oh, God, his hands! His touch. His heat. She had not wanted him to stop—all the while she had known he must. She rushed to clarify.

"For the trip, my lord? Do you mean to press on to St. David?"

He laughed, the sound drifting back over his shoulder, a snide laugh, a sarcastic laugh—knowing. "No worries, Miss Deering." His voice grew faint as he navigated the downward slope. "I will inform you of my intentions when I have formed them."

"Yes, my lord."

"Ironic, is it not?" He seemed to be waiting for her to catch up.

She plunged after him into the darkness, her legs still tingling with the memory of his touch. "My lord?"

"The trip I planned to bring me closer to my father has taken me away from him entirely—forever."

She paused a moment out of respect for his despair, remembering her own feelings after her father's death. "He is still with you in memory, my lord. In spirit."

Fallen silent, he went faster in the deepening twilight, helping her in her slipping, sliding progress as she hurried to catch up. Such grace he possessed, even in darkness. A sure-footed balance that had her thinking of his hands on her legs.

Their progress was indescribably intimate, few words said, just the communication of a steadying grip, exchanged glances, and the remembered comfort and intimacy of his fingers on stockinged feet, as she came to life, more completely than ever before.

"Steady on," he said, and, "Tread carefully now!"

The more she tried, to stop careening into him, the worse her ability to navigate became. He did not mind, indeed, he laughed, on this a day in which she had not thought to find a breath of laughter in him. A day of lost potential for both of them—a day of mourning, for fathers, and kisses, and the possibilities inherent in both.

She could not help thinking of Palmer. He would have taken advantage of the numerous collisions of arms, hands, shoulders and feet. He might have used his sorrow to bend her sympathy. He most certainly would have tried to kiss her. She could not help wishing, and then hated herself for wishing, that Valentine Wharton might be more the man she had heard described, and less the man she found him to be.

For the first time in her life, Elaine Deering longed for a man's attentions, a whisper in her ear, the strayed touch, a breathtaking kiss beneath the stars, his arms enfolding her. And yet Valentine Wharton remained the gentleman no one truly believed him to be, and that, of all things, made her long for him more.

Her whole body became rigid with desire. His every glancing touch enflamed her. Perhaps it was this rigidness made her awkward, perhaps it was the gathering darkness, but as they neared the bottom of the pathway, Elaine tripped with a little exclamation of surprise and a scrabbling noise of shoes attempting to find sound purchase.

He stopped.

She careened into him as he turned, the heel of her palms catching the bend of his arm, propelling him backward, a step, then two. She was sure he must trip and both of them end heaped in the grass.

By sheer force of will he regained his balance, and hers. They stood a moment, arms braced, breathing hard, their gazes as clinging in the darkness as his hand about her waist.

"Throwing yourself at me, Miss Deering?" he asked, with a huff of amusement.

She pulled away at once.

"No?" he murmured. "A pity. I pictured in my mind how it would be."

She blinked, a picture in her own mind that took her breath away. "Life is never quite how we imagined it, is it?"

He framed the night sky with his hands, and her in it. "True," he said, "and yet, I am reluctant to relinquish the dream."

She thought of Palmer and stepped away from the frame he would box her in.

"This is not the future you had pictured either, is it?" he asked softly, hands falling, still blocking the path, so that they lingered in the shadow of Tomen Bala.

"No."

"Do you find the life of a governess satisfying?"

Why would he ask such a question? To remind her of her place? To remind himself? She ran a finger along the frayed cuff of her poor, inadequate sleeve—grappling with equally inadequate answers.

At last she said, "It is an honorable living. I need not be a burden to my family, which is most important to me, and the work engages my mind, energies, and talents." Her voice dropped away.

"But not what you imagined yourself doing?" He spared her his amusement, his sarcasm. It intrigued her. This seriousness in him. She nodded, just as serious.

He shifted his weight and took a slow, careful step backward, as if to lead her deeper into their conversation. "What did you hope for?"

It warmed her heart that he should ask, that he should care. But did he really want to know?

He did not look away; indeed, he seemed to search the gathering gloom for her features most expectantly.

"I never pictured my father dying," she said, following his lead, examining his face as much as she might in the gloom.

That gave him pause. He looked down, as if to study his footing, as he took another step backward. "Certainly not." How heavy his voice.

"Nor that he would leave us penniless."

"Ah. He kept secret his gaming, his debts?"

"Yes." Step by step he led her. Step by step she followed.

"What else?" he prodded when she fell silent.

"I assumed my education would be put to use in teaching my own children, not someone else's."

He paused once more, head tilted. How disconcerting those searching looks. "I do understand, you know."

Did he?

His gaze remained steady. "I assumed I would watch my first infant grow, not come home from fighting Napoleon to find . . ."

Felicity. The truth hung unspoken between them.

She could not look away, from his regret, his sorrow, his face flooded with memory, open to her, so very open. "There will be other children, my lord."

He bowed his head, walls up, his mouth a bitter line. It stopped her breathing for a moment, air caught between her teeth.

"And what am I to do with her?" he blurted, then clapped his mouth shut, as if put out with himself for asking. And strode away.

"Whatever do you mean?" She followed, slower than he, falling behind.

"I cannot clearly picture her future."

The dark shape of him loomed against lamplights' pinpricks from the houses ahead. Such weight of concern in his voice, in his shoulders.

"She will never be welcomed by polite society; neither will she easily fit into a life below stairs."

Like me. "I understand your concern."

"I do not hold high hopes that she can better herself in marriage. It might happen. Stranger things have happened, and yet if marriage is not the answer . . ." He turned, held out his hand. She wondered if, in looking at her, he saw Felicity's fate. The truth struck painfully to the very core of Elaine's sense of herself.

He set off again. "I would like to think she could build some sense of purpose and independence in making herself useful. As you do."

Sops for her self-esteem. Elaine stumbled after him, a lump in her throat.

Chapter 29

So quiet, Miss Deering. So peaceful a body. No need for constant chatter. No coy glances. So polite when he offered a hand. *Like the lake*, he thought. *She is like the lake. Coolly, calmly, and reflectively she meets the world—with hidden depth, with reined in emotion.*

And yet she rouses heat in me.

He glimpsed an answering heat in her eyes. Indeed, on occasion, before her lashes fell or her bonnet shut him out, he believed he saw admiration, affection, even desire. It pleased him, warmed him most pleasantly, to think a female of Miss Deering's caliber found something to admire in him. It stirred hope where he had begun to think all hope dead.

"We must each of us find happiness where we may, my lord." They passed a window where lamplight shone, and the smells of dinner rose from smoking chimney. "Felicity will find hers when the time comes."

"Could you find happiness elsewhere, Miss Deering?"

The question startled her. He saw her surprise in the window's receding light.

"Are you still reluctant to remain in my employ?" His eyes probed the darkness, her face a pale moon whose expression he could not read. They passed a row of darkened shopfronts, the only light from the windows above, her bonnet agleam, her eyes thrown into shadow. He studied her mood in the time it took her to reply, voice low and steady.

"I cannot imagine myself anywhere else for the moment, my lord."

He pinched the bridge of his nose and offered a faint smile to the stars. "Good. You must not go when I mean to leave myself."

"Leave, my lord?"

"For Cumbria, tomorrow," he said. "Mother may have need of me."

"Of course. And Felicity?"

"You and Mrs. Olive take Felicity on to St. David's. The house awaits. I shall leave direction with the coachman." He was all business, now that his mind was made up.

"You will return to us?" Stress changed the timber of her voice, a modicum of disappointment, a trace of melancholy. Odd, how the aching hints pleased him. It must be the night, his sorrow. His father's passing. He liked to think his absence would be noted—that he would be missed.

"I should think you might be pleased to see the back of me."

"Why should you think so, my lord?"

He believed no such thing. He believed she began to like him—perhaps, too much. They walked a fine line, he and this governess.

"We shall most certainly feel your absence," she said, disappointing his need for connection, for a greater certainty as to her feelings.

"You, Miss Deering? Will you feel my absence?"

Silence met him as she considered. "Undoubtedly," she said at last.

Her honesty pleased him, the potential of more in a single word, in the tone of her voice, in the quick dart of her glance.

"I know I shall feel your absence." The inn came into view, lamplight gleaming from a half dozen windows.

"Oh?" Her breath caught.

"That surprises you?"

"Yes."

"I have grown fond of your company. I might even go so far as to call you . . . indispensable."

"My lord! You are most . . ."

"Kind?" He grew impatient with the word. "Not at all. It is not a kindness to recognize your worth, my dear Deering."

"I do not think—"

"Do not think." He stopped in the darkness, not yet ready for the inn, for sympathetic eyes and sympathetic conversation. Whatever she meant to say faded into silence. He found the glint of her eyes in the starlight. The scent of her filled his head. Almonds, sweet almonds.

"Do *not* think, for the moment, my Deering." His voice went husky as he kissed her, a breath-taking collision of lips on pale marzipan skin—not her lips, not the lips she had expected him to take. A kiss shocking for its chasteness, gently planted in the middle of her forehead. Nothing of Palmer in it, nothing of his past, nothing to make her run.

He hoped she would sway toward him, tilt her head, give him some sign of desire. He waited for it, looking deep into her eyes, hungry for warmth, the comfort of her lips, her arms. Hoping. She did not move away, did not fight or flee, simply stood there, her breathing sharp and shallow, a little shiver passing through her. A moment came and passed. He restrained the rising dragon of desire, held it at bay. Looking deep and long into starlit eyes, he said, "No running away now, on the morrow, for no more reason than a kiss farewell."

She closed her eyes, lashes dark against her cheek. "You must promise me never again to do such a thing, my lord."

"Val." He shook his head, her hair brushing his forehead, his cheek. He wished for her lips. A real kiss. A breathtakingly beautiful kiss. She deserved better memory than Palmer. And yet, what memories did he mean to leave her with? "I cannot promise, my Deering."

"My lord!" She sounded shaken. "I must have your promise, or I shall be forced to seek position elsewhere."

"But I might wish you good-bye on another occasion and would not deprive myself of all pleasure." He did not look back as he walked away. Could not look back. Too tight a rein he kept on his sudden desire for the warmth of a woman to warm his bed. Not just any woman—this woman, his daughter's governess, whom he must not disgrace with such irresponsible desires, as he had disgraced Eve—as he had too often disgraced himself. Like Palmer. He had once believed himself far better than the man. And now?

The odor of ale and whiskey met him as he passed the parlor, where two of the guests sat enjoying drinks and cards by the fire. Lord, he needed a drink! He thought of his father, of what he might have said in such a moment. He thought of Miss Deering's father, the chaos left in his wake. He would not do that to her. Steeling himself, shoulders thrown back, he passed along the corridor to the stairs.

Time for a fairy story, was it not? Something cheerful. He would read of other dragons, rather than think too much of his own.

He was gone in the morning when Elaine rose, as he had promised. She could not help but think of the times her father had ridden away, leaving wife and daughters to fend for themselves.

She wondered what she would do when she saw Valentine again. Her most prudent course lay in leaving. To imagine his lips, warm upon her forehead, was to be filled with desire for more, a true kiss, his lips to hers. She wondered if she should pack her bags and leave at once.

But then she thought of Felicity and Mrs. Olive traveling alone half the length of Wales to St. David. It seemed foolish to leave, with Valentine Wharton out of the picture.

We must each of us find happiness where we may.

She could not picture her happiness, her future, without the child in it—without Valentine Wharton.

She went to St. David's.

Chapter 30

Two months later, on a warm day so bright one must squint, even beneath a broad-brimmed hat, Elaine and Felicity went to St. David's Head to study wildflowers.

Elaine knew it was a special day because an unopened letter went with them, one more joy in a day destined to be extraordinary. She could feel it in her bones. She had heard it in the tone of Mrs. Olive's, "Halloo!" as she waved something white at them as they set out, a flag of white, as she called to Elaine, "A letter, Miss Deering!"

A letter? Elaine's heart skipped a beat. For a moment she dared hope, dared imagine, that at last a letter arrived from Valentine, some word or thought to confirm or deny his feelings for her, author of a kiss upon her forehead. The rogue who had claimed he would feel her absence, who had claimed her indispensable.

"From your sister," Mrs. Olive said as she handed over the letter.

Anne. Dear Anne, who acted as elderly Lady Hervey's companion, wrote her at least once a week. She was good about gleaning gossip and passing on word of their siblings. Anne's letters were always a welcome treat. Not so welcome as word from Wharton might have proved. Clearly, he was not a writer. Not a word had he sent since his return home.

Elaine tucked the unopened missive into her pocket, thanked Mrs. Olive, and asked her if she was sure she did not care to come with them—knowing she would say no and yet wishing her to feel welcome.

Mrs. Olive smiled and waved, and shook her head. "It is enough of a walk for these old legs just to go to the posting house and back every day, my dear. Have a lovely day."

They set off without her.

The sun was shining, the day unusually still, the ground they must cover gently sloping, along the cliff's edge, an unobstructed view of the ocean on their left, on their right the boulder-strewn rise of Carn Llidi, where burial chambers had been found beneath the stones at the top. Ahead, Carn Twic gave shoulder to the slope, behind it Carn Hen. It was a perfect day to study wildflowers, perhaps to do a few watercolor studies. Flowers bloomed everywhere: blushing mallow, and long stalked mayweed, cheery white chamomile and purple sea asters, pale blue sea holly, and star-like stonecrop. And as they walked, butterflies accompanied them, flitting white and brown and orange.

They were slowed by the weight of the two great baskets they carried, one containing the little press they used to flatten flowers, also watercolors, paper, brushes, and a book on the proper and common names of England's native blossoms. The second basket was filled with everything needed to satisfy their appetite and thirst. The potential of such a day was undeniable.

The waves made music, a great rhythmic, unending, hushing sound as the water rushed against Craig y Creigwyr, the name of the cliffs almost as musical as the voice of the ocean. Elaine was reminded of the day she and Lord Wharton and Felicity had walked the walls of Chester, and discussed why a river might change its course.

"Perhaps the river tires of one bed and decides to try another." Would I tire of such a man's bed? Could such a man be as constant and as comforting as the ceaseless sound of the sea?

She liked to imagine he could. Liked to imagine all sorts of things in connection with the memory of his lips upon her forehead. She imagined at times that he had kissed her lips instead, a magic moment that would have changed everything. She would know the taste of him, had he claimed her mouth. She would know if the rush of desire within her was real.

Her thoughts of him were like the rushing of the waves. She wished him there, and she hoped he might stay away, that the magic of his kiss might never be proved mundane or meaningless. For the present, like the waves, that kiss embodied the idea of eternity. Memory of it seemed part of a perfect day along with the heat of the sun and the brisk breeze that tugged strands from a once tidy crown of braids.

The day slowed to their walking rhythm, baskets swinging, a relaxed and liquid pulse. The water's heartbeat filled their senses, became part of them, like the keening of the gulls, the piping of the terns, the languidly rocking flight of a dozen gulls.

This, the westernmost tip of a finger of land that stuck out along the north edge of Whitesands Bay, was a favorite place to explore, first because of the spectacular views, sparkling in every shade of green and blue and silver as the sea stretched seemingly forever to the north, while to the south, the waters must wend through Ramsay Sound, fanning around the spectacularly high cliffs of Ramsay Island, where seals barked and auks nested. Here, too, lurked the horseshoe inlet to the secluded sands of Porthmelgon, where the surf curled in fine white plumes, and beyond stretched the golden sweep of Whitesands Bay.

St. David's Head made a natural outdoor classroom. Here one might see flora and fauna in abundance, birds, butterflies and moths, wildflowers and sea grasses, rocks and sand and sea. Here lurked a fascinating pocket of ancient history, too. Man had long walked these coastal pathways, leaving his mark in caves and ancient burial chambers guarded by huge flat capstones. Like Tomen Bala, great kings were reputedly buried beneath the stones. Carn Llidi loomed nearby, and in the wildflower-carpeted valley in between, if one looked carefully, ancient dry stonewall ruins, ditches, ramparts, and hut circles were still to be seen beneath the bindweed, heather, stonecrop, and gorse.

The sun warmed their faces, the sea breezes brought color to their cheeks, and the unstinting and endless beauty of the place brought smiles and a sense of great peace to their hearts. Felicity was intrigued by the notion that her father had seen this place before her, that his father before him had thought to bring him here. The child felt free to speak of the long ago death of her unknown mother at the great burial mound, the funeral that had taken her father away from her that he might honor his father's passing, the grandfather she would never know.

In the hushing rhythm of the waves, Elaine felt the pulse of the earth, the wind, the sun. She heard in the never ending purl of water on stone the passage of the days without Valentine Wharton, the days become weeks, the weeks become months. Every morning she clothed herself in dresses he had insisted she have made, dresses delivered by post—dresses he had never seen, cloth and thread that touched her skin, as he had touched her, wrapping itself around her almost as tightly as he wound himself through her thoughts.

And as each blue-gray wave rushed to the shore, turning back on its own froth of foaming white to throw itself against the rocks once more, she wondered what would become of them, of this rush of feeling, of the terrible waves of yearning, when next they met.

She waited to open Anne's letter, waited until after they had eaten, waited until Felicity was thoroughly absorbed in faithfully reproducing the delicate star-marked pink bindweed with her watercolors. Elaine saved the letter like a bonbon to savor. Once eaten it would be gone, this brief contact with her dearest sister, so far away. With fingers that trembled a little in anticipation Elaine cracked the wax seal, the paper blindingly white in the sunshine, her sister's familiar hand stirring feelings of almost unbearable homesickness.

"What is this I hear of you?" The words leapt from the page, the hand in which her sister wrote more erratic than usual. *"Rumor would have it that the notorious Valentine Wharton has made another conquest in his bastard daughter's governess!"*

Elaine stared in disbelief. A tern gave cry overhead, a lonely, worried sound, its shadow flickering over the stones of the nearby burial carn, the darkness flashing momentarily between her and the sun. She read the lines again and then again, and still they did not make sense.

Why should anyone say such a horrible thing? Could this be Palmer, rearing his ugly head again? Would he dare to so brutally besmirch her name, monster that he was?

She read on, hoping to glean some clue, and there rose from the page evidence of another monster, the three-headed kind.

"It seems the widowed Lady Wharton is pushing her son toward marriage. The odds-on favorite is one of the Biddington heiresses. Did you not meet them? Are they deserving of him? It is predicted one of them will soon take up residence at Wharton Manor. Please write," Anne bade, *"and tell me if this can be true. Are you ruined, dear sister? Are you in danger of being cast off as soon as Wharton takes a wife? If so, do not despair. I know a woman with children in need of a governess who will take you in on my recommendation, should you require another post."*

The words swam before her, the world swam, too, as the hush of the waves went on without change, unmoved by the shifting sands of change beneath her feet.

The sound of hoofbeats roused her from the swim of words. Head reeling, Elaine observed a black horse, a man astride—cape flying, horse and rider moving as one. And for a moment, Elaine felt the world fall away, the cries of the birds stilled, the ocean hushed, her heart thudding in time with the hoofbeats. Here it was, what she had been waiting for—this horse, this rider.

No mistaking him. Valentine Wharton had the finest seat she had ever witnessed. Like the knight in a fairy tale. Like a painted illustration. Lord Wharton, on a beautiful black animal with arching neck and a white starred forehead.

In the distance, following, came three more horses, pace circumspect, three women riding sidesaddle, hems fluttering, cockaded hats bobbing. No fairy tale, this, unless a three-headed Gorgon figured into the story.

Felicity abandoned her paints, left her painting to the wind, and ran toward the horses shouting, "Papa!"

In a trice Valentine Wharton swung down from the saddle, arms wide. His daughter, once so reserved, ran straight into those widespread arms. Lifting Felicity high, laughing, he swung her like a bell.

They progress, Elaine thought, and wondered, *What of us?*

*   *   *

Val saw Miss Deering first and wished that he were alone, that he might run to her in the same overjoyed manner he ran to his daughter. His dear Deering wore a blue dress, not black. A dress he had never seen before, one of the dresses he had insisted upon, he supposed. It fit the shape of her nicely. He had thought about the shape of her often in his journey, over paperwork, in the company of his relentlessly mournful mother.

Would any woman miss me so much in passing? Miss Deering had sprung to mind. Mrs. Olive had written to say his daughter missed him, that Miss Deering asked after him every day.

He had imagined the cool peace of her, like the lake, imagined cradling the heat of her foot in the palm of his hand once more, the marzipan sweetness of her forehead beneath his lips. And more—he had imagined far more.

He wondered what she would have to say to him after such a long absence, after all that had been said by those who thought the worst of them. Perhaps she knew nothing of that. He hoped that might be the case. Too painful, otherwise, and he would not bring her pain—in any way.

Because of the gossip he did not go to her first, glad that Felicity ran to him, glad that absence compelled his little one to rush into his arms. How good it felt. How pleasant the rush of words with which she meant to tell him all that he had missed.

He would have liked to swing Miss Deering in his arms just as fervently, would have listened even more closely had she rushed to spill a font of words in his ears, but she maintained her distance—the governess in the background, just as it should be—not as he wanted it to be.

She stood watching, waiting, relegated to the background part of the scenery, the cause of his troubles in the eyes of his party—two of the Biddington sisters and Penny. These women, who along with his mother had decided it was their job to keep him out of trouble—meddlers in scandal, well meaning every one.

Chapter 31

Elaine gathered together their watercolors, the brushes, and the flower press. She knew what she must do, knew how things had changed—in an instant, in a letter, in the haughty glances from the Biddington sisters, in the pity to be seen in Penny Foster's steady gaze.

She watched Deliah Biddington flirt with Val, establishing her claim on him, making sure all saw, making sure she saw.

Felicity was swept up in their gaiety, their laughter, presents, and prancing horses. She spoke to them of wildflowers, curly dock and arrow-grass, couch-grass and thistle, earning praise for her cleverness in knowing the names. No credit due the governess, who earned only arch glances and an occasional whispered comment behind shielding hands.

Elaine gathered up the baskets, their contents lighter now, the picnic eaten. No need to beg Felicity's assistance. She was packhorse-strong. She quietly withdrew from their happy gathering, headed back down the coastal path, the day spoiled, her mood spoiled.

Time to pack her bags. Time to advertise for a new position.

And yet, who would take her? A young woman made

notorious, in not one but two separate gentlemen's house-
holds.

The baskets banged her legs, heavier than she had anticipated—certainly more awkward, and yet she would not ask
for help, could not, from this group who found her wanting
in so many other ways. She shifted the weight and went
on, along the pathway that led past Arthur's burial stone
and the ancient remnants of a fort, fortifying her own resolve to be strong, to manage this turn of events with as
much competency and calm as she could muster.

I will not look back at him. She would not. She would
put one foot in front of another and make her way through
centuary and sandsedge, sandwort and evening primrose,
past the bright blue funnels of the viper's bugloss, and the
notched crimson petals of bloody cranesbill. She must remember the black and white wave-top flights of the guille-
mot and the razorbill. This might be her last chance to see
them, her last walk along the coast, back to the house
called David's Rest. She had only to pack a bag and make
her way to the posting house. A posting coach would carry
her away—to Anne—to the promised position.

"Miss Deering!" His cry brought her thoughts up short.
She turned toward the thudding pursuit of his horse's
hooves, dreading this moment, anticipating it too, the baskets like anchors, and yet she would not set them down,
would not show the slightest sign of weakness. This moment must be borne, no matter how dreadful. She would
bid him farewell. Surely Valentine Wharton understood
better than most how to say a graceful farewell.

The animal was magnificent, no less so his rider. Val was
just as she remembered, fair and vigorous, his hair guinea
gold in the sunshine, his eyes as blue as the sky, his legs—
Oh, Lord!—she must not look at his legs.

"You run away?" A statement of fact rather than accusation, and yet there was a hint of pique in his voice, in the
puzzled knit of his brow.

"I do not run, I walk."

"Do not quibble with me."

"I did not presume to consider myself necessary to the
happiness of your return."

"Is this the first thing you have to say to me?" No doubt
of his irritation now. He scowled at her from the height of

the saddle. "No 'How are you?' No 'It's good to see you?' No 'I've missed you?' "

"No, I . . ."

"How are you, Elaine? You've a sun-kissed look. A lovely color in your cheeks, my Deering. I see you thrive in my absence."

My Deering. He called her his Deering! This was going to be harder than she had anticipated. He was not going to make it easy for her.

She took a deep breath. Still her voice shook. "Thank you, my lord. It is sunshine and sea air that improve my complexion, not your absence."

He swung down from the horse, took the heaviest of the two baskets and smiled at her, really smiled at her, as if he were so very glad to hear her admit as much, as if he were extremely pleased to see her. "Sunshine and sea air become you."

"You are very kind."

He smiled, said softly, just above the noise of the waves, "You've no idea how often I have longed to be reminded."

She stifled the joy that threatened to well from her heart into her eyes. No time for tears. She must make the best of this moment. "I hear I must congratulate you."

"Oh?"

"That you are soon to be married."

"Ah." His brows rose. His eyes narrowed against the brightness of the sun, or was it against her claim. "Heard that, have you? Yes, I hope to name a date as soon as I am out of mourning."

Black. He was wearing black, for unhappy reason, and a color he hated. And yet in this moment as her heart mourned his verification that he was lost to her, black seemed the perfect color.

"Your trip. Was it fruitful?"

"Well enough. I am told Father's funeral was everything he would have wanted it to be. Very well attended. A great deal of pomp. Very conservative—even to the shedding of tears."

"You arrived too late for it?"

"A day." Regret pulled at his mouth. "I did not ride fast enough."

"How does your mother hold up?"

"She came with me. Thought the sun and sea air might do her good."

"I see you bring quite a few in your party."

"All of them hoping to boost my mother's spirits. All of them determined to"—he sighed—"visit Wales."

"You are fortunate to have such caring friends. Indeed, may I wish you every happiness."

"I hope you may."

"I hate to give you short notice, but—"

He laughed. *How dare he laugh?*

"Do not tell me you mean to leave? You cannot, you see. I shall never survive them without you." He was amused, as was his tendency, but in this moment she could not bear it that he should doubt her resolve or belittle her feelings in any way, and so she snapped out rather briskly.

"I do mean to leave. I shall. At once."

"Why so hasty?"

"I—simply think it best—most—"

"Appropriate?" A touch of anger rang in his voice as he fell into step beside her, the horse reacting to his emotion, dancing away. "You could not be more wrong. It would be very inappropriate of you to leave."

He put down the basket to soothe the horse, lowering his voice.

"I had plans to show you Grassholm Island and Pembroke Castle."

"I am sorry. I cannot stay. You cannot ask me to stay." She plucked up the basket and set off again.

He and the horse followed, noisy in the grass. "Afraid I might try to kiss you again?"

She paused to look, stricken. "This is an inappropriate topic, surely."

He reached for the basket again, his hand brushing hers. "Not at all. Quite the opposite, you see, for I am determined that we should—"

Whatever he had determined, it was interrupted by the thunderous sound of three horses bearing down on them at once, one of the Biddington sisters insisting, "You simply must show us these burial chambers Felicity claims are hereabout, Valentine."

"And prehistoric ruins!" her sister chimed in. It seemed wrong there were only two sisters present, as if they were in some way missing a limb or, at the very least, a head. "It sounds all too fascinating." Curls flew like snakes in the wind. The suggestion sounded forced.

Felicity slid down from the position she had taken behind Penny, asking, "Might I ride double, Papa, on your new horse?"

Val held up the basket in his hand. "Miss Deering requires assistance. I shall just see her to the house."

His suggestion was met with a chorus of feminine disappointment.

Penny Shelbourne silenced all complaints, saying, "I've no interest in burial chambers. I will be happy to help Miss Deering with her baskets. Val, please stay. Entertain your guests."

She caught him off guard. He could not refuse.

Very cleverly managed. They had all been very cleverly managed.

Elaine kept her eyes on the sunlit water, on the view of high-cliffed Ramsay Island and the distant sandy curve of Whitesands Bay. Beneath them, at the cliff's foot, the pleasant sheltered beach of Porthmelgon gave glimpse of sand and shale, sandpipers and gulls. A cormorant fanned its wings on a rocky ledge. Black-capped terns keened and dove above, bright red legs and beaks stark against white bellies. Great gray-backed gulls wheeled, riding the wind. Elaine took it all in with an undeniable sense of desperation, of loss, as if sand slipped from beneath her feet. She had the feeling she would never again see St. David's Head on such a day, in such a light, the wildflowers in bloom.

Penny Shelbourne shifted the basket she carried from one hand to the other. "How beautiful this place is. I can see why Val likes it here."

Elaine nodded, turning to face this woman who had been so good to Felicity, whom Valentine had once loved. "You can see why his father made a point to bring him. Why he makes a point now to bring Felicity."

"His father?" Penny Shelbourne seemed surprised, then dredged up memory. "Oh, yes, when he was a lad. About Felicity's age."

Elaine nodded.

"I begin to think the seaside suits him better than the

mountains," Penny said. "It is as wild as he. As change-able."

"And yet he is drawn to the quiet of mountains, the grandeur. He said once, 'One might find oneself in such scenery.' "

The basket swayed between them. A tern rode the breeze above, piping plaintively. "Val said that?"

Elaine paused to get the wording right, "Mountains help him 'to place himself in proper perspective to the dragons of war.' "

Penny looked at her with an arrested expression. "Strange you should say that. Cupid once called Valentine a dragon on the battlefield."

"More knight than dragon," Elaine said.

"You know a great deal, Miss Deering."

Elaine did not know what to say to that. There seemed an undercurrent in the way Penny Shelbourne said things.

"Surely you must see he comes to rescue a damsel in distress." She said it gently—too gently.

She means he comes to rescue me, the governess of ru-ined reputation.

They walked in silence, the voice of the sea constant, the song of the waves against the shore, the squabbling of the birds.

"Why tell me this? As you see, I am not in need of rescue."

"You are. You are indeed."

"From gossip? But none of it is true."

Penny regarded her a moment, very seriously. "It does not matter."

"Of course it matters. The truth matters."

"I have been the subject of just such gossip. Perhaps you knew?"

Again silence swelled between them, until Elaine blurted, "You think he would rescue me for your sake?"

"He will not allow a woman to be disgraced because of his connection with her. Not again. Surely you must see that."

"And you think that would be wrong?"

"It does not matter what I think. His mother will try to stop him. The Biddingtons . . ."

"He is meant for one of them."

She nodded.

"And you? Why tell me this? What do you want?"

"I want whatever is best for Val, for Felicity. They have endured enough gossip."

"I see."

"What will you do?"

Elaine held her head high and looked out to sea, one last look. "I shall do what I think best for Val, for Felicity. They have, as you say, endured enough."

Even as she said it, Felicity came riding to meet them, excitement lending her face a beautiful glow. "We are to take a boat to Grassholm tomorrow! To see the gannets."

And thus Valentine unknowingly managed to keep Elaine from leaving, on that first day of his return. It was the tale of gannets, after all, that had convinced her to come to Wales. She could not leave before she had seen such magic with her own eyes. Could she?

Chapter 32

Morning found them sailing across the wide mouth of St. Bride's Bay, south to Skomer Island, Valentine Wharton and his bevy of beauties: his mother sourly regarding Miss Deering, while the Biddington sisters vied for his attention and Penny spent her time providing Felicity with distraction.

Will it be as I remember? As I described? His gaze strayed away from Miss Biddington's ceaselessly moving mouth to a pair of lips he would much rather move with kisses. *What will her reaction be when she sees them? Will the sight catch hold of her heart as it once caught hold of mine?*

The weather was with them. Another few miles out to sea and they spied the island. Conditions were perfect, visibility at its best.

From a distance, Grassholm's rounded black basalt crown looked rather like a pumpernickel bun dusted with flour and poppy seeds. Only the bread was alive. The flour dusting moved. Poppy seeds took wing. Rising walls of birds took flight, stirred by their approach, birds hanging black and white in the blue sky, above acres of nesting birds. Thousands of birds. Hundreds of thousands. An awe-inspiring feathered movement.

There was no evidence of man here, no soil, no fresh water, no plant life, only birds: birds in flight, birds perched shoulder to shoulder, white and gray and black bird feathers littering the sea, bird droppings turning the black basalt white, bird voices keening and crying, overpowering the voice of water dashing against stone.

The rock rose forbiddingly from the water, no boat landing sites, only bird perches and seal sunning ledges. Black-tipped wings flapped at sight of them like rows of women fanning themselves, voices raised in a gossipy chorus, croaking and gurgling. The very rocks seemed alive, as gray seals barking and rolling, bounded for the water by the score.

Nature's nursery—beyond just gannets, there were kittiwakes by the hundreds. Black and white, smaller than the gannets, their flight more sweeping and graceful than gulls, their falsetto cry of kittiwake—ache—ache, unmistakable. Guillemots and razorbills, too, skimmed low over the water in flocks of a half dozen or so, strikingly black in contrast to so much white, but outnumbered, their voices lost among the masses of brooding gannets.

Gannets owned the island, outnumbering the others by the hundreds. Big as swans, the largest startlingly white, with stark black wingtips and yellowed head feathers, their pale eyes and beaks elegantly lined in black, were accentuated like Egyptian pictographs. The young were brown speckled with white or awkwardly splotched black and white the entire length of their wings, wedge-shaped tails edged in black.

And, just as he had once described them to her, the gannets were fishing, flinging themselves out of the sky like terns did, fearlessly falling, plunging from great heights. Val wondered if she remembered.

He watched for her reaction.

His mother had seen them before, and yet she eyed them with no less awe than when he had been a boy. He leaned close to whisper in her ear, "Leap of faith, mother. Do you remember?"

"Leap of what?" She seemed confused.

"You said that."

She blinked at him. "I did?"

He nodded. "When I was a lad. Do you not remember?"

She shook her head.

"It is very noisy!" the eldest Biddington cried out.

"I have never heard anything like it." Deliah seemed transfixed, momentarily speechless.

"I wish Alexander might have seen this," Penny said to Felicity, who turned to her father, eyes shining: "It is wonderful, Papa. Truly wonderful."

Only Miss Deering held her tongue, not a word to give him a clue as to her feelings about this image, this beauty, this courageous wildness that a young man had clung to throughout the most rigid tests of his life.

This magic was the reason sensible Elaine Deering had been enchanted by him from the start, a wild man who might ruin her reputation, a man who had proved not so wild as his memories of Wales, and yet her reputation was in question anyway.

He stepped in behind her at the railing to ask, "What do you think, Miss Deering? Were they worth the trip to Wales?"

"In they plunge," she breathed the words, as if afraid to speak too loud, her chin lifting, following the plunging flight. "Big as swans, with ink-dipped wings and Egyptian eyes. Just as you said."

His words. So long ago, and she remembered his words exactly. He had woven a tale of this magic, and here it was, larger than life, far more spectacular than she had ever imagined, far more worthy of examination than his colored past.

"Leap of faith," she said as another bird plunged.

His mother, who had drifted close, turned her head at the words, listening as Miss Deering said, "Or do they not so much leap . . ."

"As fall?" The two women spoke in perfect unison, his words and the memory linking them if only for a moment, his mother's eyes startled, as if she saw Miss Deering, really saw her, for the first time.

Chapter 33

Elaine tossed and turned in bedclothes grown wrinkled and hot, her hair sticking to her neck. The day's heat carried into the night, a time when her greatest fears and worries always reared their ugly heads. Monsters—as she had once believed Valentine Wharton to be—new monsters to trouble her now. She fretted over her sister's letter, the presence of Val's forbidding mother, the Biddington sisters' disdain, and Penny Shelbourne's watchful, knowing pity.

Elaine had known from the start this was how it would be—that she must eventually leave him. Why did it surprise her so much when life worked out as expected? Why did it tear at her heart like the cry of the kittiwake? Like the memory of thousands of birds taking wing? Like the startled look in Lady Wharton's eyes as they uttered the same words at exactly the same moment?

Elaine could not sleep.

Felicity lay curled in slumber in the next room, dreaming of castles no doubt. Mrs. Olive snored gustily from the bedroom they shared. Tomorrow they would proceed by boat from the comfortable Tudor inn in Dale, where Lord Wharton's party had taken all the rooms, to Pembroke cas-

tle, their final destination. Val's idea. He knew Felicity
adored castles.

They had come this far. It would be a shame not to
see it. A greater shame that Elaine must leave them in
Pembroke—Felicity, Valentine. Especially Valentine, who
gave her gannets.

She must make a leap of faith in leaving. Or was it a fall?

The voice of the ocean called her, promising cooler air,
a breath of a breeze, clarity of mind. Elaine went to the
window, flung wide the shutters, stared out at the moonlit
beach, the taste of salt and cooler air in her face, the sound
of the waves dashing upon the shore a comfort to that part
of her that needed it most.

Leap of faith.

She threw on a muslin wrapper, yanked on stockings,
and grabbing her shoes crept down creaking stairs. Careful
not to be seen, she laced up her shoes and followed the
moon to the beach, where she stood staring out to sea,
moonlight on rippled waves, her heart aching with the idea
that tomorrow she must leave. Tomorrow she must put all
of this behind her, perhaps never to see it again.

Leap of faith.

At water's edge she kicked off her shoes, shed her stockings, and lifting the hem of her nightshift and wrap, picked
her barefoot way across wet shale and sand to the water,
cool against her toes, surging about her ankles. Blessedly
cool, washing away her fretfulness, her worries. She took a
step deeper, lifting the bundle of her nightclothes higher,
careful not to soak them, her ankles reveling in alternating
waves of water and air, heated flesh cooled.

"Trouble sleeping?"

He came up behind her too quietly on the rocky beach,
the unexpected voice sending her heart skittering along
with the scree beneath his feet. Breath caught, she whirled,
fear looming, that anyone should be about at this hour,
that it should be Valentine Wharton—with whom her name
and reputation were now irrevocably linked.

She thought of his kiss, of so much more they might have
done—what they were suspected of doing—heat flushing
her cheeks, her neck, heat stirring lower. And not enough
ocean to cool her.

She found him strange in the night, a shape gone unfa-

miliar and gray—the shape of all that might have been—
of all that might be—his eyes catching the starlight, glinted
in the darkness. He wore nothing but an open-necked shirt,
white against the darkness, sleeves rolled high, his breeches,
stockings, and shoes the same color as the sand, so that he
seemed sprung from the night, the sea, her imaginings.

He glanced down at the shoes she had left on the shale,
head cocked, to the exposed state of her legs.

With a chuckle he kicked off his own shoes, and hopping
toward her, yanking stockings, said, "An excellent idea—
wading—in this heat."

Shocked, without thought for consequences, she dropped
her hem, a wave catching the fabric, soaking it, the wave
dragging the weight of it before and then behind her.

She made a noise and leapt away from the incoming tide,
away from the prospect of becoming even more soaked. And
in making the leap she moved toward him rather than away,
so that they collided at surf's edge, water curling around their
ankles, his arms curling about her waist, steadying her, her
drenched hem washing up around his bare ankles.

"My lord! You startled me. It is an unusual hour to be
walking." Her remark sounded so formal, proper—
preposterous.

"Indeed." He chuckled. "A dangerous hour."

Danger lived in Valentine Wharton's voice, his presence,
the moonlit sparkle of his eyes. Danger roused its head in
her own desire.

He did not release her arm, did not free his ankles from
her drenched nightwear. She did not attempt to step away,
did not attempt to look away from the link of his gaze in
the darkness, a most searching gaze, heated. Danger in that.

"Do you walk the beach often after dark, Elaine?" So
light the tone of his question, so nonchalant. And yet, his
use of her given name triggered a shiver of anticipation.
This intimacy—would it lead to greater intimacies?

She clutched her wrap, all too aware that he saw her,
most inappropriately, in her nightclothes. Not that her high-
necked plain white linen gown was revealing. To the contrary, she was most circumspect in every stitch of the sturdy
fabric she had chosen as a governess's attire. Fine lawn had
been deemed too sheer a fabric for a job in which she must
live in the homes of strangers.

The muslin wrapper criss-crossed her breasts, tying beneath. And yet water wicked up almost to her knees, the wet warp and woof of cotton plastered to her calves, wrapping his ankles, tugging at them, as though they were joined by flesh rather than fabric. She felt humid, disarrayed, her hair, still plaited, unpinned, a weighty braided rope that trailed upon her back, tendrils wisping in the breeze. The high-necked gown was unhooked, her throat exposed.

His arms, his legs seemed so very bare. The look in his eyes bare too. Needy. Wanting. Waiting. Feelings she understood too well.

She inhaled abruptly, looked down, at their legs, his naked ankles, her soaked hem. "I had best go," she said, and at last she moved, toward higher land, away from his hold on her, away from the look in his eyes.

She dragged the wet weight of fabric out of the tide, picking her way across the rocks, bruising her feet in her haste, encountering something sharp in the darkness with an exclamation of pain.

He was beside her at once. "May I be of any assistance?"

She bent, gathering wet muslin in both hands, wringing it awkwardly, ineffectively. "Turn your back," she ordered briskly, struggling with the weight, the water, her legs cold, a shiver dancing along her spine.

"Nonsense!" He grabbed up the wet hem, and gave it a good wringing. When she objected, he would have none of it. "I have seen your limbs before." He laughed, his teeth flashing white. "Rather nice limbs they are, too."

He bunched the fabric tight about her thighs as he wrung water, his movements affecting every inch of the garment, tugging, twisting, her body affected, the rate of her breathing. And yet she did not stop him. They were suspected of far worse. He could not ruin her with such behavior if she was already ruined in the eyes of the world.

She clutched the wrapper about her shoulders as if she were cold, as if she must hold it tight when in truth she longed to throw it off. He seemed so at ease, there in the moonlight beside her, sleeves rolled high, her nightclothes in his hands. She was anything but.

"This heat." He chuckled—such a devious sound. "Makes one long to throw off one's clothes and run into the sea, does it not?"

She stared at him, a trifle alarmed. Was he accustomed to young women who jumped to comply? The suggestion was strangely tempting, with her reputation already suspect. She had nothing to lose in throwing off her clothes, in running into the sea.

Nothing except self-respect and her maidenhood.

"I had best be getting back." She took a deep breath and stepped away from him, her gown slipping from his grasp.

"Wait," he said. "Your shoes."

He took two steps, bent to catch them up. "Let me help you."

"I can manage perfectly well . . ."

He laughed and knelt before her. "Stick out your foot."

She did as he bade, not because he was master and she beholden to him, not because it was a practical suggestion as there was no place to sit and do the task herself—she placed her hand on his shoulder and thrust her foot out from under the wet hem of her skirt because she remembered the intoxicating pleasure of his hands on her feet and wanted to experience it again, one last time.

He bent his head, golden threads of his hair gone silver in the moonlight. He shook out her darned stocking, plain worsted wool when he must be accustomed to silk. It did not matter. Nothing mattered but the heat of her hand on his shoulder, the movement of muscle and bone, the gentle brush of fingers on flesh. He used the stocking to dry her leg, the flat of his hand to brush away sand from the sole of her foot, from her toes, traces of salt and sand from the fat of her calf.

"A sturdy foot," he said.

She could not speak. Her none too sturdy knees almost buckled with every touch. She was glad of her grip on him, the solid support of that shoulder. He took his time, exploring between her toes, dusting away grains of sand. She did not urge him to make haste. She could not say a word, only breathe deep, ragged breaths, as she imagined allowing her hands to pass over him in similar fashion.

At last he planted the arch of her foot on buckskinned thigh, that it might not get sandy again. She could feel muscle and tendon flex as he rolled up the stocking in such a way that he might slip it over her toes without dragging it in the dirt, her heel cupped in the palm of his hand.

Deftly he smoothed the stocking over her leg, the heated friction of his fingertips traveling high, so high her breath caught on a gasp.

"Now the shoe," he said, and held it that she might step in and laced it snug and directed her, "Now the other one."

Without a word she shifted her weight, shifted the shoulder on which she braced herself, raised her wet hems and gave her other foot into his hands, abandoning it to his careful ministrations. And he, just as silently, just as thoroughly, dried and dusted off her foot, checking toes and the hollow behind her knee, his movements exquisitely deliberate, his hands and fingers languidly thorough.

This time when Valentine planted Elaine's heel upon his thigh, he paused in rolling up the stocking to murmur, "This is all wrong, of course, you know. Quite backward."

"The stocking?" she asked, voice low. "Is it inside out?"

"No." His shoulder shook. "That I kneel here dressing you when I would much rather be undressing you."

She gasped, might have pulled away, but he maintained gentle grasp of her heel.

"I shock you?" He slid the stocking over her toes, smoothing the wool into the arch of her foot, over heel, then ankle, and she knew she ought to stop him, ought to stop the deliberate path of his hands as they tugged the stocking higher, cupping the ball of her calf, nudging the wet cling of her hem higher, so that he might kiss her knee, so that he might pull her closer, by way of the hollow of that knee. "I have missed this leg," he said, "dreamed of this foot. There is something I would ask you, Elaine, while I am down on bended knee. Something I desire of you."

She tensed, unwilling to hear the request a notorious rogue would most likely make of his daughter's governess.

"My dear Deering." His hand drifted higher, abandoning the stocking, smoothing the bare flesh of her thigh. "Will you . . . ?"

"My shoe," she gasped, hoping to halt his question, hoping to distract his hand.

He sighed. "Your shoe. Yes. It is here, somewhere." But it was not her shoe he reached for, his hands delving deeper beneath the damp folds of her nightshift, finding trembling inner thigh, seeking higher still, ever so gently, the most private and aching parts.

She ought to have bolted away from this forwardness before it went so far, this intimate invasion, and yet as shocked as she was, she was equally seduced by the delicious sensation, by the magic of his touch. By the answering magic of her own body.

Alarmed by her own willingness to allow him liberties, Elaine inhaled abruptly and stepped away at last, abandoning her shoe, wet fabric catching in his hands, wet fabric slapping her legs.

"Wait," he said, unmoving. "Your shoe. Do not go away without it."

She hesitated, breathing hard, legs shaking, the intensity of her desire frightening. She wanted so much more from him than her shoe. She held out her hand for it, forced her voice to steady in saying, "All I desire of you is my shoe, my lord."

He rose, dangerous at full height, dangerous and enticing in the moonlight. He passed a hand over his mouth, took a deep breath, sighed, shook his head, and smiled knowingly. "A lie, that."

He dusted off his knees, and took a step closer to hand her the shoe. "You wear the perfume of the sea, the scent of your desire."

She reached for the shoe, a little off balance with one foot only stocking-clad. He handed it over. She jammed her foot into it, watching him warily, shaken to her very core.

His eyes glittered dangerously.

She had no idea what he meant, knew only that she had allowed things to go too far, to get out of hand. *Here it is. The monster in him roused at last. Will he consume me? Will I let him?*

No leap of faith, this. This was unquestionably a fall.

She had allowed him to touch her inappropriately. In so doing she had committed herself to leaving. No turning back, now. She—they—could not go on as governess and employer as though nothing had happened. She must go.

Chapter 34

She set off for the inn, laces trailing, shoe sliding, rubbing her heel as raw as her nerves, her emotions, her heart.

He fell into step beside her, matching stride. "Shall we to bed then, my Deering?"

To bed? His Deering? Too bold his choice of words. She took a deep breath, swept by contradictory desires—to throw herself at him, or to flee.

He crouched to pick up a stone, somehow much less threatening so low to the ground. "Will you sleep? I found that I could not."

She dared to stop, to tie the loose lace of her shoe. Perhaps he had meant his remark to be suggestive of nothing more than sleep.

He chuckled, rising smoothly, muscles uncoiling, beautiful to behold, skimming a pebble into the moonlit glitter of the sea. "My mind would not be still."

Her own mind would not still—the questions—the doubts. "You were thinking of her, weren't you?"

He turned, attention caught. "Her?"

"You still love her, don't you?"

Silence hung between them.

"Why didn't you stop Penny from marrying your friend?"

He scooped up a handful of sand and held it out to her. "Grab this."

She grabbed. His servant, ready to obey.

"Can you stop the sand from sifting through your fingers?"

She shook her head as it trickled between every finger.

He cupped his hand around hers. "Penny was sand." He stared into her eyes, a starlit look of such delving intensity it took her breath away. "Are you sand, my Deering? Do you mean to slip through my fingers?"

His words shocked her. Their implication.

He leaned forward, as if he meant to kiss her.

Her hands spasmed, away from his, sand flying.

"I fear you are," she heard him whisper as she ran away.

He came after her, caught her by the shoulder, turned her as he said her name, gently, his voice like the tide, washing over her. "Elaine."

"My lord."

"Val, my Deering."

She could not look into his eyes, could not voice his name. He would sweep her under with a look, a gesture, a touch. She could feel the undertow of desire—ready to sweep her off her feet.

"I am not your Deering."

"You are," he said harshly. "At present I pay your keep. Or are you determined to leave me again?"

"Like she did?"

"Like you have been set on doing since the moment I met you."

She said nothing, could not tell him how much it pained her to stay in his keep, his pay.

"Thought of you keeps me awake, my Deering. Your face today watching the birds, I could not get it out of my head."

She collected her wits, her breath coming fast. "An unforgettable image, my lord."

"Yes, it was, and is again this evening, here in the moonlight, the silver of this tear upon your cheek." He touched the damp trail, sending waves of agitated anticipation through her.

She eyed him warily, nerves on edge, a shiver passing the length of her spine, his eyes hard to read, dark wells of shadow. His silhouette loomed against the moon, against the silver dance of light upon the water. When starlight at last unveiled his features, he was smiling. He reached out to catch a flyaway strand of her hair.

She flinched.

He slowed the movement, his fingers transfixing her as he smoothed it away from her face, fingers catching in her hair, grazing the curve of her ear, coming to a stop at the nape of her neck.

She shivered and closed her eyes, so delicate was the sensation, so provocative. Her hand rose to stop him.

"It takes courage to take a plunge." He caught her fingers, parrying her move. She opened her eyes as he drew her closer, grasping her hand to his chest. She could feel the rise and fall of his breathing. She could feel the beat of his heart.

"Elaine, will you . . . do you dare?" His lips brushed her fingertips, nuzzled her wrist, planted a warm kiss where her pulse beat hardest. She closed her eyes, his touch delicious, the movement of breath and mouth and tongue mesmerizing. She ought to have withdrawn her hand from his, and yet it never even occurred to her.

"Leap of faith?" he asked, the wind fingering his hair, starlight in his eyes—and desire, a terrifying heat.

"Leap of faith, my lord?" she reminded him. "Or fall?"

He chuckled. Oh, how the sound ran through her. "You must learn to call me Valentine, Elaine."

"It would be inappropriate, my lord."

"Just as this is inappropriate?" He kissed her, lips warmer than the night, humid as the breeze, as laden with potential.

"Yes," she breathed.

"I like the sound of that."

She ought to have objected, to have stepped away, but she could not, did not. Another yes implied.

Hands linked he drew her closer.

She offered no resistance, curious of all that he was known for, of all that her heart held, of all that she was suspected of doing—wanting another taste of his lips.

He pressed his cheek to hers, murmured against her hair, her hand curled in his, held tight against the fine white lawn of his shirt. She could feel the warmth of flesh beneath.

"I do not think . . ."

"Do not think. Feel." He pulled her deeper into his arms, lifting hers to encircle his neck. Her fingers caught the tossed waves of his hair, the warm, silken wonder of it. Her breasts found the solid comfort, the warm resistance of chest muscles. Such a perfect position, such a perfect fit. The friction of their clothing seemed small resistance, the sound of his breath in her ear as endless as the sea. He chuckled, the low rumble of his laughter provocative. "Just feel. Can you not feel it? I know you do."

Of course she felt it, the charged quality of the air, as if thunder must rumble and lightning flash between them. She took a deep breath.

"Say yes," he murmured, hands encircling her ribs, sliding lower, into the small of her back, drawing her closer, rousing the throbbing heat he had touched upon earlier between her legs. What was this unfamiliar ache? So intense, demanding. It seemed to crowd out all other thought and feeling—certainly all good sense.

Her hipbone nestled his thigh. He adjusted his stance, accommodating her curves. Her belly, through the fabric of her nightshirt, found contact with his flank, muscles stretched taut. Desire pulsed deep within, throbbed within lips and temple, crashed over her like waves dashing on rock. She did not pull away as he nuzzled her neck, as he gently tugged the end of her braid, tilting her head so that she must look at him, her mouth only a fraction of an inch from his. Her lips hungered for his, for that humid connection of aroused flesh.

"Say yes," he whispered, waiting, poised, teasing her with the heat of his breath. He pressed the curve of her waist tighter to his, the flat of his right hand passing slowly along her ribs, as if he would count them.

"Say yes," he whispered against her cheek, the satin of his lips, the velvet of his breath too heated to refuse.

"Yes," she said, and turned her head that he might more easily find her lips, as though seeking the perfect placement, the perfect fit. "Yes," she whispered as he drew her closer, the flats of both his hands pressing downward from the small of her back, so that the hard muscle of his thighs met hers, so that aching heat found something harder still, nudging her, as his finger had nudged her, this time confined by the fabric between them, that friction tantalizing, adding to the sensation.

His mouth tested hers with a similar pressure, a similar heat, his lips parting, hers parting, his tongue tasting, testing, seeking.

He took her breath away and gave it back again, and never had she imagined kisses such as these. Like the sea he swept over her. She opened up her mouth to him, clung tight, stepping into the embrace as tightly as barnacle clings to stone.

She did not want to let go, to disconnect lips and tongue, and straying hands, and yet with her passion came the flicker of a memory—Palmer—Palmer's lips—Palmer's hands. She had to escape. Too fast, this tumble of desire and confusion. Too heated the flame of desire that sprang within. She pushed away, arms stiff, body resistant.

"Stop. We must stop. I must go back."

He stopped, arms still claiming her, eyes searching—surprise there—disappointment—receding heat. "Elaine." He sounded crestfallen.

"Please do not stay me." She pressed both hands to his chest, holding him at bay.

He released her reluctantly, wistfulness teasing his mouth. "I go too fast. Before I have even asked . . . Just one more question, Elaine. One more yes."

"No." She tried to steady herself. She must be steady. Strong. Unswayed by the wash of feeling that left her dizzy. Aching. Needy. Wanting more. She took a step away from him.

"You would say no when you've no idea as to the question?"

The tide washed in. The tide washed out. Her heart seemed to beat too hard. She took a deep breath. "What question, my lord?"

"Val. Surely you feel free enough to call me Val?"

She shook her head, shook away the lure of his voice, his name. "My lord. It is wrong of me. To say yes. To kiss you."

"Did you not enjoy our kisses, Elaine?"

She could not lie. Could not deny the wonder of those kisses. The bliss. Neither could she give in to him, to the lure of more such kisses. "It is not my place to enjoy kissing you, my lord."

"Who better?"

She closed her eyes. Closed out the moon and the stars and the silvered sea. "Better to kiss the woman you would take to wife, my lord."

"Indeed." His tone was seductive. He meant to kiss her again. She could hear his intent in every word. "Who better?"

"One of the Biddington sisters." She heard his step in the shale, and still she did not open her eyes to the truth, for then she must step away.

He laughed gently, laughter lost on the wind. "I've no desire to kiss a Biddington, and every desire . . ." He stopped only inches away, and yet he did not try to touch her.

Her damp gown billowed out to wrap itself around his legs as it had in the water, now driven by the wind. She felt the tug and opened her eyes, dizzy with the scent of him, swaying. "It is unkind to tease."

"My dear Deering, I have resolved never to do any woman an unkindness, most especially not to you. I would not tease, my dear. I have every intention of kissing you."

He did just that, an infinitely gentle kiss, just one, and then he pulled back, lingering close enough that, resolution wavering, she closed the gap, bowing her forehead to rest upon his chest, hands clutching windblown white shirt linen.

He laughed and pulled her close, finger crooked beneath her chin. And then his fingers sent fresh shivers down her spine, plucking at the bow tied beneath her left breast, loosing the criss-cross of fabric that bound her wrap, the wind catching the fabric, lifting it like wings so that it wrapped them both. His arms slid beneath the wings, encircling her waist, cupping the softness of her breast through the softness of muslin. As his lips sought hers he murmured heatedly. "I am a man of wicked reputation, my dear."

"I know," she said, and lifted her lips that he might kiss them again.

"Well-deserved," he said, and trailed his fingers along her spine so that she arched her back, fitting her body more tightly to his.

He chuckled wickedly in her ear, and shifted his hips that he might accommodate the depth of their embrace even more.

She pushed away, breathing hard. "What motivates this sudden ardor, my lord?"

His brows rose. He smiled playfully. "Proximity, Elaine. Would you not agree?"

She would not allow him to embrace her again. She held him at arm's length, breathing hard, trying to regain decorum, self-control. "A letter arrived. My sister. She says that my name is now inextricably linked to yours."

"I would have it so linked." He stilled, only his eyes moving, focused on hers, intent in their regard. "And you? What would you? I have endangered your reputation. And so you must marry me."

He made this proposal matter-of-factly, as if it were already decided, and kissed the tip of her nose, as if she were a child to be placated.

She stared at him in disbelief. "You wish to marry me?"

"I must marry you. Surely you see that."

She heard only the word "must", as if this decision were thrust upon him rather than chosen. She pulled her wrap close, retied the strings.

It pained her to think he would marry her because he "must", rather than because he wanted to or longed to or loved to. It hurt deeply to think he asked out of a sense of duty rather than true desire. It piqued her pride that he did not ask her if she wished to marry him.

"I confess myself astounded, my lord, at such a suddenly posed question." Pain spoke, her voice dropping away, "Is it a question?"

"Is it?" he repeated, stepping back, as though she surprised him. The breeze ruffled his shirtsleeves and tossed his hair. The sea washed in, inevitable as his response. "Is there any question that you must marry, Elaine? I think not. Is there any question that you must marry me?"

She did not answer at once, and now his voice evidenced pain, even a trace of anger. "Do not try to convince me you hold me in disgust, even disdain, for I will not believe it."

"No, I . . ."

"Would you have me go down on bended knee?" He

gave every indication that he would do just that, right there in the sandy shale.

"No," she caught at his arm. "Please."

With an expression of growing pique he pulled free from her grasp. "What is it that makes you hesitate to say yes to my proposal, Miss Deering?"

"I—" She struggled with the words. "I must know . . . I must know if you would marry me rather than see me ruined as Penny was ruined."

"Penny?" He grew irritated, seemed compelled to take two strides away from her, voice rising. "Penny has nothing to do with this."

"She has everything to do with the man you have become. You loved her. I know you loved her. Love her still."

He went very still a moment before he said, carefully, "You think me irrevocably heartbroken?"

"I know you are loath to let anyone in, other than Felicity."

"Who else needs letting in?"

She blinked, hurt by the question. Was he blind to her feelings? Could he not see the truth whenever he looked into her eyes?

He asked again, tone softer, "Who else needs letting in, my Deering?"

Truth hovered between them, in her silence, in his expectant waiting. She found she could reveal no more than she already had. "You wouldn't see another woman's name smeared due to your actions," she said at last—an accusation. He waited for soft words. She gave him hard.

He laughed, a snide sound. "And so you think I offer marriage as a kindness?"

"Do you? While I would hold such an offer in deepest respect, I could not accept. It would not be a kindness in me to saddle you with a wife for no more reason than gossip gone awry. It would not be a kindness to Felicity."

"She loves you."

"And you?"

Silence hung heavy between them.

"Do you fear I do not love you?" he asked. "That I would seduce you, as I have just seduced you, without some affection involved?"

She could not look at him. "I would suppose there is some sort of affection involved with any seduction."

He wrapped his arms about his torso, as if to shield himself from her opinion. "Fair enough. I am deserving of all doubts. My history provides you with reason enough to question my intentions, does it not?"

"I think, my lord, your intentions are . . ."

He threw up his hands. "Do not say kind. I beg you."

She bowed her head, shaken. "My experience has been that you are capable of great kindness. And yet, I would not have you offer me marriage as nothing more than that."

Silence stretched between them, and the unbroken song of the sea. Despair rising, she turned once more to go. Only then did he find voice.

"Wait."

She stopped.

"I will not deny the past came to confront me again in you. In unfounded rumors." He pulled a wry face. "Unfounded until this evening, of course. But, you see, I cannot turn my back on the harm I once blithely walked away from. It is a good thing, I think, to atone for past mistakes."

Her spirits fell. A cloud covered the moon. It seemed right, and timely, that its light should be doused.

He took a step toward her. She took a step away.

"You are mistaken in assuming I marry you for no other reason." His voice swept over her, as it always had. Dangerous waters.

"Oh?"

"I ask that you do me a great kindness. Make a leap of faith. *Sublimiora petamus.* Marry me."

Let us seek the sublime. The moon shook off its shroud.

She turned, tears in her eyes. "You will give me time, my lord? To consider your . . ." she stopped herself from saying kind, took a deep breath, finished lamely, "your offer?"

He nodded, moonlight dancing in his hair.

She ran to the inn, tears streaming, wet nightshift slapping her legs, moonlight and possibilities in pursuit.

Chapter 35

What to do next? Two events helped Elaine make up her mind.

The first occurred when she returned to the room she shared with Mrs. Olive. The older woman stood at the window, fanning herself with a bit of paper and dabbing her upper lip with a damp handkerchief.

"A warm night," she said, her gaze passing over Elaine rather searchingly. "I see you have been out, Miss Deering."

"To the beach. For a breath of air."

"These windows are too small for much of a breeze, though not too small for a bit of a view." She cocked her head, as if waiting for more.

"I went wading."

"Wading is it? With whom? Up to no good he was, you can be sure."

True enough. I was up to no good, and Lord Wharton no better. And yet, she would not undo a moment of it. Not one single heated moment.

"Ruined, is it?" Mrs. Olive waved an agitated hand.

The gravity of Elaine's situation reared its ugly head. *Am I ruined? By a touch? A kiss?* Funny how it did not feel like ruination at all. Quite the opposite. She felt newly made, clothed in a new skin.

The hem of her wrap. Mrs. Olive meant her hem. Was it ruined?

Elaine slipped the wrap from her shoulders, thinking of his hands steadying her in the swim of the tide, sending her reeling in a swim of extraordinary feeling. He wrapped himself around her, clingy as a wet hem. Her skin burned. She studied the dirtied garment by the window's dim light. "Sand. Salt," she said. "Nothing that cannot be washed away." It was a lie. She could never wash away the memory of this evening.

"And you, my dear? You look . . . flushed."

So worried the older woman looked. As if she knew.

Elaine pressed the back of her hand to flaming cheek. "Almost as warm without as within." She hung her garment to dry. On the beach a man walked. Lord Wharton.

"Are you ruined, my girl?" Mrs. Olive asked, the question startling.

Elaine flushed with guilt. She steadied her voice and managed to say, "No more ruined than my gown. Why would you ask such a thing?"

"I've eyes in my head, haven't I, and ears to hear the gossip that is bandied about. I know that you care for the master, and he for you."

Elaine sat to remove her shoes, caught off guard. She could silence the woman in an instant. All she had to say was, "He asked me to marry him. To be his wife." Why did she not proclaim it from the rooftops?

It did not seem real. She, the penniless daughter of a drunken gambler, might marry a known rogue and womanizer—father to an illegitimate daughter? A man far above her in wealth and station and yet a man like her father, like Palmer. Could it be true that he loved her? Wanted her? That he was a changed man? A page out of a fairy tale. *And the damsel is much confused. Definitely in distress. The knight offered rescue. It is his duty. And yet, is there love? Magic? Or does the tale turn in on itself?*

Mrs. Olive turned from the window. "It will not do to care too much for him, lass. If you take my meaning."

Elaine's right shoe dropped to the floor with a thump as she unlaced it. "I am well aware of my place, Mrs. Olive."

"Good," the older woman said briskly, and crawled back into the bed. "You must not take offense that I have warned you in such a matter." Her voice came muffled but firm as the second shoe dropped. "He can be a winning lad when he turns on the charm, our Valentine."

"Yes, he can," Elaine murmured, remembering the dance of his hands upon her feet and the taste of his lips upon hers.

The second event that helped Elaine decide what she must do occurred on the way to Pembroke Castle.

They took a sloop-rigged barge. One might walk around if one were careful of the rigging. Felicity, agile as any sailor, followed her father wherever he went. Elaine avoided him, knowing he expected an answer to his proposal. Just as well. His mother seemed bent on positioning herself or the Biddingtons between them.

They had just sailed past Dale Point, a bony finger of rock that pointed their direction into the inlet known as Milford Haven when Deliah Biddington, who seemed most unhappy when conversation ceased, asked, "Are there legends associated with the castle?"

"Pembroke?" Val's mother shrugged and adjusted her hat that it might more fully protect her face from the sun. "I've no idea. You had best ask my son. I am unfamiliar with it. However, there is a sad legend connected to the Norman castle of Haverfordwest, which we passed on our way to St. David. Do you remember the place?"

They assured her they did. It overlooked the Cleaddau did it not?

Lady Wharton glanced over her shoulder then, as if to be sure Elaine was listening before she began. "A Welsh bowman was captured by the English there, long ago, when Welshmen and Englishmen fought one another. While in captivity this commoner befriended none other than the governor's son, whom he entertained with tales of his prowess."

Again the glance over her shoulder. For a moment she looked right at Elaine—not through her—but directly into her eyes. She did not look as if she particularly cared for what she saw.

"One day the bowman lured the nobleman's son to the

top of the castle wall, from which he threw the lad to his death."

"Oh my!" The Biddington sisters' faces were twin pictures of shocked fascination.

"How dreadful!" Their eyes glittered like matched emeralds with a need to know more. "What happened to the despicable bowman?"

"Was he hanged?" Deliah asked.

"Perhaps drawn and quartered?" Her sister speculated.

Lady Wharton shook her head sadly and looked away. Once again Elaine felt blessedly invisible.

"It would seem he loved the lad, after all, and regretted his revenge. He followed the lad, leaping to his own death."

"Goodness. That is indeed a shockingly sad tale."

"The most affecting I have heard in an age."

And meant for my ears. She believes I lead her boy astray.

"Imagine the governor's wounded feelings," Lady Wharton said.

As she is wounded.

"He built a monastery nearby and named it—can you guess?"

"After his son?" Deliah suggested.

"Certainly not after the dreadful Welshman?"

Sad eyes fixed on Elaine. "Sorrowful. He called it Sorrowful."

Deliah laughed. "One cannot hear the name without growing melancholy."

Her sister did not seem in the least melancholy. "Shall I go and ask Lord Wharton if there are any similar tales of Pembroke?"

"Oh yes, let's do."

With that, they scrambled to the other end of the boat.

Without turning from the rail, Lady Wharton said, "My son tells me he means to marry you, Miss Deering. That you have captured his heart."

Elaine was surprised by her directness. "So he tells me."

"He brings much to a marriage. A fine name, a worthy title, a life of comfort for the one who wins his heart. Tell me, what do you bring him?"

Elaine was taken aback by such a question, but gathered nerve to say, "Love. Understanding. Commitment. Trust. A faithful heart."

"I think you bring more, Miss Deering, perhaps all unknowing."

"What would that be, my lady?"

"A fall, Miss Deering."

Leap of faith. Or is it a fall?

"As deadly as from the top of a Norman tower. You see, he will fall from favor with such a marriage, from power, from social standing, from the respect of his peers. All in an effort to protect your name he will lose his own. The pity of it is, you see, you will fall with him, and I—like the poor governor of the story, shall be left with nothing but sorrow."

Harsh words. Devastatingly harsh. They shook Elaine, tore at any confidence she might have had in the success of a marriage.

Lady Wharton, it would seem, had nothing more to say. And Elaine, in her own right, had no words with which to defend a marriage she questioned as much as the widow.

She could see how it would be with Lady Wharton if she accepted her son's proposal. She had behaved with unvarnished disdain from the start, and yet now that this woman stood in a position to act as her mother-in-law, her displeasure in such a match took on new significance. Lord Wharton was willing to displease his mother for her sake. He was willing to alienate friends, family, and social contacts.

Such sacrifice. A fall? Perhaps it was. Women like the Biddingtons would always look down their noses at her. They might speak to her, but only as they spoke to Felicity—condescendingly.

Val's willingness to sacrifice himself revealed the depth of his kindness. He cared for her enough to make this noble gesture, a slaying of quiet dragons. She shivered to think of such a love, to think how greatly his peers underestimated his kindness—she would not flinch from the word. It was a wonderful characteristic—rare—cherishable. And she would cherish it always, from a distance. Once she had recognized the extent of his affection, Elaine, who loved Valentine Wharton with the entire depth and breadth of heart and soul, could make no less a noble gesture. She made up her mind to go. Out of her love for him she would give him back his friends, his family, his potential to marry well. She could do no less, no matter how painful.

She stepped from barge to pier with firm intention: she must say her farewells—to Felicity, to her father—and then she must slip away. A post coach in Pembroke could take her anywhere she desired.

Chapter 36

The deep throat of Milford Bay led them to Pembroke
Castle.

The castle did not appear much ruined when viewed
from a distance by way of the water's approach. Situated
on high ground, the old stone lady looked sprung from the
sea, white swans her handmaidens. Breathtaking. Magical.

Val thought of his old hip flask without thirst, the castle's
image haunting, breath of the dragon.

He smiled, pleased, and wanted to share his thirst for
a new future with Miss Deering—he could picture it all
so clearly.

The steep inclines leading to the bailey were covered in
shrub. A little forest seemed to grow in its canopy a magical
tree tower, a gatehouse, and crenelated stone walls. It
looked an impregnable spot, highly defensible, a jewel set
in green velvet against a blue silk sea.

"As if we have sailed into a fairy tale," Felicity said, the
remark meant for Val.

It warmed his heart to think they two shared confidences.
It made him long to make her life more like a fairy tale,
the kind that ended happily. And yet, such longing was
futile. He must content himself with the idea that dear Fe-

licity would find moments, like this one, in which to be happy. Was it not all anyone could hope for in life? Moments of happiness? Of connection? Fairy tale moments. They were doing well, he and his daughter. He had hopes that they would continue to do well, perhaps more than ever with Elaine Deering as his wife.

If she agreed to be his wife.

His own fairy tale moment of happiness last night had withered into a state of puzzled confusion. She had responded so readily to his touch, to his kisses. There was no doubt she enjoyed both. He had been so sure she must say yes to his proposal, without doubt, without hesitation. Why had she not accepted his offer immediately?

"A magnificent sight," she said when he looked her way.

He nodded, words stuck in his throat, anticipation rising. Finally she spoke. All morning it had seemed she avoided him. After last night's romp on the beach, his awkward proposal, he had been left unsure just where they stood. Her silence had compounded his confusion.

Would she understand? About the castle? His dragons?

"Most impressive to see it first from the seaward side."

He smiled as Felicity tucked herself beneath his arm and said, "May we climb the tower, Papa?"

A castle cupped in liquid and still I feel no thirst. It is a miracle, this thing called love. "But of course we must climb," he said.

They disembarked, a starry-eyed Felicity swinging his hand playfully as they moved in a gaggle between two towers, one fallen, one in good repair, following a pathway other wanderers had etched across a dry ditch moat, stone arches rising where once had stood a bridge.

Here the castle's decay was more pronounced. Arched windows stared emptily at the town. Rubble made walking a challenge. Vines and weeds encroached upon the grayed face of walls unbuckled by routing forces, vandalism, or time. A tired hulk of ancient glory, this castle Pembroke, hunchbacked, the jagged walls an open maw against the sky.

They had to pick their way carefully, Val offering his hand to the ladies as they scrambled over piles of fallen stone and mortar.

"How very safe they must have felt," his mother said,

when they had gained the clearing of the inner ward and stood staring up at the great keep. "Once a position of power, of strength—only look at it now."

"It has lost its roof," he said, "but amazing, nonetheless, to see what remains standing after more than five hundred years."

"Closer to seven," Miss Deering said tentatively, and when their party turned to stare at her, she clarified. "The castle was built in 1105."

"What else?" Val asked with an encouraging smile, glad she braved his mother's disapproving glare. "The Misses Biddington were asking me earlier if I knew of any wonderful histories in connection with the castle."

"Oh, indeed." Deliah Biddington fluttered her lashes at him. "Any great tragedies or tales of torture?"

A smile lurked in the corners of Miss Deering's delicious lips. He wanted to kiss her right here in front of everyone to hear her say, "I know nothing of torture, but I can tell you of romance and conquest."

"Do tell," the Misses Biddingtons begged. His mother turned and walked away as though disinterested.

"It seems that the same Gerald de Windsor who built Pembroke fell in love with and married a Welsh princess named Nest."

"Like a bird's nest?" Felicity laughed. "What a strange name."

"Yes. And with the building of this . . . nest for Nest," Elaine waved at the castle before them like a sorcerer with magic wand, "de Windsor and his wife built one of the greatest Norman strongholds in Wales."

"Very clever," Deliah said, "to link families of power and influence."

"Indeed," his mother chimed in rather abruptly from where she stood examining an archway a few yards away, listening after all.

"What else?" the elder Miss Biddington prodded.

"Henry VIII was born here," Felicity announced proudly.

And when everyone, including Val, eyed her with some surprise, she too blushed and said, "Miss Deering told me on the way here."

"And a most attentive pupil you are," Elaine beamed at her.

"And conquest?" he asked when it seemed she meant to say no more.

She wore a wary look in turning to face him. No. Not wary. This was a look of uncertainty, of awareness, as if she, too, thought of conquest in a context none but they understood.

"You mentioned a tale of conquest," he reminded her gently.

"Cromwell," she said a trifle too hastily. His mother regarded them most searchingly.

"Cromwell ordered the tower destroyed," his dear Deering went on, "following a starvation siege that lasted months."

"And yet it still stands." He wanted to hear more, wanted to observe her interaction with his mother, with the Biddingtons. He wanted them to understand how clever she was—well-spoken, well-read, a woman of spirit and poise. He wished to show them in some small way his regard for her mind, her opinion, her thoughts.

"It is damaged," she said, and looked at him. *Like me. Like her.*

"They made every effort to destroy it." *As they would destroy us.*

"And yet, its makers had done a most worthy job," she went on. "It was meant to withstand anything." *Will we? Can we withstand disfavor, gossip, snobbery, and misunderstanding?* "The walls are almost twenty feet thick at the tower's base."

"A sturdy foot," he said wryly.

She blushed, understanding his flirtatious message, and then, expression grown serious, said, "An unshakable foundation."

Surely love was just such a foundation. If she loved him they could face anything. But he had yet to determine if she truly loved him—if she meant to marry him.

Lady Wharton was in no mood for climbing, and the Biddingtons agreed that the walls of the tower looked to be in far too unsound a state of disrepair to go climbing about, dirtying one's gloves and hem. They met with dismay Lord Wharton's intentions to climb the stone stairway to the top. He had promised Felicity. Their brows rose even higher to hear him second Felicity's plea to the governess. "Come, Miss Deering. You do mean to come and see the view, do you not?"

Elaine's answer stuck in her throat, at the prospect of a moment alone with Lord Wharton. But in the end, just as she had on the beach after midnight, she uttered that most magic of words, "Yes."

Inside the tower they picked their way, past fallen stone, and weeds grown high. Birds beat wings above them as they entered, evidence of breaches in thick stone walls that cooled the air like a cave, the smell musty and dank, wet stone, damp earth—the smell of the past peppered in bird droppings and rain-spawned moss. Above them a glimpse of what might have been a stairway long ago clung to the wall just beneath a patch of sky, all that was to be seen by way of the hole that opened up one side of the tower. A stairway to the heavens, no way up, no way down. They saw it at the same time, knew at once its implication. There was no climbing this tower to see the view. And yet neither of them stopped Felicity, who ran ahead, calling, "Be careful. The ground is most uneven."

Here Lord Wharton had a perfect opportunity to reach out to Elaine, to help her over fallen mortar and stone. She did not want to avoid that contact. It might be her last.

One hand grasped her elbow, the other braced the small of her back, and with sudden dexterity she was swept into his arms, and his lips were on hers—she did nothing to fight the lightning taste of his lips, the kiss of damp heat, shocking in its haste, in its very public nature.

As quickly as they had come together they parted, for Felicity called out, voice echoing with disappointment, "There's no way up. A single step, that's all; a single step that leads to nowhere."

Elaine caught her breath, stepped away from the dizzying embrace, tried to regain her equilibrium. A single step that leads to nowhere. Was that what their marriage would be?

His lordship, who looked none the worse for wear, called out to his daughter, all the while looking Elaine directly in the eyes, "Never mind, my dear. We shall find something else to do." ·

Then he was kissing her again, her neck, her temple, her nose, her lips. And she, as desperate as he, kissed back with matching passion, until she regained sense and reminded them both, "Felicity."

He backed away reluctantly, breathing hard, eyes fired with desire.

"Where shall we go?" Felicity scrambled back to them, enthusiasm undiminished. "There is a secret hidey-hole that goes under the castle."

They went to the hidey-hole, just the three of them, by way of a turret in the northern hall of the castle, as directed by a little sign, through an arch and down a winding staircase. Wogan Cavern it was called, a natural, rounded cave. The opening to the sea was walled in, leaving an archway big enough to accommodate a boat, and several windows for hoisting things through. Light streamed through the openings. Moisture streamed from the ceiling. The floor was uneven, damp, and littered with fallen rock. Mineral sediment stippled the walls and ceilings. The place smelled of damp and the sea. One might imagine all sorts of things making their way into the castle thus.

Felicity delighted in the echo that bounced back to them from the cave walls. Val and Elaine stepped out of the archway, and stood looking out upon the inlet on a little apron of an embankment, while Felicity remained within, shouting her name that she might hear its repeat.

Elaine's gaze turned toward the water.

Valentine stood waiting for her answer. She must say yes. Anything else seemed senseless.

Words spilled from her mouth at last, as though they were very important. Not the words he expected.

"I find myself in despair."

The word caught at his heart, toppling his confidence. "Despair?"

She nodded. "Considering my life, and what I thought to do with it, the dreams of a future like a castle that was built, brick by brick in my imagining, stone upon stone, fair to look upon and live in, defensible against any foe, and yet, in the end, I find it is a castle made of sand."

Despair did not sound like a yes. He expected nothing less than yes. Surely a penniless governess could not refuse his offer: half of his future, brick upon brick. Not sand to sift through her fingers. He would not sweep security from under her feet. Like her father had. *Like Palmer had.*

"You might be describing my life," he said. "Anyone's, really."

Her hands moved about in an agitated fashion, not the calm hands he had come to expect of Miss Elaine Deering. "The waves of life come to wash my dreams away, to undermine their imagined stoutness, to wash the path of my life smooth, so that not so much as a trace of the imaginary castle remains. It is heartbreaking, enough that I would wail, as children wail when their creations are destroyed by the inevitability of the waves."

He did not know how to respond. Did she think he sought to undermine the walls of her castle? Had he swept away the imagined stoutness of her future?

"Will you rebuild?" he asked.

She tried to smile and failed. "Pick up bucket and shovel, and begin again? Children do, I know, time and time again, caught up in the fascination of building. And yet, with time, children mature, and recognize the impermanence of dreams, and sand castles."

"The question is then, do you choose something stouter? Or do you stand back, and watch other children playing, and shake your head at their folly?"

"I do not know. I do not know. I think there is something of despair so dark and incapacitating that on occasion it hides answers from me. Even simple ones."

"But together we shall make all right again."

She looked at him a long moment before she nodded, and said with resigned determination, "Yes, of course. All shall be made right again."

Chapter 37

The Howard children broke Elaine's teapot on a rainy day that reminded her vividly of the day she had met Valentine Wharton.

Tossing brightness out of the single window of her tiny, tip-tilted garret room, the boys—four of them—and the girls—six high voices shrieking—stomped upon the floor above with undisguised glee as the gilded, fire-breathing dragon took wing, soaring high before it fell, smashing into glittering pieces on the courtyard cobbles.

They argued over who got to have a go next as the cloud-filled cups followed, one after another. Not enough to go round and thus a source of squabbling discontent, as all of the magic that was left in Elaine Deering's mean existence sailed into oblivion onto the drive, just as a carriage arrived. A passenger disembarked amid glittering shards, horses uneasy, heads tossing, the coachman shouting, "Stop that nonsense! At once!"

Elaine, watched helplessly from Mrs. Compton's room. She gave the old lady her bath, a task she could not abandon, lest the old woman slide down under the water and drown, or stray from her room without a stitch of clothing on. She had been known to conduct herself in the oddest fashion since her eighty-fifth birthday.

Elaine recognized the teapot as it flew past the window, her only precious possession left to destroy. She had hidden it away when her mirror was shattered, her perfume vial emptied onto her mattress, the shells she had brought from the seashore flung into the fire, her dresses spattered with ink. Mrs. Howard's children wished to scare the new governess away. They had scared away half a dozen before. Elaine wished with all of her heart she might oblige them. But where would she go, without use of her references? She dared not use her precious references. Lord Wharton might come after her. And she would not say no to him a second time. She couldn't. She hadn't the strength.

This position, obtained at a moment's notice on her sister's recommendation, had seemed, at first, a godsend. Ten children, a large family, and yet she knew she could handle the task. She came from a family of six, after all, and had handled classes far greater in number. However, ten children grown wild and unruly from their father's neglect, their mother's cosseting, and the eldest boy's mean-spirited control over his younger siblings had proven daunting. Especially when she had been informed, on more than one occasion, that it was not her place to discipline Mrs. Howard's brood.

"You must not expect too much of them," Mrs. Howard advised. "They are only children."

Elaine had underestimated their tenacity in finding ways to encourage her leave-taking. She had not hidden the dragon carefully enough. In watching it shatter, in knowing she could do nothing to save it, something inside her seemed to shatter as well.

Dazed, she helped the old lady from the tub, gently drying arms and legs. Numbly she watched a well-dressed young woman climb from the coach and bend to regard the broken china, the shattered dream cups. Only when she looked up did Elaine recognize Penny Shelbourne.

So beleaguered was Elaine's frame of mind, her soul so despairing, that she immediately assumed the worst. She hastened to dress Mrs. Compton, rang for a maid to take her, and was down the stairs and striding into the sitting room before her mistress could reach for the bellpull, before the raindrops had dried on Penny Shelbourne's hair.

"What is wrong?" she demanded. "Is Felicity ill? Injured? Has he . . . ?"

"Calm yourself, Miss Deering." Penny Shelbourne took her hands in her own, and as Mrs. Howard made no effort to vacate the room, asked, "Might we go somewhere private to talk? Your room, perhaps?"

Her room? Her room was three flights up and very small, with a leaky, sloping roof that did not allow one to stand. There was nothing to sit on but the lumpy mattress, and that would be damp today. "The schoolroom," she suggested.

Penny Shelbourne followed her up the narrow back stairs to the gloomy, ill-lit, ill-furnished room designated as schoolroom. She paused in the doorway to look about the dark buff walls, traced a finger across one of the outdated maps Elaine had drawn new boundaries on, and thumbed through one of the dog-eared books left splayed on one of ten mismatched, saggy-bottomed chairs. She went to the window, to lean against the sill and examine the rain-dappled view of the garden wall, almost tripping over the basket of unmended linen.

"What was the object that almost hit my horse in the head?"

"A teacup." Elaine's voice shook, ever so slightly. She squared her shoulders and set her chin resolutely. "I trust you suffered no injury?"

Penny shook her head, expression thoughtful.

"You must come," she said simply.

"Come?" Elaine looked at her stupidly. "Where?"

"Back to St. David."

Elaine hated to admit it. "I cannot afford to lose my position."

Penny looked down at the mending basket. "Not even for the saving of a soul?"

Elaine's heart jumped. "Felicity?" She sank into one of the dreadful chairs, hand to mouth, fearing the worst.

"No. Val."

Elaine shivered. The room was cold without a fire in the chimney.

Val? She came about Val? She stared in disbelief at her visitor, who looked back at her with evidence of strain and profound concern.

"His soul is in danger? Has he taken to drink?"

Penny squared her shoulders, took a deep breath, looked her in the eyes, and then regarded the sodden view. "No. He has sent Felicity to me."

"What?" Elaine felt she swallowed the word as much as said it. It made no sense to her. "To visit?"

"To stay."

"But why? They were getting along so well."

Penny nodded, stricken. "He means to buy colors."

Elaine was struck dumb. She half-rose from the chair with a harsh exhalation and then sat back down, as though someone had punched her in the stomach. "Sharpshooting? No!"

Penny nodded.

"But what of his property? His father's estate?"

She made a frustrated sound. "Leaves it in his mother's care. Says it means nothing. Will not listen to reason, entreaty, pleading, or threat."

"But fight again?" Elaine stared bleakly at the mending pile, a pair of boy's breeches on top. The knees needed patching. She shook her head in disbelief. "Why? He once said he hated to leave everything behind."

Penny nodded, understanding in her eyes. They were the most unusual shade of blue, these eyes he had once held dear.

"Felicity is heartbroken. She asks for you," she said, as gentle as the rain.

Elaine rose and paced the length of the room she had grown to consider a torture chamber. This room was a blissful haven compared to a battlefield. "It will drive him to drink again." How bleak her certainty.

"I fear the same."

"He will drink to still the voices of the dead."

"And I am to blame."

"You? How? Because you did not love him?"

"No." Penny tried to smile, her mouth crumpling in the attempt. "Because I helped chase away the one he loves."

Elaine knew not what to say to that. She clasped hands about her shoulders, cold, suddenly so very cold. "But you were right. He wished to marry me out of pity. Not love. It would have meant the loss of the love of his mother, the loss of his friends, his place in society. I could not take so much from him with nothing to offer in return."

Penny pushed away from the windowsill to stand in the way of her pacing. "No, Elaine. I was wrong. He is more than willing to sacrifice all as unimportant to him. You see, he does love you. "

"You cannot be sure of that."

"I can." She presented a folded page from her pocket, the broken seal, the dash of his hand familiar. Elaine stood by the window to read, rain blurring the pane. She could see him in her mind's eye, astride a horse—a centaur, a mythical beast.

She skimmed a letter not meant for her eyes, fixing on three lines, tears springing hotly to her eyes, his voice in the ink.

"I cannot seem to hold onto the women I love. A heart mending—is torn asunder again. Felicity is best left to your care in such circumstances."

Could it be true? Women. Not just Penny. Did he really love her? Had she broken his heart as much as her own in abandoning him?

"It was entirely wrong of me to interfere," Penny said, "to encourage you to leave. It is probably wrong of me to go on interfering, but once upon a time Val brought my true love to me. It seems only appropriate that I should return you to him. Can you find it in your heart to forgive, Miss Deering? To mend Val's broken heart?"

"You were not the only one to discourage me."

"His mother? Will it please you to know she encouraged me to find you? She loaned me her carriage to come and fetch you."

Hope rose in Elaine's throat like a bird on the wing. Too sudden, too wonderful this news. She burst into tears.

Murmuring soothingly, Penny offered up her shoulder for comfort and gave Elaine's back a gentle patting, as if she were a child.

From the door came a stifled snickering, then the snide voice of Alfred, the eldest of the Howard children. "She weeps," he crowed. "I told you we could bring her to tears—drive her away."

Penny handed over her handkerchief, brows raised, a mischievous glitter in her eyes. "Shall we grant the little darlings their dearest wish?"

Elaine laughed though her tears. "With pleasure."

Chapter 38

Val stood on the clifftop at St. David's head, a bottle in each hand, looking out to sea, prepared to get soused to the gills. He found no joy in the prospect, and yet there was nothing left for it but to get drunk—to forget. He had trusted in St. David, who had found his inspiration here, trusted his own inspiration must return to him here, where she had left him. But she had escaped him, Miss Deering. All attempts to find her had failed.

Her mother, her sisters, refused to respond to letters. He had been turned away from six different doorways by young women who resembled her, as though they offered her up to him in pieces: hair, hands, mouth. They listened to his pleas with the same wariness once found in her eyes. What had she said? How had she warned them to send him away?

Gatehouse, the girl's school, had no idea of her whereabouts. The gentleman he had hired to hunt for her came back empty-handed but for word of Palmer. She had not reconsidered his scurrilous offer. The scoundrel did not have her tucked away in private rooms. Thank God for that much.

She filled his thoughts, his memory. He could not look

at Felicity without thinking of his dear Deering: her gentle way with the child, the light in her eyes on a moonlit beach, the change in her wary attitude. He thought of her mouth, their kisses, the press of her body to his. She had wanted him, cared for him, cared for his daughter. She had, he thought, loved him, and still she had left him. It made no sense, this knife to the heart from the last person in the world he had thought capable of bringing him pain—quiet, biddable Miss Deering. His heartache's ease.

Why had she turned her back on him? Fled without so much as a fare-thee-well?

He thought of her father, of Palmer. Had she in some way found him as contemptible? Unworthy? He knelt amongst the wildflowers to uncork the bottle, hands awkward, shaking. The cork did not come easy, and yet its popping sound was a familiar friend. He lifted the cork to his nose, the smell beckoning, full of promise. He tossed it into the grass, stared at the open bottle, mouth watering.

The glass was cold against his lips—as cold as his memories. He would forget, shut out the voices of the past, of love's abandonment. He would drown his sorrow.

And yet, something within him raged, persistent, a voice that would not be silenced. A warning.

Dragon's breath. False courage.

Felicity.

The spirit of the grape never touched his lips.

With a burst of anger, with a shaken, wind-caught cry of "Damnation!" he tossed the bottles from him, one after another, twin glittering arcs over the edge of the cliff, falling, twisting, catching the light, contents spilling, tinkling in destruction on the rocks below. Then, head bent, bowed by the weight of a heart and soul aching sorrow, he thought of Miss Deering, who had abandoned him and his daughter.

He whispered fiercely, "Damn you!"

Elaine watched him rage against the wind, the wine bottles given to the rocks, to the sea. She heard his anguished cry and knew at last how much she had hurt him. It was a scene she would never forget, a moment in which sight and sound and smell imprinted indelibly on her memory.

She had once believed this man a monster, but in the

end she had proved monstrous in leaving him, without a word, without an explanation, without apology.

He stood near the burial stones known as Coetan Arthur, an ancient cromlech, resting place of a much loved king, his hand upon the tilted cap stone, his shadow long, hair tossed in the wind, face bright with the sun. Then he turned, hastening down the slope into the valley, through ruined walls that spoke of man's dwelling here long ago. Circles raised the grass, heather, wildflowers, walls—long gone—the people long dead and buried. It struck her how brief life was, how precious. How futile were the walls with which man tried to hem it in.

Valentine Wharton was precious to her—she had allowed him to breach her defenses, to storm the walls with which she had long held the world at bay—a notorious womanizer and rogue, repulsed for imbibing too freely. Not a monster but a man, the kindest of men. A kind-hearted Valentine. How foolish she had been to believe all that was said of him, how foolish to turn her back on the gift of his willingness to change, his affection, his offer of marriage.

He looked up, caught sight of her, paused, and then he flung up his arms, as if to stay her.

"What are you doing here?" he shouted, hair and eyes wild.

She went to him, her feet gaining speed as she slid downhill, her skirt belling behind her, caught up on swaying flowers: broom, bindweed, stonecrop, and gorse. She came to a halt a few arm's lengths away.

The tide rushed against the rocks below them, and yet she could not throw herself as wildly against his stone-like stance, his arms crossed over his chest, jaw rigid, his expression unwelcoming.

"Is that the first thing you would say to me?" she asked.

Birds scolded from above.

His tone was just as brusque. "What do you do here, Miss Deering?"

She said nothing for a moment, out of breath, unsure if, after all, he wanted her, so darkly did he scowl at her, so distant was his look.

"I wanted to be the hero." She laughed uneasily.

That changed the knit of his brow. "You wanted what?"

"In your fairy tales. I wanted to be a women who conquered dragons, who did the right thing. For you. For Felicity. No matter the cost. As you intended to."

He rubbed his hand across his mouth, his tone angry, resistant. "And I was the cost?"

She exhaled heavily, let the sighing breath of the sea fill the silence, and then explained, "I believed you meant to play hero, saving a damsel in distress when you could not save Penny Foster or Felicity. I was not sure that you loved me."

He raked an impatient hand through windblown locks and turned away. "You made that all very clear to me. And yet you return. Why?"

He wasn't going to make this easy. She couldn't blame him, only try to reach him. "A kind gentleman once told me . . ."

He frowned.

She swallowed hard and moved closer, that she might see his face more clearly, that he must look at her. ". . . not to say no when I meant yes."

His frown deepened. She did not know what to do with this hard, unwelcoming expression. She did not know what to say next.

"Y-you mean . . . ?" He seemed as breathless as she, with anger rather than exertion. "You have the gall to come to me . . . now . . ."

"Yes."

His lips pressed tight, as if at a bitter taste. "To say . . ."

She nodded, the word catching in her throat, tears as salt as the sea in her eyes. "Yes."

He shook his head like a bull, still angry, still raging. She had never seen him so angry. "Yes, what?"

Her eyes burned. His anger seemed completely undiminished. It had been a mistake to come, to leave a perfectly good position, to risk all, even rejection, and yet she had. She must throw her heart at him, let the walls down, let her pride smash as completely as the wine bottles he had flung from the clifftop.

"Yes, I love you, Valentine Wharton." She whispered, the words caught on the wind, raw with feeling. "Yes, I would kiss you. Yes, I would tear off my clothes and run into the sea with you. Yes, I will marry you, if you will still have me. I love the kindness in you, the strength, the intelligence, the decency." Her voice shook. She steeled herself to go on. "I love the fact that you stood ready to sacrifice all for my honor. I love most of all the way you look at your daughter with love in your eyes, the way you have looked at me. I wonder if you can find it in you to look at me that way again. If you cannot find it in your heart to take us home with you."

He stood a moment, breathing hard, as if they ran a race, as if his anger were a new wall he would build between them.

Above the sea a bird hovered, a single gannet, poised to plunge.

"Leap or fall?" she asked, the words a challenge.

Val loosed a little huff of breath and flung open his arms. With a tearful cry Elaine flew into them.

"My dear Deering," he murmured against her hair.

"My kind-hearted Valentine." His shirtfront muffled her words.

"How I have longed to hear you say it." He kissed her ear, her temple, her forehead. "I have missed you, dearest Elaine, how I have missed you."

They did not speak again for quite some time, communicating their feelings in a number of other ways, breaking down all sorts of walls, generating all sorts of heat.

Breath of the dragon. Blessed breath of the dragon.

Epilogue

Valentine Wharton never did buy his colors. He was much too busy attending to preparations for a wedding, a Valentine's Day wedding.

His beloved wife, Elaine, insisted they make a point of spending their anniversaries in Wales, if not every other year, at least as often as time, and the births of their children permitted. They always took Felicity with them, the eldest of their brood, even when she was a woman grown, with a husband and children of her own.

The years passed, and with them came a growing flock of children. Thrice, Cupid and Penny and their own band of four nestlings, were lured into the wilds of Wales, where over steaming cups of Darjeeling tea, served in beautiful cloud cups from a Chinese dragon teapot, very much like the one that had been smashed, they heard, again and again, tale of a Widnot who struck fear into many a Welshman's heart, and of the magical palace at the bottom of Bala lake.

There, too, they learned to build elaborate sand castles on the beach near St. David's Head, and learned the names of all of the wildflowers there, and were encouraged to explore the vine-draped ruins of Pembroke Castle with its dripping cave and heaven-bound staircase. Best of all, they clamored every visit to take the boat to Grassholm Island to watch the seals slide into the sea at their approach, and listen to the voices of the kittiwake-ache-aches, and watch, again and again, the gannets' leap of faith. Thousands upon thousands of them.

And never a fall. On that they were in complete agreement. Never a fall.

Author's Note:

Setting locations throughout the book are real, as are the historical details concerning the sites.

An exception: While the fictional Caxton Castle is inspired by, and modeled after, the real Chirk Castle, the fictional Biddington and Myddulph families are modeled in name and motto only after the very real Myddelton and Biddulph families, whose admirable mottoes are indeed *Sublimiora petamus* and *In veritate triumpho*—"Let us seek higher things" and "I triumph in the truth." In paying homage to this fascinating castle, its history, and its owners, I would in no way imply the story actually took place. The Biddington sisters and their families are entirely fictional creatures.

Pembroke Castle is no longer quite the vine-draped ruin of the Regency period. In 1880 a Mr. J. R. Cobb spent three years restoring what he could. Additional extensive restorations were made in 1928 by Major-General Sir Ivor Philipps, KCB, DSO.

Both castles are well worth a visit, as are the islands along the coasts of Great Britain, where hundreds of thousands of beautiful coastal birds nest every year.